LOVE IS FOR LOSERS

WIBKE BRUEGGEMANN

MACMILLAN

First published 2020 by Macmillan Children's Books
an imprint of Pan Macmillan
The Smithson,
6 Briset Street, London EC1M 5NR
Associated companies throughout the world
www.panmacmillan.com

ISBN 978-1-5290-3372-4

1 3 5 7 9 8 6 4 2

A CIP catalogue record for this book is available from the British Library.

Printed and bound by CPI Group (UK) Ltd, Croydon, CR0 4YY

Visit www.panmacmillan.com to read more about all our books
and to buy them. You will also find features, author interviews and
news of any author events, and you can sign up for e-newsletters
so that you're always first to hear about our new releases.

For Brittain, Luci, and Sophie.

Did you know that you can marry yourself? How strange/brilliant is that?

It's called 'sologamy', and here's why it's such a good idea:

- The only person you need to actually, like, answer to or tolerate is you.
- No one is ever going to leave you, disappoint you or hurt you.
- We all die alone anyway.

The reason I'm considering sologamy at this point in my life is not because I was secretly hoping to marry Polly one day (euw!), but because the sudden and rather unexpected end of our friendship is teaching me all sorts of vital life lessons. And never let it be said that I'm not a fast learner.

For as long as I can remember, it's been Phoebe and Polly, Polly and Phoebe – the two Ps in a pod.

Neither of us existed without the other – BFFs since birth.

And suddenly, *ding dong*, Big Ben strikes midnight, and Tristan Can't-Even-Ride-A-Bicycle Murphy pops the reality-altering question: Polly, will you be my girlfriend? And just like that, I've been literally erased from Polly's brain.

I'm not even angry about Polly losing her mind. I'm angry about being angry, because I knew (and I did know) it would come to this.

I knew that when she was like: 'Let's all go to Embankment

and see the fireworks.' What she actually meant was: 'Please, Phoebe, can you come along so that it isn't obvious I'm asking Tristan on an actual date, even though I basically am, because all I actually want is to be alone with him so that we can take whatever it is we're doing to the "next level".'

Bleugh!

I never should have gone.

Polly didn't even wish me a Happy New Year.

Possibly because she couldn't see me at that point, because the moment the Thames erupted into the meteor-shower-like fireworks extravaganza that must have cost the taxpayer millions, all that existed for her was Tristan's mouth.

And you know how in films, kisses are always really hot and gorgeous (mainly because the people are hot and gorgeous)? Well, Tristan looked like he was trying to swallow Polly's entire head.

I was literally sick in my mouth.

Good thing was, though, that I fought my way back to the Tube station as millions of people stood glued to the spot looking the other way, which meant that, apart from the driver, I was the only person on the District line at 0.08 a.m.

I'm at Kate's until tomorrow because Mum's at work attending a Syria crisis meeting, and when I let myself in, Kate was like: 'What happened to you?'

Me: Polly's got a boyfriend now, so she didn't need me to stay out.

Kate: I was going to pick you up from the station.

Me: I walked.

Kate: You should've called me.

Me: I didn't.

Kate: Wrong answer.

Me: Sorry. And sorry.

Kate: Better text Polly to say you're home safe.

Me: She doesn't care.

Kate: Text her.

Me: I'm going to bed.

Kate: Happy New Year, Phoebe. I love you. Text Polly.

I'm so not texting her.

2.05 a.m.

Polly just called me from the District line.

She was like: 'I didn't realize you'd gone.'

And then she was like: 'Tristan this, Tristan that, Tristan says hi, OMG, Tristan and I are so happy.'

And I was like: 'Who is this? Can you get Polly, please?'

What happens to people when they fall in love?

It's like their brain short-circuits. Like they've had a stroke.

It's been the shittest NYE in fifteen years.

It's been even more shit than last year when Polly puked in my lap after too many Apple Sourz.

3.30 a.m.

I just researched sologamy a bit more, and even though it is a brilliant idea, the people who've done it look like proper dicks.

P.S. Polly still hasn't wished me a Happy New Year.

P.P.S. I think people turn crazy the moment they turn sixteen. Polly was literally normal until her birthday in November.

P.P.P.S. I swear I'm not going to fall victim to love when I turn sixteen, if it's the last thing I do . . . or should that be 'don't do'?

TUESDAY 2 JANUARY #THEHAPPYNEWYEARCONTINUES

There are 7 billion people in the world.

That's 7 thousand million. So why, oh why, does my mother think *she* has to be the one helping out whenever there's a major catastrophe?

This is how it always goes down:

Earthquake in Italy:	Sorry, Phoebe, I'm off to dig some nuns out from under the rubble.
	(Dumps me at Kate's house.)
Hurricane in Haiti:	Sorry, Phoebe, I'm off to help all those who didn't get blown away.
	(Dumps me at Kate's house.)
Cholera in the Democratic Republic of Congo:	Sorry, Phoebe, I'm off to rehydrate the Third World.
	(Dumps me at Kate's house.)
Ebola in Africa:	Sorry, Phoebe, a deadly disease that may or may not be airborne just broke out, and I simply must be there.
	(Dumps me at Kate's house.)

So guess what happened when Mum collected me from Kate's this morning?

Yep.

I knew what was going on as soon as I got into the car, but I didn't say anything, because I was like: If you think I'm going to make this easy for you, you've never been more wrong.

And when we got home, Mum was all awkward like: 'Sit down with me for a minute, Phoebe.'

Me: . . .

Mum: Look, I have the opportunity to go to Syria for six
        months and help build a medical centre at a refugee
        camp.

Me: . . .

Mum: I know six months is a long time, but I promise I'll
        be back for your birthday.

Me: . . .

Mum: I've spoken to Kate, and she can't wait to have you.

Me: . . .

Mum: Phoebe, talk to me.

Me: What about? You've already decided you're going, so
        go. Bye.

Mum: Phoebe, I . . . The people in Syria need help, and . . .
        I'm a doctor. I help.

Me: When do I have to be packed?

Mum: I'm flying to Ankara tomorrow.

Me: (leaving the room) . . .

Mum: Phoebe—

Me: What? I said it's fine, so it's fine.

Mum: I'm sorry, Phoebe.

Sorry? Oh, LOL.

    We're way past sorry.

    When I tell people Mum works for Médecins Internationaux,
they're always like: 'Wow, that's so amazing – you must be
so proud.' But no one's ever like: 'That must really suck
when your mum goes away for MONTHS at a time ALL THE

TIME to places where BOMBS ARE DROPPING and EVERYONE'S DYING.'

No one cares about what it's like for me.

I grew up literally without a mother or a father, although Dad's dead, which is a much better excuse for being absent than Mum's constant Mother Teresa complex.

Why have a child if you don't want to spend time with it?

It totally runs in the family too. Nan and Granddad moved back to Hong Kong where they grew up when Mum started uni because: 'We'll always be expats, toodle-oo, and God save the Queen.'

I'm never having children.

I wish I could call Polly, but I'm definitely not speaking to her after last night.

And she still hasn't wished me a Happy New Year.

WEDNESDAY 3 JANUARY   #SEEYOUORNOT

Mum dropped me off at Kate's this morning.

In the car she was all like: 'Phoebe, I know the timing of this is terrible. I know you've got GCSEs coming up, and I know how stressful that is, and please, if you need me to stay, I'll stay. Please, can you just talk to me?'

But I was just like: 'I don't need you to stay. In fact, I don't need anyone to do anything.' And then I pretended to be doing something important on my phone.

At Kate's, I took my things up to my room (I'm the only

7

person I've ever known to have their own room at their godmother's house) and shut the door behind me. I didn't even say goodbye to Mum, but she clearly didn't care, because she never

a) knocked, or
b) tried to kick the door in.

Mum's a doctor first and a mum second.

I've always known that.

And I stopped doing goodbyes a long time ago.

THURSDAY 4 JANUARY   #FURBALLCENTRAL

I don't actually mind staying at Kate's house. The positives outweigh the negatives, as follows:

Positive things about staying at Kate's house:

- Unlike Mum, Kate no longer works for Médecins Internationaux and is therefore able to provide me with food, shelter and emotional support.
- She treats me like a flatmate, not like a five-year-old.
- When she goes off on one, I struggle to be offended because she turns so Scottish that I basically can't understand what she's saying.

Negative things about staying at Kate's house:

- I have to take the bus to school.
- The designer cats.

How is it possible that I've known those cats forever, but I still can't tell which is which? I can only ever tell them apart when they're sitting right next to each other. Just like Kayleigh and Melody Sessions (school uniforms do nothing for identical twins).

The designer cats are going to be a bigger pain in the arse than usual too, because they are currently

- in heat, and
- under strict house arrest (and therefore going nuts), because Kate has scheduled a shag-fest in High Barnet for them so they can have designer kittens at the same time.

And because the cats think my room is actually their room, they're continuously scratching the door trying to get in and whining because they can't.

This place is like a mental asylum run by a bonkers Scottish woman.

Cat 1: *Meow, meow, whinge, whinge, scratch, scratch.*

Kate: Mimi, Mimi, leave Phoebe alone. Mimi, Mimi, good girl. Who's a good girl?

Cat 2: *Meow, hiss, scratch, whinge.*

Kate: Sassy, Sassy, come to Mama. Good girl, Sassy. Who's a good girl?

Cat 1   (throws massive tantrum, knocking over everything that's not glued to a surface): . . .

Kate: For goodness' sake, ye total crazy fuckwit. Do I need to put ye in yer carrier?

Me: . . .

Mum always jokes about Kate ending up as a crazy cat lady, but hello – newsflash – it's already happened.

Who drives their cats all the way to High Barnet to get shagged?

There's a designer boy cat up there (also Persian, obvs) who's going to shag the designer cats all weekend, and then Kate is going to sell the designer kittens for, like, £500 each.

Imagine there are eight of them. That's £4,000.

This place is going to be furball-central.

Oh, and FYI, the creepiest thing is that the cats are mother and daughter. Imagine a sex orgy with your mother, and then think about this: if you had a baby with your mum's boyfriend, and your mum had a baby with him too, then your child would have the same dad as your brother/sister, and basically, how gross is that?

FRIDAY 5 JANUARY #FAMILY

Mum sent an email from Ankara telling me about all the fabulous people on her team. How nice for her to be surrounded by such a great bunch. And how equally wonderful for them to be spending so much time with my mother. Maybe they can tell me everything about her one day.

Still nothing from Polly.

This is the longest we've gone without speaking to each other. Maybe I should check if Tristan Training Wheels Murphy is holding her against her will.

SATURDAY 6 JANUARY   #HORMONALCOCKTAILFROMHELL

I never texted Polly.

I was thinking of asking her to go to Starbucks, but then I thought I'd feel even worse if she were like: 'Oh, sorry, Phoebe, I'm already going to Starbucks with Tristan, because Tristan's my boyfriend now, which means life's all about Tristan.'

4.00 p.m.

Get this.

I found Kate's old medical books, and they're changing my life.

Turns out Polly is the victim of a chemical shitstorm in her brain.

Out-of-control levels of phenylethylamine are basically giving her a personality change. Before her brain chemicals started boiling over, she was a normal person who saw someone like Tristan for what he was/is: a sixteen-year-old loser who can't ride a bike.

But suddenly – *crash, bang, wallop.* Love hormones are being released, and now she's like: 'OMG, Tristan's so hot, Tristan's so wise, Tristan's everything.'

So here's what I'm thinking. It's obviously too late for Polly (may her hilarity, her gorgeous mind, and her infinitely stunning personality RIP), but I can totally prevent myself from becoming a victim of this unfortunate condition, because I'll recognize the chemical process in my own brain and therefore will be able to react accordingly.

SUNDAY 7 JANUARY   #DISPROVINGTHETHEORYOFEVOLUTION

Polly's attraction to Tristan Training Wheels Murphy makes no biological sense.

Apparently we subconsciously fancy people we can make superior babies with so the genepool can be enriched, and the human race can grow stronger and better.

But Tristan can't even ride a bike.

Now, this wouldn't be bad/questionable/problematic if he could, for example, fly a plane. But he can't. So what's going on?

And how has Polly not called me in a week?

Maybe her brain is actually broken.

P.S. Back to school tomorrow, and I'm sure all will be revealed.

P.P.S. I hate that I have to take the bus because I have to get up an hour earlier than usual.

Thanks, Mum.

I've sunk so low that I had to sit with Miriam Patel and her minions at lunch.

She saw that I was lunching solo and invited me to her table like she was Jesus hosting the Last Supper, all gracious, with her arms wide open.

Everyone had to squeeze past Polly and Tristan kissing outside the library.

Bleugh!

Seriously, Polly's hormonal brain cocktail must be not only potent but also off, because Tristan's gross. Compared to Polly, anyway.

On our way to biology, I told Polly that her mentionitis was already getting on my tits, because normally she'd be saying things like: 'The only reason I remember the term *chloroplast* is because it sounds like an adhesive, but it isn't.' And all she'd said to me all day today thus far was: 'Tristan thinks, Tristan says, Tristan wants . . .'

Me: Can you say one sentence without saying Tristan?
Polly: You don't get it, Phoebe, Tristan and I are in love.

My God.

Miriam Patel has new fluorescent-pink braces, which she's loving more than life. She's fake-smiling all day like those teenage twats off Nickelodeon who pretend to be twelve but are actually eighteen.

Miriam Patel: Oh, hi, Phoebe.
Me: Oh, hi, Miriam.
Miriam: I'm so happy for Polly. Aren't you?
Me: Ecstatic.
Miriam Patel: (grinning, because she's evil) . . .
Me: (grinning, because I'm choked with hatred) . . .

I suppose I could always have watched Polly and Tristan make out while eating my sandwich, but then there's the gag reflex.

Tonight when I was watching telly, Kate sat down next to me on the sofa and poked me with her foot until I looked at her.

Me.   What?
Kate: Why haven't I seen or spoken to Polly? She usually
        moves in during weekends when you're here.
Me: I told you. She's found someone she likes better. He's
        called Tristan.

Kate: Oh, I see.

I told her that Polly doesn't even know Mum's gone to Syria, and how she still hasn't wished me a Happy New Year, and that Tristan basically ruined everything Polly and I had, and that he's always there and touching her, and that I don't ever get her on my own any more. And that he doesn't know how to ride a bike.

Kate was just like: 'What an absolute wankpot.' And then she put one of the designer cats on me and told me to stroke it because apparently that makes you feel better.

It didn't.

THURSDAY 11 JANUARY   #NOTHANKS

I locked myself out this morning and had to go to Kate's charity shop after school to get keys.

Apart from Pat, who I've known all my life and I can't remember not hating, here is the other main issue I have with the charity shop: most of the clothes that they're selling people have died in. Relatives then shoved those clothes, plus the contents of the dead person's home, into bin bags and dropped them off outside the shop in the middle of the night (and we all know what happens when bin bags are left in front of shops or homes: vermin, vomit, vandalism).

You should see their assortment of bric-a-brac (FYI, *bric-a-brac* is a fancy term for 'random shit nobody needs'). Examples:

- Ancient Royal Wedding mug featuring a washed-out Princess Diana with a massive chin. (Vile.)
- Arsenal salt and pepper shakers. (Just crap.)
- Thimble with IBIZA written on it. (What?)
- Christmas soap collection from Boots circa 1971. (Rancid.)

And last but definitely not least, my personal favourite, and a genuine bargain at only £3:

- A dried-up yet fully inflated puffer fish with plastic googly eyes stuck on. (Why?)

When I walked in, I was like: 'Yes!' Because it wasn't Pat behind the till, but a guy with Down's syndrome who was a bit older than me.

He didn't say hello, and so I didn't say anything either, which I thought was fine because it's a charity shop and not Lush, where the sales people are all like 'Hiya' and in your face for half an hour.

I could hear Kate through the open door to the stockroom, and I thought I'd walk straight in. When I passed the till, the guy took a deep breath in, then shouted: 'Kate! Customer!'

I literally had a heart attack and swung around to look at him and say something, anything, and our eyes locked.

Him: (so loud) Kate! Customer!
Me: . . .
Him: (even louder) Kate! Customer! Kate! Customer!

Me: Shut up!
Him: . . .

Then a girl in a school uniform with the bluest icy-blue eyes I've ever seen in all my life appeared from the back room, and she looked at me like: *Did you just tell a person with Down's syndrome to shut up?* And I looked at her like: *Well, yes, because why would I discriminate just because he has a learning disability?*

Then she went: 'You OK, Alex?' to him. And to me: 'Can I help you with anything today?' And I told her I was there to see Kate, and suddenly she looked at me like she totally had me figured out, and she was like: 'Are you Phoebe? I'm Emma. Kate's in the back – do you want to go through?'

I nodded, and the second I moved, Alex shouted: 'Kate! Customer!' again, so loudly, I swear it made all the shitty bric-a-brac rattle.

I flinched, which I know Emma thought was hilarious because I saw her biting her lip like she was afraid to laugh in my face.

Me: (to Alex) Do you have to be so shouty?
Alex: I'm Alex.
Me: I know.
Alex: Hello. Nice to meet you.
Me: . . .
Alex: Those who aren't seen must be heard.
Emma: (nodding) . . .
Me: . . .

18

Turns out, I didn't escape running into Pat after all, because she was in the back with Kate. Apparently she doesn't really do the till any more because she has now taken on a more 'administrative role' (pricing bric-a-brac).

She looked me up and down, as usual, and it was so obvious that she had a million things to say about:

- my hair,
- my face,
- my school uniform, and
- my mere existence.

I was just like: 'Pat.' And she was just like: 'Phoebe.'

Kate tried to talk me into staying and helping out, but I was like: 'No thanks, I'm busy' (lie).

She told me that Emma and Alex are really nice, and wouldn't it be great to make new friends, but I was like: 'Thanks, but I don't need friends, because, you know, lesson learned. Besides: Pat.'

P.S. On my way out of the shop, Emma was all friendly like: 'Nice to meet you, Phoebe,' which confused me, because looking back now, maybe the way I spoke to Alex wasn't ideal.

I ended up not saying anything to either of them when I left.

P.P.S. I think I'm socially awkward.

It appears that now we no longer have to hunt for food, some people have become too stupid to even purchase food, and in my opinion, this should affect evolution.

I watched a woman throw a massive tantrum at the shops today when she was asked to use a self-service check-out machine.

She was like: 'I simply refuse to use these!'

I bet she wouldn't 'simply refuse' state-of-the-art keyhole surgery, though.

I wanted to message Polly about it, but I didn't.

P.S. Mum sent a WhatsApp this afternoon, but I haven't looked at it.

SATURDAY 13 JANUARY   #DESIGNERCATHELL

Since I've been seen taking the bus to and from school for a week, Polly has cleverly deduced that I'm at Kate's, and so today, she was like: 'Is your mum away for long?'

Me: She's gone to Syria, so who knows when she'll get back. If she gets back.

Polly: Phoebe, don't say that. You can't say that.

Me: I just did.

I honestly expected more from Polly. What's everyone's problem with the truth? Mum's job is dangerous; we all know that. But instead of admitting it, everyone's always like: 'She'll be fine.'

According to the internet, over four hundred thousand people have died so far in Syria. That's almost the population of Manchester. And I'm sure all their friends and family were like: 'Oh, they'll be fine.'

It's always other people, until it isn't.

Like, I hate it, but at least I don't bury my head in the sand about that, so if anything were to happen to Mum, I'll be emotionally prepared.

In other news, the designer cats broke into my room and went to sleep on my school uniform.

And how is it possible that Kate doesn't own lint roll?

It took a whole roll of Sellotape to get those beige designer cat hairs off.

I should lock my door, but then Kate will think I'm antisocial (which is probably actually true, and maybe the real reason I secretly love the idea of sologamy, and self-service check-out machines).

SUNDAY 14 JANUARY   #HELLOFROMTHEOTHERSIDE

Mum called.

She's still in Ankara, and apparently it's freezing, and she's not having a nice time.

Good.

P.S. Polly hasn't messaged me all weekend.

Instead, she's posted a new Instagram story of her and Tristan feeding each other pizza.

Everyone's like: 'Aww! You're such a cute couple.'

Lies.

Tristan's vile.

Also, what's wrong with you? Just eat your pizza like a normal person.

Today, we were in the toilets, and Polly was being all dramatic, like staring at herself in the mirror, and then she was like: 'I love Tristan. Do you think it's too early to tell him?'

I was like: 'It's literally been two weeks, so yes, it's way too early.'

And then Polly got proper angry like: 'Why would you say that, Phoebe? You're my best friend.'

WTF is wrong with everyone?

I googled *true friendship* and came across this definition: *True friendship is when someone takes a position in your best interests in a crisis.*

Polly was having a crisis, and I was taking a position in her best interest.

Seriously, everyone needs to calm down.

And I refuse to lie to people about insignificant crap like that.

The cat got out. No!

Which means I destroyed Kate's dream of an early retirement, because the cat's most likely being shagged by a feral non-designer cat as I write this.

I only left the door ajar for a millisecond because I had to put the bin out, and next thing I knew, it bolted out of the house like Wolverine on speed. I tried to catch it – but try catching a horny cat.

All I could do was stand by and watch its beige designer-cat ass disappear over the fence.

Noooooooo.

I tried calling it for ages. I even walked up and down the street looking for it for, like, an hour – but nothing.

So when Kate got home, I was like: 'I'm totally sorry, but the cat got out, and I can't find it anywhere, and I promise I tried.'

Kate: Oh no. Which one?
Me: . . .
Kate: (shaking her head, tutting, because she knows I don't know which is which) . . .
Me: I'm so sorry.
Kate: I'm sure it was an accident.
Me: I actually think the cat planned it.
Kate: . . .
Me: Not funny, I know. I'm really so, so sorry, Kate. It just got out.
Kate: (taking a deep breath) Well, it can't be helped now.

You know when people say: *I'm not angry. I'm just disappointed.*
   That.

Kate says the cat will only come home once it's been shagged. Natural instinct, apparently. So now only one cat will have designer kittens, and all the others will be cheap knock-offs.

Instead of Chanel they'll have to be called Shanel.

P.S. I realize it's actually not funny.

WEDNESDAY 17 JANUARY   #ONWARDSANDUPWARDS

I feel so bad about the designer-cat debacle that I've decided I need to get a job ASAP and pay Kate back the money she lost.

In an ideal world, the designer cat could have had four designer kittens and, according to the internet, your average squishy-faced Persian designer kitten costs £500, which means I owe Kate £2,000. Though it's probably going to be more, because Kate's probably not going to be able to sell the knock-off kittens. And then she's going to have to feed them too, because I've concluded that if she can't find owners for them, she would never

a) give them away to Battersea, or
b) drown them.

So this is what I was thinking:

Minimum wage for people under eighteen is £4.20 per hour (rip-off alert).

$$£2,000 \div £4.20 = 476.19$$

So I'm going to have to work 476 hours to make up that money.

If I get a weekend job, let's say for twelve hours, that would mean earning £50.40 per week.

$$£2,000 \div £50.4 = 39.68$$

Conclusion: It's going to take me just under forty weeks to pay back the money I owe Kate.

That's almost a whole year. How depressing.

THURSDAY 18 JANUARY #CURRICULUMVITAE

I've done my CV, and it's proper shit.

Phoebe Alexandra Davis
Curriculum Vitae
3 Rochdale Close, Wimbledon, London SW19 1AL
Phone: 07965500713, Email: phoebead666@gmail.co.uk

I am fifteen years old and am currently looking for part-time employment on evenings and/or weekends.

Education
Currently attending Kingston Academy. Straight-A student (apart from English Lit, Art and History).

Other

I was awarded my cycling proficiency diploma in Year Five

In my free time, I enjoy going to the cinema.

References are available on request.

I wouldn't even give myself a job, but what can I possibly put on it that makes me sound interesting? I've done nothing in my life.

FRIDAY 19 JANUARY   #RETURNOFTHEDESIGNERCAT

The runaway designer cat is back.

Apparently it took no more than seventy-two hours for it to get shagged.

Today, Polly said that she feels like she hasn't really seen me for ages.

I can't think why she would feel that way . . .

Anyway, I figured I'd give her a break because of her hormonal imbalance, and I agreed to go to the cinema with her and Training Wheels tomorrow.

Only now I feel like *I'm* the one with the hormonal imbalance, because why would I agree to that?

I got to Kingston ridiculously early because I forgot that on a Saturday, the bus only takes fifteen minutes versus an hour during school traffic. I went into the Bentall Centre to kill time, and guess who was there, right outside Starbucks, pretending to talk on her phone?

Miriam Patel.

And she was wearing the teeniest, tiniest belly top and no coat, even though it was, like, minus three outside.

Me: (thinking, Whyyyyy are you everywhere?) . . .
Miriam Patel: (ending her pretend conversation) Oh, hi, Phoebe. Are you on your own? I'm meeting the girls at Starbucks. Feel free to join us.
Me: Oh, hi, Miriam. No, thanks. I'm going to the cinema with Polly and Tristan. (Why, oh why, did I even have to mention him?)
Miriam Patel: (scrunching up her face like she's sucked on a lemon) Really? Because you know what they say: Three's a crowd.

I know that she only says these things because she's trying to get a reaction, and I really wish she didn't annoy me so much, but she does. She makes me bilious. I hope beyond hope that she froze to death in her teeny, tiny top.

Unsurprisingly (because deep down, I knew) things got worse. From the moment we said hello, it was awkward-central with Polly and Training Wheels. How is it possible that two people who used to talk all day every day since the beginning of time suddenly have nothing to say to each other?

Polly was trying so desperately to start a conversation between the three of us, but all I could see in her huge, dark eyeballs was her silent apology for no longer loving me the most.

And that's fine.

I get it.

Things change.

But what happened next wasn't fine at all.

Turns out, Polly and Tristan didn't really want to watch the film but spend one hundred and twenty minutes snogging instead.

All I could hear in my left ear was wet, juicy, tongue-y kissing noises, and at one point, I swear she actually put her hand on his crotch, which, like, no!

I'm never going to forgive Polly for this.

Before Tristan, she never would have been that person. She never would have invited someone out only to then exclude them. She was the best person I knew. And now she's just like everyone else: self-absorbed and wanting to have sex, sex, sex.

When I got home, I went straight to my room and shut the door. Kate knocked a bit later to ask if I was OK or if I needed to stroke a cat. I told her I was fine, but I think she knows I'm not.

I'm not even sure what's upset me most: Polly reaching for

Tristan's crotch, or Miriam Patel being right about three being a crowd.

SUNDAY 21 JANUARY   #MEDECINSINTERNATIONAUX

Mum WhatsApped from Ankara.

She looked like shit already, and they're not even in Syria yet, but they're going tomorrow.

She said she doesn't know when she'll be able to WhatsApp next. Same old, same old, blah blah blah, yawn.

I'm not going to watch the news any more.

I mean, diseases spreading is one thing, same with earth-quakes, hurricanes, typhoons, erupting volcanoes, etc. But wars?

They flew drones around Aleppo, or maybe I should say around where Aleppo used to be when it was still an actual place with houses and shops and schools, because now it's just a pile of rubble. The place has literally been bombed to shit.

They showed a legless woman being wheeled down what once upon a time could have been a road in a shitty, broken wheelchair to a makeshift hospital that was basically just a room where people were lying on wooden planks.

Why are we doing this to each other?

And then it's on telly, and we casually watch it over dinner.

P.S. I think Polly knows Saturday didn't go well, because this morning she was like: 'Do you want to have lunch together?'

But I was like: 'Sorry, can't. I have to go to the library.'

I don't even know why I made that up, and I contemplated changing my mind for a moment, but then I saw her feeding Tristan carrot sticks, and I congratulated myself on my life choices.

I bought individual plastic wallets for my CVs.

Kate was like: 'A lot has to be said for presentation, Phoebe. Well done. Maybe also smile when you talk to people.'

OMG.

January must be the worst month of the year to go job hunting.

No one is looking for staff.

I went round the entire Bentall Centre after school, and in every single shop, they were like: 'Sorry, we just had to let all our Christmas temps go, so we're not recruiting right now.'

Whyyyyy?

I did the whole CV thing again in Wimbledon today.

At this rate, I'm going to need someone to drop dead the moment I'm sliding my CV across the counter.

Another complication is that a lot of people don't hire anyone under sixteen, which is really unfair, because I'm in the same year at school as all these people who are already allowed to work but don't want/need to.

On the way home, I walked past the charity shop, and I looked in the window to see if Kate was there, but she must have been in the back.

Alex was behind the till again, and he was chatting to Emma, who was holding an armful of blouses on hangers.

They caught me peeking in like a crazy stalker person, and Alex waved at me. I waved back, and then Emma gestured for me to come in, but I gestured like: *Sorry, I have to go.*

Maybe I should have said hello.

Mum messaged saying it's taking them forever to travel through Turkey. Apparently the weather is really bad, and their cars and vans keep getting stuck.

I told her I was looking for a job because the stupid cat got out.

FRIDAY 26 JANUARY   #BOXESTICKED

I gave my CV to Kate to have a look at, and she was just like: 'Yes, but no.'

Half an hour later, she emailed me this:

Phoebe Alexandra Davis
Curriculum Vitae
3 Rochdale Close, Wimbledon, London SW19 1AL
Phone: 07965500713,
Email: phoebead666@gmail.co.uk

Enthusiastic and experienced customer service professional who enjoys being part of a team. Strong work ethic, ambitious, goal oriented and quick to grasp new concepts and ideas. Able to work well on own initiative and can demonstrate high levels of motivation. Even under significant pressure, possesses ability to perform effectively. Reliable and punctual with exceptional organizational and customer service skills.

Currently looking for part-time employment on weekends.

Education

Kingston Academy

I am in Year Eleven and will sit my GCSEs in June. Next year, I am looking to going into sixth form to prepare for my A-level exams in Mathematics, Biology, Physics, English Literature and Language as well as History and Sociology.

Work Experience

Cancer Charity Shop, Wimbledon

I have been a regular volunteer for many months. My duties include sorting through donation bags, steaming and tagging clothes behind the scenes, as well as customer service on the shop floor. I thoroughly enjoy working with such a diverse clientele, and I am always looking to build a positive rapport with my customers.

References are available on request.

Me: I thought you're not supposed to lie on your CV.

Kate: We're stretching the truth, Phoebe. It's not the same.

Me: *Always looking to build a positive rapport with my customers?* I hate people.

Kate: You're the one who wants to venture out into the corporate world, pet, and let me tell you, there are rules. You need to walk the walk. You need to talk the talk. It may all be a big bucket of bullshit, but the only way to success is by ticking all their boxes.

Me: (looking at my CV) This ticks boxes?

Kate: (making ticks in the air) Tick, tick and bloody tick.

P.S. I'm not sure I want to tick boxes.

SATURDAY 27 JANUARY   #INCESTALERT

I tried to apply for jobs online today, but I ended up accidentally Instagram-stalking Emma. I've been thinking about her, but only because I basically don't get why she'd want to volunteer at that place. First I thought she was doing her Duke of Edinburgh, but Kate told me Emma's been there for months, and I think for the Duke of Edinburgh, you only have to be there for a couple of hours.

It took me ages to find her on Instagram.

Annoyingly her account is private, and all I can see is her picture, which is of her and what must be her boyfriend dressed up as Luke and Leia from *Star Wars*, which is a bit wrong, because Luke and Leia are actually brother and sister.

I wonder how long they've been together.

P.S. Emma looks amazing as Princess Leia.

P.P.S. I wonder who Luke is.

SUNDAY 28 JANUARY   #MYOWNBESTFRIEND

I asked Kate if she thinks it's OK Mum's always dumping me at her house, and she was like: 'I actually love it when you stay with me, Phoebs. So yes – it's better than OK.'

Then I asked if she thinks it's OK that Mum's currently en route to Syria of all places, and she said: 'Your mum's my best friend in the whole wide world, and I may not always agree with her, but I'm always on her side. Do you know what I mean?'

I don't.

And I'm not just saying that to be difficult.

Miriam Patel invited me to Jacob's party next weekend, and because I was standing with Polly and Training Wheels (who are now one singular entity because they are literally always attached) at the time, I was just like: 'Thanks – I'd love to come.'

Later, Polly said she thought I hated parties, but I was like: 'No, I don't.'

Which is a blatant lie, because there's literally nothing that repels me more.

Today at lunch, Miriam Patel went on and on about how she and Jacob are sleeping together, but aren't "official", and that that's totally OK for them.

And I hate to admit she has a point, but she does, because why should she have to be like Polly – all 'I love you, I love you, I love you' like a crazy person? Maybe Miriam just enjoys having sex. Everyone is different.

Then she got half a pine nut stuck in her braces, but I didn't tell her, and let her prance right into her geography presentation.

Tonight, Mum WhatsApped and was like: 'How's Polly?' And I was like: 'Brain-dead and floating in an oestrogen-induced delirium.' And Mum was like: 'Oh, don't be mean, Phoebs. It's a nice thing for her. Just wait until you fall in love.'

I was just like: 'I will never fall in love.'

And what a stupid expression that is in the first place: To *fall in love*.

Like you fall into a ditch or something.

Maybe people need to look where they're going.

THURSDAY 1 FEBRUARY   #WORSTNIGHTMARE

I told Kate I was invited to Jacob's party hoping she'd say I wasn't allowed to go, but of course, she was like: 'Great. I can drop you off and collect you if you like.'

I told her I'd take the bus because, let's face it, it's not like I'm going to be there for long.

I have nothing to wear, and everything I do have is covered in cat fur.

I hate my life.

Now that it's February, everyone has jumped on the bandwagon that is the pointless frenzy about Valentine's Day. I reckon Valentine's Day was only invented so people don't die of absolute boredom in winter.

After the Christmas sales, everyone's like: 'Now what?'

Enter: Saint Valentine. And off we go again, spending money on meaningless crap, chocolates that now have hearts on them instead of Father Christmas, and stupidly overpriced cards.

I actually saw a card that said, *Happy Valentine's to a Great Sister-in-Law*.

What does that have to do with anything?

Oh, and because love is in the air, the much-less-horny mother designer cat of the very-horny-escapee daughter designer cat is going in for the shag-fest.

Kate's decided to only take that one up to High Barnet now because the other one is most definitely already up the duff, and the dirty weekend costs, like, £500 per cat.

I wonder if you can buy shares in designer cat sperm, because Kate should.

In fact, I should.

SATURDAY 3 FEBRUARY   #PARTYHELL

I knew I'd have a terrible time at Jacob's, and I did.

If it's at all possible, I hate parties more than ever now that people have turned them into communal make-out sessions.

Tonight, we played this game called Seven Minutes in Heaven, which is actually seven minutes in the toilet.

Miriam Patel: (dressed like she's forgotten to put on actual clothes and looking at me specifically): 'I would just like to mention that not everyone in this room is sixteen and therefore old enough to be legally sexually active. That means intercourse, FYI.'

Me: (dressed in actual clothes) 'Intercourse. LOL.' (Because who says that?)

Miriam Patel: (giving me a death stare): . . .

Me: (considering her sky-rocketing levels of phenylethylamine): . . .

Anyway, I ended up spending seven minutes in the loo with Travis Monahan.

I suppose it was OK. Not that I would EVER have sex with him, because I basically don't even know him, and why would I want to snog a random person right next to a toilet? But we both like *Doctor Who*, so we talked about the latest series, and we agreed it was excellent.

When we came out, it was clear that no snogging/sex had taken place, and the only person who spoke to me all night after that was Annie, who also has no friends, although I think she's a bit more tragic because she never had any to start with, and she only gets invited because she brings booze (and nobody knows where she gets it from, which adds mystery, and people love that).

We sat on the sofa together and watched one happy couple after the other disappear into the toilet and reappear again seven minutes later.

Yawn.

Miriam Patel and Jacob went in together, and when they came back out, Miriam was all like: *Look at me, don't look at me*. And then Annie went: 'Miriam, come here.' And Miriam obviously thought that Annie wanted to hear details, but then Annie gently raised her hand to Miriam's face and casually picked a pube off of her cheek.

I was like: 'Euw, you have a pube on your face?' And you know what happened next? Instead of everyone going: 'That's disgusting – a pube was stuck to your face,' everyone went, 'OMG, how amazing – Miriam Patel had an actual pube on her face.'

I left thirty seconds later.

On the bus, I was thinking, you know, there I was, sitting with Annie, wishing for a millisecond that I was popular, but if I was the popular girl, I'd be the girl with a pube on her face.

Also: I can solve a complex mathematical equation, I know about the chemistry behind love and lust, and I have a deep understanding of the difference between *there*, *their* and *they're*. I don't want a medal or anything, but why are people being idolized for having pubes on their face?

Polly texted to ask how the party was, and I was going to be all hateful like: 'Maybe you should have gone instead of joining Tristan's family on a daytrip to his grandparents' house not even five weeks into your brand-new relationship.' But I ended up telling her the party was actually really good.

I don't know why I'm lying. It's not that I'm desperate to become best mates with Pube-Face Patel.

Miriam Patel has turned into some sort of celebrity after getting the pube stuck to her face, and Polly is still wandering around like a zombie looking for Tristan if she's not already latched on, so my goal today was to speak to no one at school.

At lunch, I went to the library to print off CVs again.

Then I sat on the floor behind the *Classics* (where nobody ever goes), trying to eat a packet of crisps, but Mrs Day busted me straightaway.

Mrs Day:	Phoebe Davis. Hiding?
Me:	(swallowing a giant not-fully-chewed Kettle Chip, almost slicing open my trachea) . . .
Mrs Day:	I was going to have a word with you anyway.
Me:	(coughing) I've done nothing wrong.
Mrs Day:	There's no eating in the library.
Me:	Everyone does it
Mrs Day:	And if everyone jumps off a bridge, do you jump off a bridge too?
Me:	. . .

I honestly thought I was in trouble for a minute, but turns out, she just wanted to tell me how pleased she was I decided to take 'mathematics' (who says that?) for one of my A levels.

Of course I'm going to do maths. I mean, it's easy, and I like that there's only ever one answer. Not like in English, where it's all *blah blah blah*, and if you're not a communist like Mr Harris, you get a shit grade.

On my way to history, I ran straight into Polly and Training Wheels, who were entangled in a tight embrace just by the first-floor toilets. Polly had her back to me, but Training Wheels looked me straight in the eyes and pulled her just that little bit closer.

I don't even care any more.

P.S. I wonder if Emma and Luke Skywalker are like that when they're together. Emma seems too grown-up to be that basic. But to be fair, so did Polly until it all went wrong.

TUESDAY 6 FEBRUARY   #GOODNEWSATLAST

Yes! I got an email from Dream Bear Factory inviting me to an 'audition' on Saturday.

I suppose *audition* is their happy-clappy word for *job interview*.

Bring it. Seriously, how hard can it be?

P.S. The designer cat's back from High Barnet and has been asleep ever since, totally sexed out. I can't even look at it.

WEDNESDAY 7 FEBRUARY

Kate told me not to make fun of Dream Bear Factory, even though they call a job interview an 'audition', and the email says: *Thank you* beary *much for your interest in dreaming with us.*

Mum's still in Turkey. I looked at a map because I was, like: *How long can it take to drive to Syria?* But Turkey is actually huge, three times the size of the UK to be exact.

Mum said they passed through a village today, and the locals offered them goat udders to eat, and all I'm thinking is: You could work at any London hospital, eat Pret, or itsu or Marks and Spencer's for lunch every day, sleep in a nice warm house, in a nice soft bed, spend time with your nice only child, and yet here you are trekking through shitty Turkey in the middle of winter eating goat udders.

I swear she thinks she's the New Messiah.

THURSDAY 8 FEBRUARY

I don't know what to wear to the Dream Bear Factory audition.

Kate told me to put on something 'bright and cheerful, maybe with unicorns'. *Now* who's taking the piss?

Everything I own is black featuring designer cat hair. I could always put on my school jumper, but that's just cringe.

I suppose I should ask Kate to drive me home-home so I can raid my closet. But to be honest, I don't even know what

I've got at home-home any more.

I could also go to Primark and buy something, but I hate Primark. Not because of child labour, but because the average customer appears to lose control of all motor functions, and when you go in there after school, everything's on the floor.

P.S. Child labour is also not OK. Obviously.

FRIDAY 9 FEBRUARY   #TICKTICKBOOM

Kate did a pretend audition with me earlier, in preparation for tomorrow. She's totally serious about it being serious, and even though she's usually crazy and scary, she got *very* crazy and *very* scary (and *very* Scottish).

She pretended to be Miss Dream Bear Factory, thanking me 'beary' much for my application. She even printed off my CV and had a pen at the ready.

Kate: Is it Phoebe Alexandra or just Phoebe?

Me: Just Phoebe.

Kate: All right, Phoebe. I'm going to ask you a series of questions. They're all pretty standard, but you're welcome to take your time answering them.

Me: OK.

Kate: (rolling every *r* in the most ridiculous way) Describe a time you had a disagreement with a fellow team member. What did you do to overcome it?

Me: I'm at school, so I don't really have team members.

Kate: (writing something down) OK. Tell me about a time you went above and beyond to meet a customer's expectations.

Me: I'm at school. I don't really have customers. I don't know how to answer that.

Kate: (writing something) Would you consider yourself a team player or do you prefer working on your own?

Me: I don't know.

Kate: What are you most proud of? Please elaborate.

Me: Oh my God, Kate — I don't know. These are stupid questions. Seriously, what do you want me to say?

Kate put her pen down and was like: 'For goodness' sake, Phoebe, just make something up. What did I tell you about ticking bloody boxes? Tick, tick, tick. Tell them what they want to hear. *How did you solve a disagreement with a fellow team member?* "Well, Miss Dream Bear Factory, I think communication is at the heart of a functioning working relationship." *Are you a team player?* "Yes, but I also enjoy working on my own." *What are you proud of?* "That time I helped a blind person across the road." Jesus Christ, pet, pull yerself together.'

At that point, she'd gone so Scottish that the BBC would have given her subtitles.

Then she said: 'Might I suggest you think long and hard about how you would answer those questions?'

I sat there for, like, an hour thinking: This is too extra.

When I stopped thinking, it was way too late for Primark, and I didn't want to ask Kate to drive me over to Kingston.

Shit.

SATURDAY 10 FEBRUARY   #PHOEBESGOTNOTALENT

8.00 a.m.

The internet says to dress 'smart casual' for job interviews, which apparently means fancy trousers or skirt, and a blouse. I don't own anything like that, apart from my school uniform.

Someone help me.

8.25 a.m.

I told Kate that I've got nothing to wear, and she was like: 'You're telling me this *now*?'

So I'm going to the charity shop with her to see if we can find me something from a donation bag.

You know that saying, *Life is hard, but it's even harder when you're stupid?*

Totally me right now.

7.14 p.m.

Things did *not* go well.

I ended up going to that ridiculous audition in a dead man's skinny-fit lilac shirt from M&S and my school trousers. I looked like an absolute dick.

When I got to Dream Bear Factory, it turned out that I wasn't the only person being 'auditioned'. There were, like, twenty people there, and they all looked as if they'd been up for hours doing their hair and make-up.

The store manager, a horrendous woman called Sandra, spoke in one of those high-pitched voices old people put on when they talk to babies.

Sandra (forcing a smile that gave me sympathy face-ache): 'Welcome, everyone, and thank you beary much [not even lying] for coming. There's quite a few of you, and unfortunately I only have two weekend positions to give away, but I wish you all the best of luck. Now, let's all introduce ourselves using a word starting with the first letter of our name, followed by our name. That's going to make it much easier for us to remember who we are. I'll start, and I am "Silly Sandra".'

In all my life, I've never wanted for the ground to swallow me up more. I didn't even listen to what anyone was saying, because I was trying to

a) think of my word, and
b) not think about how ridiculous that game was, because

Phoebe may start with a *P*, but you say it like an *F*, so whatever *P*-word I was going to choose would probably make it more difficult for people to remember my name.

When it was my turn, all I could come up with was 'Pointless Phoebe'.

The guy next to me was 'Marvellous Max', then there was 'Terrific Tiffany', and one girl was 'Beary Enthusiastic Bella' (aka Buttkiss Bella).

Next, we were given a guided tour of all the different stations of bear-making.

It's basically like a shit droid factory: Select the empty shell, take a handful of fluff, make a wish, shove it all in, sew it up, and that's £25. *Ka-Ching!*

FYI, isn't it absurd that we live in a world where a child in Africa or India is starving and, at that precise moment, a brat in Wimbledon is spending thirty quid on a chaise-longue and flip-flops for their stuffed Pikachu?

Anyway, after the stuffing malarkey, things escalated.

Silly Sandra: 'Now we're going to take five minutes each outside to engage with potential customers and actively invite them into our store this afternoon. Our mission as a company is to bring a child's imagination to life.'

Me: 'And make money for your shareholders.'

I only said it because it's true, but Silly Sandra did not appreciate my insightful comment at all, and her face contorted into the most ridiculous grimace yet, her fake grin forever expanding outwards. She didn't say anything though –

just clapped her hands together twice. Then she pulled a purple Easter bunny on roller skates out from behind the till. She gave the leash to Terrific Tiffany, who tottered off outside in her six-inch heels.

I was temporarily positioned at the fluff-stuffing station, and my brain was like: OK, you've been here thirty minutes, and already you want to kill yourself. But it could be worse, you could be Terrific Tiffany, looking like an absolute tit out there, interacting with a toy on roller skates while people from school are walking past. Next thing I know, Silly Sandra has called Terrific Tiffany back in, and goes to me: 'Your turn, Pointless Phoebe.'

I looked at Tiffany, at the leash, at the Easter bunny, at Silly Sandra, and I was just like: 'I don't think so.'

Then I walked out.

Terrific Tiffany let out an outraged, high-pitched yelp, but I knew that deep down, she wanted to be me right then.

I left the shop quite casually, but as soon as I passed the juice bar, I ran. I ran out of the shopping centre, down the Broadway, and back to the charity shop, where I collapsed into the flea-infested armchair.

Emma was in the process of tidying the mess I'd made earlier, when I'd emptied ten donation bags onto the floor looking for an outfit, and she looked at me like: *What the hell have you come as?* And I was just like: 'This isn't my shirt.'

Kate (totally in my face): 'Phoebe. Explain to me, precisely, what possessed you to apply for a job there in the first place, because I can't think of a single place on Earth that's less like you. Except, perhaps, Mothercare.'

Me: It's just a job.

Kate: But you do realize that once you get a job, you will actually have to *do* that job?

Me: Yes.

Kate: And you saw yourself stuffing teddy bears?

Me: Not really.

Kate: And what can you see yourself doing?

Me: Something where I don't have to talk to people.

Kate: And this is why retail was your obvious choice? You think those people get paid just to stand around? You think this is a joke?

Me: The woman's name was Silly Sandra.

Kate: And you think Silly Sandra has got nothing better to do than conduct group interviews on the busiest shopping day of the week for people who don't want to be there? The woman has a shop to run, sales targets to meet, bills to pay. You wasted her time today, and that's not OK.

Why is everything so hard?

I changed back into my hoody, and because I had nowhere to go, I stayed at the charity shop all day and alphabetized the book donations in the stockroom.

Now, that's something I can see myself doing. Menial, mundane, mindless. And I didn't have to speak to anyone. Except for Emma. I still can't get over the colour of her eyes.

They are the palest blue; it's insane.

Tomorrow, I'm going to make a new plan regarding the job situation.

It *cannot* be this difficult!!!

SUNDAY 11 FEBRUARY   #JOBSEARCHTAKE345219

Here are jobs I found in the *Wimbledon Gazette* that don't involve talking to the general public:

- Nanny (but I don't like children).
- Papergirl/boy (but I don't want to get up at 4 a.m.).
- Dog walker (but I don't want to pick up shit for a living).

I also looked if there were any jobs at the library, but the only 'jobs' they're advertising are voluntary, and let's face it, a job you're not getting paid for isn't a job. It's a hobby.

Maybe I should work my connections. Tyler Johnson works at that crap cafe by the train station; I could ask him if they're looking for anyone. I went in there once, and the woman literally didn't even acknowledge my presence when I paid for a Coke. I can do that.

Matilda Hollingsworth works at Hollister, but there's no point me even asking, because you have to be proper fit to work there. Like Matilda – oh, and Jason Goodman. I swear if those two had children, they'd be like the next master race (not in a Nazi way, though).

The Valentine's countdown is getting real.

Last year, I got a card from Polly, but since she still hasn't even wished me a Happy New Year, I reckon I'll be cardless this year.

I really hate that it bothers me, because you're not a better or worthier person just because someone felt pressured into buying you some meaningless crap.

5.43 p.m.

Should I make a card for Polly just in case she's got one for me?

I could use watercolours, but instead of water, I'll use my own tears. LOL.

Annie asked Polly if she and Tristan have had proper sex yet (i.e. intercourse).

Luckily Polly did the classy thing of saying: 'I'm sorry, Annie, but I don't discuss my sex life in public.'

Miriam Patel cut in immediately and was like: 'Oh, I know. It's so tacky – neither do I.'

How is she missing the irony?

Kate's such a weirdo. She gave me a massive handmade Valentine's card from the designer cats, including actual pictures of each one. She made the writing all different and crooked to try to make it look like the cats actually wrote it. (She's so insane.)

Dear Phoebe,
Will you be our Valentine?
Lots of love,
Mama Mimi

Sassy

When I got to school, Miriam Patel already looked like Miss Universe, holding bunches of flowers and 3 million cards.

And to think it's all because of one pube . . .

I didn't get anything from Polly. Lucky too, because the card I made her last night looks horrendous. I put it in the recycling when I got home. Maybe it can be a shiny new card this time next year, and the person getting it may even give a shit.

Tristan got Polly a gigantic teddy bear holding a heart that reads: *Girlfriend, I love you to the moon and back.* Surprisingly, instead of actually dying of

a) laughter or
b) embarrassment,

Polly grinned like an idiot all day.

I have thought about her reaction long and hard, and I've concluded that it must be the hunter-gatherer instinct that's somehow engrained in our DNA.

So Polly, in a very cavewomanish way, thinks that Training Wheels has hunted and gathered this huge love token (possibly also symbolizing a giant penis), and is thus worthy of her love and of fathering the next generation.

FYI, when I say 'our DNA', I mean *Polly's* DNA, because *I* have actually come out of the cave, crossed the valley, discovered fire, and invented the wheel, etc, etc.

6.54 p.m.

Looks like I'm going to spend tonight with a crazy Scottish woman.

Kate and I are going to the Goat Tavern for dinner because they've got a special Valentine's 2-4-1 curry night. I don't really fancy it, and it's clearly for couples, but Kate was like:

'You listen to me now, Phoebe. I'm not going to be punished for not having found love, and neither will you, so put on a frock, chin up, shoulders back, and let's go.'

I don't have a frock, so I'm wearing black skinny jeans as usual.

P.S. According to my research, Valentine's Day actually had nothing to do with love until love came into fashion in the eighteenth century, when lovers (not friends or distant relations) sent each other cards and maybe flowers. What this basically means is that the human race hasn't evolved since then. Nothing ever stays in fashion that long, except maybe God.

Seriously, everyone needs to calm down about love.

Besides, tomorrow, all Valentine's tat will be £1 and in the bargain bin. If nothing else, that should really put things into perspective.

THURSDAY 15 FEBRUARY   #GASTROPORN

The Goat has got to be in the bottom three 'romantic eating establishments' in SW19, coming in just ahead of Pizza Hut and KFC. Weirdly, though, everyone was dressed like they were on *Love Island*.

When our waiter brought the food, he was all like: 'Hi, I like your T-shirt. I'm a huge fan of the Stones.'

I honestly only wear it because it's a tongue that's constantly sticking out at people. It's the socially acceptable way of holding up your middle finger all day long. But I was like: 'Yeah – yay them.'

Kate was all: 'Wish I was wearing a Stones T-shirt. That boy is beautiful.' And I was like: 'Ew.' Because he's like twenty-five, and his biceps were bursting out of their short sleeves, and Kate's almost forty, and she was wearing a jumper that literally read: I Heart Cats.

When he came to collect the plates, Kate was squinting so badly trying to read his name badge that her eyes disappeared, and then she was like: 'James, this is my friend Phoebe. Phoebe, this is James.' He was like: 'Nice to meet you.' And then he shook my hand.

He also shook Kate's hand, and she took it as an invitation to tell him her entire life story: How she manages the charity shop; how I often come to help out (total lie, FYI); blah blah blah.

When we were leaving, James was like: 'See ya, Phoebe. Bye, Kate.' And outside, Kate was just like: 'Gosh! Beautiful people like that serving food is pure gastroporn.'

Gastroporn.

Oh my God.

She clearly fancied him.

FRIDAY 16 FEBRUARY   #COMPUTERSAYSNO

This afternoon, I failed the online application test for Boots. What a total joke. Like, an actual joke, because the questions were all like:

A customer walks into the store. Do you:

a) welcome them,
b) ignore them, or
c) immediately inundate them with questions and shove the latest No.7 wrinkle cream in their face?

I clicked on a), obviously, because I'm not an idiot, and I'm ticking boxes. But guess what? Computer says no, thank you.

And to think that Miriam Patel did her work experience at Boots.

I'm never shopping there again.

It's half-term next week, and Kate was like: 'Any plans, Phoebe?'

I told her I'm going to have another go at handing out CVs, because you never know, someone somewhere somehow may have croaked it.

SATURDAY 17 FEBRUARY   #EFFRIGHTOFF

Kate's been discussing my life with Mum, who started a WhatsApp-intervention conversation with me at six in the morning.

Mum: *Sorry!!!! I know it's early where you are, but I missed you.*
        (Lie.)
Me: *Hi.*

Mum: *How's the job hunt going?*

Me: *Not great.*

Mum: *How do you feel about that?*

Me: (thinking: What does it matter how I feel about it?) *Sucks.*

Mum: *I know you feel responsible for what happened with the cat, but it sounds to me like it was an accident, and I'm sure Kate doesn't expect you to reimburse her for it.*

Me: *I know.*

Mum: *I think you should concentrate on school, darling. GCSEs are going to be full-on, and they are rather important. Why don't you wait and get a summer job instead?*

Me: *I don't need to concentrate on school. School's fine.*

Mum: *I believe you. I'm just saying, you don't need to get a job.*

Me: *Fine.*

Mum: *How's Polly?*

Me: *Still in love.*

Mum: *Kate says she hasn't been around at all. That's not like Polly.*

Me: *She's in love with* Tristan, *so she's probably at* his *house.*

Mum: *Why don't you ask her to come over for a few days in half-term?*

Me: *Because I don't want to.*

Mum: *She's your best friend, sweetheart.*

Me: *Was.*

Mum: *I know it's hard when relationships change, but make sure you don't cut her off now. I know what you can be like, Phoebe, and just don't, OK?!*

Me: *OK.*

I only said OK because I needed her to go away, because how dare she be all 'I know what you're like' when she's not even here?

She *decided* to not spend this time of my life with me.

She *decided* there were more important things.

She *decided* that it is acceptable she may be killed on the job, just like Dad, and that I end up on my own.

And that's fine – it's her life; I get it – but don't WhatsApp me at six in the morning under false pretences with a load of textbook advice just so you can tick the 'Mum' box and sleep at night.

Today is one of those days that I wish I never have to see her again, because what's actually the point?

SUNDAY 18 FEBRUARY   #MOTHERS

I told Kate to never gossip to Mum behind my back again, and we had this super weird moment where we just stood in the kitchen looking at each other, and then Kate went all parenty on me and said: 'I know you're not happy, Phoebe, and I thought Amelia should know. She's your mother.'

I think mothers are overrated. Mine certainly is. She does nothing apart from caring about other people and making me absolutely furious.

I remembered that Polly did her work experience at Toni & Guy, and all she had to do was sweep up hair and make cups of tea. *That's* a job I can imagine myself doing. It's not like being one of the actual hairdressers all like: 'Blah blah blah, and where are you going on holiday this year?'

10.41 a.m.

I've decided to categorically never like a picture of anyone on social media who poses pretty much in the nude.

I'm happy that Chloe Brenton is #simplyloving her new @MacCosmetics Highlighting Set, but why does she have to have her tits hanging out?

What's wrong with everyone? Why are they so obsessed with being photographed nearly naked? Because do you really want to attract people into your life who like you purely for the way you look? Because Chloe is actually a nice person.

1.41 p.m.

I can't believe I'm printing off CVs so I can apply to sweep hair off the floor.

7.45 p.m.

I went to the charity shop this afternoon on my way back

from every hairdressing place in Wimbledon.

When I walked in, Alex and Emma were behind the till, and Kate and an old lady with a massively long white ponytail were standing in front of it, and they were all laughing so hard, they were literally dying.

When Kate saw me, she was like: 'Oh, Phoebe, perfect timing. Come here – you'll love this.'

Turns out someone had donated picture frames, but with their pictures still in them. They were all family snapshots – like at Chessington, in front of the Eiffel Tower, by the seaside – but the man's head had been cut out of all of them and replaced with the head of Mickey Mouse.

The old lady with the ponytail was wiping her eyes, going: 'I should threaten to replace Bill's head with that of Harrison Ford if he doesn't behave.'

'Or someone really cool like Barack Obama,' Emma said. And Pat went: 'Hmm, or George Clooney. I've always had a thing for George Clooney.' And then Alex went: 'Or Batman.' And they all lost it again.

Kate then introduced me to ponytail lady, whose name is Melanie. Apparently she and her husband volunteer at the shop when they're not travelling the world, but he wasn't there today because he had an eye appointment.

Instead of shaking my hand like any other old person would have done, Melanie kissed me on both cheeks, and then hugged me. She was like: 'I'm so pleased we're finally meeting. I feel like I know you already from hearing so much about you from Kate.' I was just like: 'Oh.' Because, TBH, I don't think anybody actually really knows me.

Emma was like: 'You're on half-term as well, then?'

Me: Yes.
Emma: Are you doing anything exciting?
Me: I'm trying to get a job.
Emma: Why don't you just work here?
Me: No – I mean an actual job.

OMG, why do I say these things? I didn't even mean it in a derogatory way or anything. All I meant was: I need to actually earn money. I can't work for free.

TUESDAY 20 FEBRUARY   #BIRTHDAYDATE

Kate asked if me and Emma would mind taking Alex out for his birthday on Thursday as it's half-term.

Apparently Kate usually takes him to Sprinkles, because ice cream is his favourite thing ever, but she was thinking that maybe he could socialize with people his own age for a change, which is obviously bullshit, because he's actually turning twenty-one. Apparently Emma was all for it, and I said OK as well.

I've never been out with anyone with Down's syndrome.

I've heard nothing from the hairdressing places. How depressing is all that?

When Kate got home, I was reading up on Down's syndrome in preparation for tomorrow's activities, and she was like: 'Phoebe. It's Alex. It's ice cream.' But I'm so glad I read up on it, because I knew nothing.

According to www.downwithfriends.org.uk:

> Down's syndrome is not a disease, and therefore people don't 'suffer' from Down's syndrome. A person who has Down's syndrome may be referred to as, 'Linda is twenty-four, and she has Down's syndrome.' People with Down's syndrome are all individuals, and Down's syndrome is only one part of the person.

One in one thousand people can have Down's syndrome, and the really interesting thing is that at the moment of conception, the very instant of sperm meeting egg, an extra chromosome joins the mix, and no one knows where it comes from.

THURSDAY 22 FEBRUARY   #HBDALEX

Emma is everything neither Miriam Patel, nor I, nor anyone else will ever be: entirely effortless perfection.

She had on a fake-fur coat, skinny jeans, and red high-top

Converse. She'd done nothing to her hair, apart from maybe brush it, and she wore zero make-up. I swear, I almost didn't recognize her, but she was walking up with Alex, and you can't miss him in his long military coat. I must have looked so incredibly basic in comparison.

When we sat down, Emma was like: 'Alex, what should I order?'

Turns out Alex knows the whole menu off by heart, including prices.

I told them I'd never been to Sprinkles, and Emma was like: 'I'm not sure we can be friends with her, Alex. What do you think?' And Alex was like: 'I don't know.' And then Emma was like: 'We normally only let fun people into the inner circle.' Alex laughed, but Emma just smiled and looked at me like she knows something I don't, and I swear I forgot what we were even talking about.

I suddenly couldn't read the menu like a normal person and ended up ordering a Banana Split, because it was the only thing I recognized.

Emma (who ordered Butter Popcorn Extreme) was like: 'Banana Split. Classic choice.'

Does she think I'm boring? What does 'classic' actually mean, anyway? So, of course, now I'm thinking that instead of researching Down's syndrome, I probably should have looked up the Sprinkles menu online.

And then Alex was like: 'The banana split was invented in 1904.'

Emma and I just looked at each other, and he went: 'You

can check.' And Emma was like: 'No, I believe you. I'm just fascinated by your knowledge.'

As am I. Plus, I love people who know random shit.

Emma was like: 'Have you opened your birthday presents yet, Alex?' And Alex was like: 'Yes, I got a KitchenAid.' Which apparently is a big deal, because he's majorly into baking, and when he's not at the charity shop, he goes to a college where he's learning how to do it professionally.

Emma: Lucky us. Now you can make us cake every week.

Alex: Not every week. I'm busy.

Emma: Just putting it out there.

Alex: I'll make a coconut cake.

Emma: I can't wait.

Alex: Phoebe, do you like coconut?

Me: Yes, thanks. My mum likes to bake. When she's at home. Which is never.

Alex: Where's your mum?

Me: Working in Syria.

Alex: Do you miss her?

Me: Not really.

Alex: I would miss my mum.

Emma: I think what she does is so cool.

Me: (shrugging) . . .

Emma: Really? You don't think that?

Me: I hate that I think she's dead every time the phone rings.

Emma: Yeah, I get that.

Me: No one gets it. Not really.

Emma: No, I absolutely get it.

Me: (thinking: But you don't) . . .

Alex: Where's your dad?

Emma: Alex—

Me: No, don't worry about it – it's fine. My dad's dead.

Alex: Sorry.

Emma: I'm very sorry.

Me: It's honestly fine. I never met him.

(Awkward silence. Everyone eating for a minute.)

Emma: Do you know much about him?

Me: Not really. My parents weren't like *together*-together.
         Mum only found out about me after he'd died.

Alex: That's cool. He died, and you were born. Death is
         not the end.

Me: Well, it was for him.

Alex: I don't think so.

Me: I do.

Alex: (to Emma) What do you think?

Emma: I think you should tell us more about your KitchenAid.
         Because it's your birthday, and today is about you.

Alex: I'm going to make ice cream in it.

Emma: That's cool.

Alex: Did you know that Neapolitan ice cream should
         actually be green, white and red? Because that's the
         Italian flag.

We sat at Sprinkles for almost two hours. Partly because Alex takes his time ordering and eating, but mainly because we had a really nice time.

Afterwards, I walked them back to the charity shop, and guess who we ran into outside Tesco?

Miriam Patel.

And Mrs Patel, who must've had a facelift since I last saw her, because no one can possibly be that surprised to see me.

Miriam: Oh, hi, Phoebe.

Me: Oh, hi, Miriam.

Miriam: I'm out shopping with my mum. What are you doing here?

Me: I'm just out with my friends.

Miriam: (looking at Emma and Alex, clearly judging) Oh, hi. I'm Miriam.

Me: Miriam – Emma, Alex. Emma, Alex – Miriam.

Emma

and Alex: Hi.

Me: Anyway, we've got to go.

Miriam: Yeah, we have to go too. Bye, Phoebe. See you next week.

Me: Yes, bye. See you next week.

And then I dragged Emma and Alex away, and I was just like: 'Oh my God, that was Miriam Patel. She's in my year, and she's horrendous. She's always really nice to your face, but as soon as you've turned your back, she'll slag you off.' And then Alex went: 'Takes one to know one,' totally suggesting I was doing the same thing. So I was like: 'Oh, shut up, Alex.' And then Emma started laughing, and she ended up laughing so hard that she literally cried.

Thing is: of course he's right. I was doing a Miriam Patel on Miriam Patel, which means I can sink no lower.

And now I'm really worried that Emma thinks I'm actually like that, because I'm not. I'm the least two-faced person I know. Fine, I often say things, and people are like: 'OMG, Phoebe, you can't say that.' But nine times out of ten, they were thinking it too.

11.44 p.m.

Found this, written by a person called Thomas Moore: *Eyes of an unholy blue.*

FRIDAY 23 FEBRUARY   #SOCIALMEDIAHELL

Yes!!! Instagram follow-request from Emma. She doesn't hate me. But I obviously can't accept straightaway, because that'll make me look proper desperate.

I'll wait until midnight.

I'll finally be able to stalk her.

Four hours to go.

Why is this so stressful?

8.59 p.m.

Bored.com.

Three hours to go.

11.10 p.m.

Watched crap telly with Kate and already fell asleep once.

Fifty minutes to go. I can do it!

SATURDAY 24 FEBRUARY   #LUKESKYWALKER

4.15 a.m.

I can't believe I fell asleep. Emma's gonna be like: *Why has she accepted my follow request at 2 a.m.?* Anyway, I did, and now I can't go back, and apparently I can't go back to sleep either.

The last time I went to such lengths to Insta-stalk someone was with Polly when she needed to know every last detail of Training Wheels' life.

Thing is, after spending all that time I'll never get back looking at Tristan's Instagram, I knew everything about him.

Miriam Patel's the same: nothing's secret, nothing's sacred, nothing's even slightly intriguing any more, because she has visually and verbally vomited her entire being onto the page.

Emma is the exact opposite. There's nothing there. She

only has 175 followers, which is way below average, and her last post is a picture of a Christmas tree from 25 December. I mean, I never really post anything either, but I've got 503 followers, and I don't even like people, nor do I ever follow-request anyone myself, because it stresses me out.

In order to find out who Luke Skywalker is, I went through all her followers and everyone she follows, but I can't see anyone who looks even remotely like him. Unless, of course, he's an ex, and she's unfollowed him, but then she wouldn't have that picture up any more, would she? It's also the first ever picture she posted, but he's not tagged in it. Lots of people have commented, but it's all like: *Lovely picture of you two*, or *Love, love, love*. So that's not really telling, either.

I'm giving up Insta-stalking for Lent, because the stress of not accidentally liking a picture from months ago (at three in the morning) or follow-requesting someone's random cousin twice removed is just too much. I mean, I love social media, but my God, I'm losing my mind.

And seriously, who's Luke Skywalker?

SUNDAY 25 FEBRUARY   #GETMEOFFINSTAGRAM

I Insta-stalked Emma again.

I think I need help. Social media addiction is an actual thing.

According to the internet, it affects 210 million people. That's 3.2 times the population of the UK!

But I swear, as soon as I know what Emma's all about, I'll stop.

Here are the updates: Emma's got three more followers since I last looked, all of them old, like forty, and there's more comments on the Luke and Leia picture, but again, nothing that gives me a single clue as to who that boy is or when the picture was taken.

And still no posts.

WHY?

Where does she go, and what does she do?

And then there are people like Miriam Patel, and I can give you a detailed account of every single mundane thought they've had over the past twenty-four hours, as well as the nutritional value of their breakfast, lunch and dinner.

Miriam Patel and I are over.

When I got to school, Polly was waiting for me by the gate, and she was like: 'Miriam Patel is telling everyone you're dating someone with Down's syndrome.'

Me: Did she actually say that?
Polly: She was like: Isn't it sweet that Phoebe is dating a guy who is suffering from Down's syndrome.
Me: (thinking: This is too good) . . .
Polly: Tristan knows someone with Down's syndrome.

OMG! Why do people always have to say things like that? 'Yeah, like, I know someone who's, like, disabled too, like . . .' Shut up!

So here's what I did: I waited. Until lunch, when I sat down at Miriam Patel's table.

Miriam: Oh, hi, Phoebe.
Me: Oh, hi, Miriam. Just FYI, Alex isn't my boyfriend.
Miriam: (clearly regretting her life choices) . . .
Me: He's a friend I know from Kate's charity shop. And also, people don't "suffer" (I actually drew speech marks in the air at that point) from Down's syndrome. They *have* Down's syndrome, which basically means they have an extra chromosome. The only thing they *suffer* from are ignorant fuckwits like yourself.

God, she's such a dick.

Tonight, when Kate asked me to sit down with her in the
kitchen, I was like: 'Who died?'

Kate: No one died – don't be daft. It's about your job hunt.
Me: I know it's not going well, but—
Kate: No, no – I'm not having a go. I wanted to make a
        suggestion.
Me: . . .
Kate: Your mother told me that you think you need to get
        a job because of me.
Me: Not because of you, but because of me. Because the
        cat is pregnant with illegitimate kittens, and my
        research has shown this means a financial loss of up to
        two thousand pounds for you.
Kate: (super Scottish) Och, don't be ridiculous. I'd never
        expect you to pay me anything because the bloody cat
        got out.
Me: . . .
Kate: But, if you feel like you need to make it up to me,
        which you really don't, and besides, you need to be
        focusing on your GCSEs, why don't you come and
        volunteer at the shop? I can't pay you, but I suppose
        we could always pretend.

Me: . . .

Kate: Look. You want a job, and I'm short-staffed.

Me: How many days would you need me?

Kate: Six, of course.

Me: . . .

Kate: Joking, you idiot. One or two afternoons. But only if it doesn't interfere with school.

Me: What days?

Kate: Any days you like. You can do Thursdays and Saturdays if you want to hang out with Emma and Alex.

Me: . . .

Kate: We can even pretend I give you ten pounds an hour.

Me: If I work every Thursday afternoon and Saturday all day, that would mean, like, twelve hours a week.

Kate: (clutching her chest) Which would be tremendously helpful.

Me: That means I have to work for you for sixteen point seven weeks in order to make up the money I owe you.

Kate: Is that a rough estimate, or did you just work that out?

Me: . . .

Kate: All right, clever clogs — but please don't think you owe me money.

Me: But I do.

Kate: Phoebe, you owe me nothing. Look, it's just an idea. You really don't—

Me:	I'm not doing the till.
Kate:	(snapping to attention) Back of house only.
Me:	I don't want to talk to customers.
Kate:	Naturally.
Me:	Or Pat.
Kate:	. . .
Me:	Or any of the other old people.
Kate:	What's wrong with talking to old people? You've met Melanie. She's a hoot.
Me:	(because, let's face it, I'm proper out of options) OK.
Kate:	(clapping her hands, then kissing my face) I love you! I love you! I love you!
Me:	Get off.

9.15 p.m.

I'm regretting my hasty decision already, and here's why:

Cons of working at the charity shop:

- Pat.
- Other hateful/crazy old people.
- Rummaging through the clothes of the dead.
- Rummaging through general household goods of the dead.
- Alphabetizing the books of the dead.
- The wee smell.

Pros of working at the charity shop:

• Emma.
• Alex.
• Repaying Kate the kitten money at an imaginary £10 an hour rather than slaving away for actual minimum wage in a job I hate.

Six to three, I shouldn't do it.

How do I go back and tell Kate no?

WEDNESDAY 28 FEBRUARY   #KITTENALERT

Both designer cats are preggers.

Kate texted me when she got back from the vet's.

'Congratulations! You're going to be an auntie.'

Fuck off.

In other news, Miriam Patel's still ignoring me. Turns out she didn't like being called a fuckwit.

She can go to hell.

And Polly can go to hell too, because today she actually said to me: 'You know, Phoebe, I think it's really cool you're hanging out with people from the charity shop.'

What are you even talking about?

Mum sent an email saying they're still in Turkey. I swear by the time they get to Syria, there'll be no one left who needs saving.

P.S. I'm going to the charity shop after work tomorrow.

THURSDAY 1 MARCH   #HNY

Polly still hasn't wished me a Happy New Year. It's now March.

This afternoon, I had my first official shift at the charity shop, despite the six-to-three majority against the endeavour. When I got there, Emma was already working. She goes to Wimbledon High, and it only takes her ten minutes to walk there.

Kate was like: 'I'm so glad you're here. We had our Easter card delivery this morning, and we need to get it out ASAP.'

There were ten huge boxes of cards containing approximately twenty-five thousand different variations on the Easter theme:

- Photograph of daffodils.
- Daffodils in watercolour.
- Daffodils in oil.
- Daffodils featuring a tree.
- Daffodils featuring a lamb.
- Daffodils featuring the Easter bunny.
- Daffodils featuring daffodils.
- Daffodils featuring daffodils featuring daffodils.

I had to fill three spinners with cards, and I couldn't shove them in just anywhere (even though who actually cares?) because I had to follow a plan they'd sent from the cancer charity's head office, and it took me, like, three hours.

So at one point, I was like: 'How is it there's six of us, and yet I'm the only one dealing with this?'

Emma said that she did Christmas cards and had told Kate that if she ever made her do cards again, she'd never come back. And Alex doesn't ever do cards because, according to him, he's a 'customer service specialist' and therefore *must* be on the till.

Melanie and her husband Bill – who, FYI, is one hundred per cent hilarious and wears brightly coloured corduroy trousers – were also there, and Melanie was like: 'Oh no, darling. I'm not here for that.' And then Bill said: 'And I've got bad eyes, so they all look the same to me.' Funny, because he could see the tiny price labels just fine that he

a) wrote on in tiny writing, and
b) gingerly attached to the equally-as-tiny tie labels on the back of the ties.

Pat was off sick, which initially made me happy, but I quickly realized that she blatantly called in sick because *she* didn't want to do Easter cards either.

It turned out to be the worst job on the planet ever.

I'm not being funny, but maybe communism is a good idea after all. There's a lot to be said for people not having a choice.

Kate was so happy I was there to do the shit job nobody

wanted to do that she got us all Starbucks. I had a vanilla latte as usual, and Emma was like: 'I didn't take you for a vanilla latte kind of woman.' And then she winked at me.

Is the vanilla latte a stupid drink?

Emma got a chai latte with soy milk. Maybe I'll get that next time.

On the way home, I asked Kate why Emma volunteers at the shop, and Kate was just like: 'Why don't you ask her yourself? I'm sure she'll tell you.'

Yes, well, I'm sure she'll tell me too, because I'm sure it's not actually a very interesting story, except it is now that Kate's made a drama out of it.

I really wish life was a lot more straightforward.

What's Emma all about?

9.08 p.m.

And just one more thing about Emma: I've never known anyone with bigger, more beautiful eyeballs.

According to the internet, blue eyes are a mutation that occurred between 6,000 and 10,000 years ago. Until then, all humans had brown eyes. Also, only 8 per cent of the world's population has blue eyes, and there actually is no blue pigment in blue irises, and they only look blue the same way the sky looks blue but isn't.

When Kate got home tonight, she was like: 'James came to the shop today.' And I was like: 'Who's James?'

Kate: You know James.
Me: . . .
Kate: *James* James. Beautiful James. From the Goat.

Turns out Gastroporn James visited the charity shop and was casually browsing the non-fiction book section when Kate recognized him.

Apparently working at the Goat isn't his life. He's at Wimbledon College of Arts, where he's doing a BA in Fine Art, and he's twenty-three. Kate said she asked him to volunteer for her because she's got a chronic volunteer shortage, and he said he'd think about it. I swear if he starts working at the charity shop, I'm never setting foot in there again, because Kate would be so gross as she clearly fancies him, and I don't need to be subjected to another couple being all cringe, kissy and coupley right in my face.

SATURDAY 3 MARCH   #THECANCERSHOP

Pat was back at work today. She sat on her usual chair by the big table pricing bric-a-brac, and I swear she looked me up and down like three times. I only glared at her. I wish I knew why she hates me.

My first job was sorting the Easter card spinner, because apparently people are

a) too blind, and
b) too stupid to put the cards back into their correct slots.

And, of course, the whole time I was trying to sort them, people were spinning the spinner round and round, taking out cards, and putting those back incorrectly too.

I was literally like: 'Please ask for assistance if this is beyond you.'

Afterwards, I had a lesson in how to use the clothes steamer, which is basically a massive industrial strength iron. It boils water like a kettle and then blows it out through a nozzle, which you use to run over the clothes to take the creases out. Sadly, it doesn't make anything smell better, but Emma was just like: 'For tough jobs, there's this –' and she spritzed Febreze – 'fragrant floral freshness.'

I was just like: 'Now it smells of public toilet.' And Emma went: 'Hmmmmmm, delicious.' And she smelt the crusty armpit of the shirt we were steaming, and we laughed.

Pat didn't speak all morning, and she seemed genuinely inconvenienced that Emma and I were having a nice time. When she finally snapped out of it, she was like: 'Phoebe, I hear your mother is in Syria at the moment.'

Me:	Yes.
Pat:	Kate says she's helping to build a hospital?
Me:	(thinking, why are you asking me this when you already know the answer?) Yes.
Pat:	She's ever so brave.
Me:	. . .
Pat:	And your father was ever so brave too. You must miss him.
Me:	Not really.
Pat:	(jaw literally hitting the table) . . .

I'm sorry, but I really hate it when people say shit like that. It's like saying: 'Oh, it must be so difficult living without that third arm you never had.'

I'm really annoyed that Kate can tell the whole world about *my* life, but when I ask one thing about Emma, she's all like: 'Oh, sorry – I can't possibly open my big Scottish mouth.'

Maybe I should tell Kate I don't want to work for her after all.

You know what they say: *Don't shit where you eat.*

SUNDAY 4 MARCH   #WWW.HELL

Still no posts from Emma I could like. A post I chose *not* to like was Polly's: *Lazy Sunday with the boy*, and a picture of their feet sticking out from under a fluffy blanket. I can't even.

I spent an hour trying to WhatsApp call Mum, but the connection was so bad, we had to give up.

Kate was like: 'I'm sorry, Phoebe.' But I was like: 'It's not your fault. Plus, I don't actually care.'

Kate looked at me, and she was like: 'You do care, Phoebe. Amelia's your mum.'

I really don't, though. Mum only calls because she loves to hear the sound of her own voice. I get it, the whole ticking-boxes-at-work thing – but ticking boxes at home? Forcing conversation with people just because you're related? I don't think so.

Teacher training day tomorrow, so I'm going to the charity shop.

If you're rubbish at telling lies, you shouldn't do it.

Polly 100 per cent never lies to me because

a) she knows I can always tell immediately, because her left eyelid twitches, and her voice changes, and

b) because she's always like: 'Lying to you would be like lying to myself.'

Also, if you insist on being all hush hush about something, but it's making you feel guilty, and you have therefore decided to rid yourself of that guilt at some point in the future by telling the truth, why aren't you just being honest in the first place?

People are pathetic.

So today I found out that Mum has never told me the whole truth about Dad.

And, of course, just like every other vital fact about life, like periods, penises, and how to assemble IKEA furniture, I had to learn it from Kate. Because my mother sucks at being a mother.

Apparently – and rather disappointingly, if I'm honest – not sharing details of my father's demise with his child (!) was a joint decision between my crap mother and my crap godmother.

But, of course, they were going to tell me one day . . .

They just figured that finding out I've been lied to since always would be so much less disappointing than having known the truth from day one.

My life is literally one of those talk shows where people find out family members/loved ones have been keeping secrets from them, and at first everyone's shouting, but in the end everyone's crying. Or leaving.

So this morning, Kate and I had to go the charity shop early because someone was coming to service the fire alarms.

We stopped at Starbucks to get coffee.

Kate: (yawning) Remind me why I've chosen to run a charity shop?

Me: Because you didn't want to be a trauma nurse any more?

Kate: (rubbing her eyes) Oh, yes. Of course.

Me: Why did you give it up?

Kate: (shrugs) Many reasons.

Me: Name one.

Kate: I couldn't do it any more.

Me: Why?

Kate: I couldn't do it any more.

Me: What, you woke up one day and were like: "OK, that's it"?

Kate: Yes. I woke up and was like: "OK, that's it."

Me: You're lying.

Kate: And what if I am? It's seven in the bloody morning.

Me: So something happened.

Kate:	Phoebe. Things always happen when you're a trauma nurse. And they're never good. Especially in a war.
Me:	So tell me.
Kate:	(looking at me like it's on the tip of her tongue, then breathing out, and in again) I'll tell you one day, Phoebe.
Starbucks person:	(shouting, even though we were the only customers and standing right there) One black Americano, and a soy chai latte for Kate.
Kate:	Thanks.
Me:	(holding the door open for her) Have you noticed that you don't treat me in a consistent manner?
Kate:	Whatyaonaboutnow?
Me:	One minute, you talk to me about ticking boxes and cat sex; and the next minute, you're like, *Oh, no, Phoebe. I can't possibly share this information with you.*
Kate:	(stopping in the middle of the pavement, then pulling me into the alleyway that always smells of piss just between the pet shop and the pound shop): OK, Phoebe. So, first of all, not everything is about you. Maybe, on this occasion, I'm not ready to share information with you, because even though I am an adult, I am a person with feelings. And, second of all – fine, I'll bloody well tell ya.
Me:	. . .

Kate:	I watched your father die.
Me:	. . .
Kate:	I've watched many people die, but this was different, because he was my friend. And your mum loved him, and I couldn't save him.
Me:	(piss alley literally spinning) . . .
Kate:	I'm sorry. I shouldn't have said anything . . .
Me:	(piss alley still spinning) . . .
Kate:	I'm so sorry, Phoebe. I . . .
Me:	(Kate also spinning) . . .
Kate:	(reaching for my free hand) I suck. I'm sorry.
Me:	(pulling away my free hand) Don't touch me.
Kate:	Phoebe—
Me:	And don't talk to me.

I left her standing in piss alley and walked on ahead to the shop where I waited for her to come and open up. I think I was too confused to throw a tantrum. Or run away. It was totally pathetic.

Kate eventually caught up with me, unlocked the door, and I went straight to the back and started sorting clothes. When the fire alarm guy came and was like: 'Hiya, you all right?' I was just like: 'Not really.'

Later on, Pat was like: 'Have you fallen out with Kate?' And I was like: 'Yep.' And I swear she looked pleased.

I can't believe nobody has ever said anything.

The one good thing about it is that there's genuinely no one left who could disappoint me now.

Kate just told me the whole story.

She was outside my locked door like: 'I'm sorry we never told you, and I'm sorry I blurted it out like that. It was a very difficult time, and we don't like to talk about it. Please don't tell your mother I behaved like a five-year-old. I'll do that myself. I'll email her in a minute. Phoebe?'

I was like: 'Fine.' And I opened the door.

I knew Dad died when he worked at a hospital in Iraq and it got bombed, but I never knew Kate and Mum were there too.

Kate said she was still in the building the doctors and nurses lived in, and my dad had just left to go across to the hospital where Mum was already working.

Kate said the thing with bombs is that you don't hear them because of the speed at which they are dropping. So suddenly there was this insane explosion, buildings were shaking and collapsing, and everyone was thrown to the ground.

Kate said that she ran out into the courtyard, and that most of the hospital building opposite had been flattened, and that people were screaming and running, and apparently all she could think was: 'Shit, Amelia's in the hospital.'

She ran across, and then she saw my dad lying on the ground.

She said a big piece of roof had blown straight into his stomach and that he was bleeding out so fast that he was already lying in a puddle of his own blood by the time she got to him.

She said that she thinks that he knew he was going to die.

And she said that he probably knew that she knew, and so she just knelt down beside him and held his hand.

Kate said it was the most horrendous moment of her life, and that the whole thing was over in less than thirty seconds, but that she remembers it like it was hours and hours.

Me: Why did they bomb a hospital?

Kate: (shaking her head) Wars, Phoebe. You can't imagine what it's like — you just can't. People become evil.

Me: Did Dad say anything before he died?

Kate: (shaking her head again) No, pet, he didn't.

Me: What did you say to him?

Kate: (shrugging) I . . . Gosh. I think I told him not to worry about anything.

Me: I'm sorry.

Kate: (hugging me) No, I'm sorry, Phoebe. He was your dad. And he was a wonderful human. Just like you. And it's not fair.

Kate said fifteen people died in the bombing.

Mum was knocked out and suffered a head injury. She was evacuated to Cyprus, and Kate went with her. That's where they told her she was pregnant with me.

Kate resigned as soon as they returned to London.

Dad's body was flown to his family in Tel Aviv, where he was from. Kate said that Mum didn't speak to anyone or do anything for five months. When I was born, she decided to say on the birth certificate that my father was 'unknown', because she couldn't deal with it.

I've thought about this, and it's such a typical Mum thing to have done, isn't it? Just like always, it was all about her. She didn't even consider that maybe Dad's parents would have liked to have known about me, because to be honest, that probably would have been a pretty big deal when your own child's just died. And Mum obviously didn't care at all about me either (standard), and the fact that I actually deserved better than to have an anonymous, dead father.

I asked Kate if she thinks Dad's family might want to know about me, and she said that she doesn't know how Mum would feel about trying to contact them, but that she'd back me up all the way if I wanted to.

She told me my dad was the funniest person she'd ever met, and that I've inherited his 'crazy' sense of humour. She said he was very warm and welcoming, but that I hadn't inherited that trait at all (rude).

I was never really interested in my dad.

I suppose because I never saw him as an actual person.

But now I do.

I'm glad that he was funny.

I wonder if he'd like me.

Imagine if he'd had a Facebook account. I could be stalking him right now.

According to the internet approximately 20 million dead people are still on Facebook. Not literally, obviously, because they're dead. But just imagine I could see pictures of Dad, befriend his family, check what he liked to eat for lunch, what films he watched at the cinema, where he went on holiday . . .

P.S. I never thought about it before, but I'm actually really sorry he died.

TUESDAY 6 MARCH   שלום#

Tonight, Kate and Mum WhatsApped each other, and Kate told her about telling me about Dad.

I'm glad it's all out now.

I'm glad because, in a way, people only become real people when we hear a story that features them. All my life, I've been like: My dad's dead. He worked as a war doctor, and he got killed before I was born.

And now I think I'll be more like: My dad was called Ilan, and he was from Tel Aviv. He was a war doctor and died when a hospital he was working at near Mosul was bombed. We never met, but apparently I'm just like him. Without the beard.

Kate was like: 'Phoebe, ask me anything you like about him. I'm sorry we've been so weird all those years.'

Me: So my dad was Jewish?
Kate: Yes.
Me: But I'm not.

Kate: I don't know – you tell me.

Me: Ha ha.

Kate: Not by birth, no. Jewishness is passed down by the mother. So I suppose you're only half Jewish.

Me: And he spoke Hebrew?

Kate: (looking at me like I'm an idiot) Yes. Him being an Israeli person, who was born and raised in Israel, and went to medical school at the University of Tel Aviv, he did in fact speak Hebrew.

Me: I think I should learn Hebrew.

Kate: Phoebe, if you want to learn Hebrew, I will personally finance your studies.

(But then I googled it and, oh man, have you seen the writing? *Hello* is also *hello*, which is easy, but it's spelled like this: שלום.)

Me: Am I more like Mum or Dad?

Kate: You, pet, are the best of both.

Me: Hashtag cliché.

Kate: All right, stroppy. Let me tell ya. Your beautiful eyes are your dad's, as is your quick wit and often questionable sense of humour. From Amelia, you've inherited the ability to take no shit. But your clever brain is all me. As are your good looks. And your luscious hair. And—

Me: Oh, shut up, Kate. I was being serious.

Kate: (clutching her chest) I'm being *very* serious. Nature, nurture, Phoebe.

Me: . . .

Kate: (grabbing me and kissing my face like a thousand times) You, my darling, are the perfect combination of those two.

Me: Why did we never talk about Dad?

Kate: Sometimes things happen that are so big that it becomes impossible to find the right words. And it's not that your mum doesn't want to speak about it. I honestly think she can't.

Me: . . .

Kate: But let me tell you, Phoebe, your dad was a wonderful man.

Me: I'm sorry you lost your friend.

Kate: Not as sorry as I am that you two never got to meet each other.

Me: . . .

Kate: (kissing my face again, then holding me too tight, laughing into my hair) His English was perfect, but it was never *Hello* – it was always *Shalom*.

Me: Maybe I should greet people like that. Being half Israeli and all.

Kate: But warn your mum before you say it to her.

Me: . . .

Kate: She loved him. Maybe she still does.

9.32 p.m.

Shalom [exclamation]:

Used as salutation by Jews at meeting or parting, meaning 'peace'.

10.00 p.m.

I think I may want to find Dad's family.

I mean, it'll probably give them a heart attack, but wouldn't you want to know if your dead son/brother/bff had a child somewhere? I get that Mum's upset, but not everything can be about her.

WEDNESDAY 7 MARCH #THATSGREATPHOEBE

When I saw Polly at school, I was like: 'Shalom.' And she was like: WTF? So I told her that, since Dad was Israeli, I'm going to find out a lot more about their culture, and that I was thinking of learning Hebrew (which is bullshit, because I've already decided that I won't actually be doing that).

Polly was just like: 'That's great, Phoebe.'

I don't know what I expected her to say to that, but this was such a non-reaction. I swear if I'd been like: 'I'm thinking of throwing myself under a bus.' She'd have been like: 'That's great, Phoebe.'

She just doesn't care, and I hate that, and I hate that I hate it, because *I* want to not care as well.

The fact that Miriam Patel is still basically ignoring me because of me calling her a fuckwit totally doesn't bother me. On the contrary – it's making my life a hundred times better. But Polly's indifference is making me want to be sick.

How can a boyfriend replace a best friend?

P.S. I just googled the above question, and the answer is: A boyfriend *cannot* replace a best friend because

a) you need your best friend to talk about your boyfriend;
b) your best friend is objective when you are not, and
c) boyfriends are temporary, but best friends are for life.

Doesn't Polly realize any of this?

P.P.S. Life would be so much easier if we didn't have feelings. Like Data in *Star Trek*. I know he's not an actual person, but an android, but he's a proper genius until Geordi installs the emotion chip, at which point Data basically breaks.

I'm really trying to not have feelings, but when I look at Polly and I think that I don't know her any more, some fragments of emotion literally eat their way through the iron shield around my soul. Like acid, all burning and stinging.

This afternoon, a customer complained to me that our selection of Easter cards lacked those featuring Jesus on the cross. She then went on ranting about how even Easter eggs don't say *Easter* any more but are now labelled *chocolate* eggs, and how political correctness has gone too far, because at the end of the day, this is still 'our' country.

I'm not being funny, but unless once upon a time Jesus laid a chocolate egg, I really don't know what that woman was even talking about.

I wish I'd said something clever, but because I was so shocked by her casual racism, I ended up not saying anything.

Gastroporn James came to the shop this afternoon, and here's my question:

Do people think they look good when they're flirting?

Because Kate looked like she had nits, forever running her fingers through her hair.

Emma and I were watching them for ages, and then Emma went: 'He is very good-looking, isn't he?'

I was going to ask her about Luke Skywalker then, but I didn't.

Now, I feel physically weighed down by all the words I didn't say today.

My life would be so much easier if I wasn't this awkward.

FRIDAY 9 MARCH   #ITSAMADWORLD

I just spent an hour looking at Emma's Instagram trying to figure her out.

Maybe I should google her.

11.55 p.m.

Googled her. Nothing.

SATURDAY 10 MARCH   #LIFESUCKS

I wonder what Polly is doing. How is she not missing me? Half of the time, I can't work out if I'm sad or just offended. How can ten years of friendship have been this inconsequential?

It's not even that I feel the need to tell her all about Dad, but it would be nice to just go and get Starbucks together. Thing with Polly is, she always has something to say, and sometimes, when I don't feel like talking, which I admit is often, she'll just read me something boring from the *Metro*. Or she'll pretend to be doing the Sudoku, but because she hates it, and doesn't understand how numbers work, I end up doing it all for her.

I hate that my life's so shit.

And I know that I have sort of made new friends, but I can't exactly ask Emma if I can sit with her in Starbucks in silence and do a Sudoku.

I reckon I could ask Alex, though.

But he's got the busiest social life out of everyone I know, plus I don't want to force myself on to people.

It's Mother's Day tomorrow.

Emma says they're driving down to Brighton for the day to go shopping and have lunch. Mum and I have never done anything like that. I mean, not that I want to – I'm just saying.

SUNDAY 11 MARCH   #HAPPYMOTHERSDAY

I never really thought about it before, but Mother's Day is actually totally offensive to people who haven't got mothers. Like Valentine's Day is offensive to single people.

Every Happy Mother's Day card/bouquet/selection of pralines is literally laughing in your face going: *You've got no one to give me to.*

I suppose I should have gotten Kate something.

Nature was all in my face too, with daffodils and birds and so much sunshine that my retinas ached.

Kate and I went out to have a pretend Mother's Day dinner at the Goat, and because Gastroporn James wasn't working, Kate was like: 'Well, they've just lost five stars on their TripAdvisor rating.'

P.S. Not looking forward to school tomorrow.

It's all about GCSEs now, which is so stressful because

a) the teachers are losing their minds over it,

b) the parents are losing their minds over it, and

c) everyone else is consequently also losing their minds over it.

And I know GCSE stands for General Certificate of Secondary Education, but it really should stand for Great Compulsory Scholarly Evil, because how is it not evil to make us take up to two exams a day for, like, six weeks?

Magda Jennings said that her cousin, who's Italian and lives in Italy, doesn't have to do GCSEs at all. Apparently they have quizzes and three main exams in every subject, but spread over the year, and the average is your overall grade. Which is so much fairer. Because what if you happen to have a really bad week in life, and all the important GCSEs happen to be in that exact week? Like: What if you're 100 per cent hormonally challenged because you're on your period, or you feel like shit because you've got a cold, or a headache that won't go away? All exams that week could potentially be ruined, indicating that you suck, which isn't true.

P.P.S. I hadn't actually really thought about it, but I just worked out that I'll be taking twenty-seven exams in six weeks.

And yes, they may be idiotic, because you mainly have to just learn things off by heart without needing to understand what they actually mean, but twenty-seven exams in six weeks?

It's cruel.

Interesting development with Polly today.

She asked me if I wanted to go to Starbucks with her after school tomorrow.

I was like: 'Yes, sure, why not – I'm not working tomorrow.' And she was like: 'I didn't know you got a job.' And I was like: 'Oh, didn't I tell you? (Obviously, I hadn't.) I work at Kate's charity shop.'

I can't wait to see what she wants. Does she finally miss me, or is she feeling super guilty for being such a shit friend?

I'm sure all will be revealed.

I don't know what I was thinking, but I honestly thought Polly wanted to see me because she missed me, but it turns out she wanted to see me because of her.

I suppose I should at least be a little bit flattered because Tristan wasn't there and literally hanging off of her.

When we got to Starbucks, Polly ordered her usual, and I was like: 'Soy chai latte to have in, please.'

Polly was like: 'Since when do you drink that?' And I was like: 'Since always.' Which was obviously a massive lie.

We sat on our favourite brown leather sofa, and for, like, a millisecond of a moment, things weren't even awkward at all, but more like we'd been teleported back to a year ago when we were still perfect.

Then this happened:

Polly: It's about Tristan.

Me: (thinking: Are you fucking kidding me?) . . .

Polly: The sex isn't working.

Me: Are you fucking kidding me?

Polly: I know! How's that possible? We've got so much chemistry, and I really, really want it, but when we're doing it, nothing, like . . . happens.

Me: No. I mean, are you fucking kidding me wanting to talk to me about this? You don't call or text or speak to me unless in passing for, like, three months – you never even wished me a Happy New Year, FYI – and *now* you ask to spend time with me so you can tell me your boyfriend is shit in bed? What did you expect from a guy who doesn't know how to ride a bike?

Polly: Phoebe—

Me: No! I'm leaving. I don't have the brain capacity to deal with your crap sex life right now. Why don't you talk to Tristan? You talk to him about everything else.

And then I left.

Kate made us jacket potato with baked beans for dinner, but I literally felt sick. She tried to feed me two forkfuls, but I told her I'd vom if she made me eat more.

I can't deal.

11.47 p.m.

I think it's great Tristan has no clue what to do with his penis/ mouth/fingers.

I think I'd actually hate him more if he was orgasm-central.

WEDNESDAY 14 MARCH   #TALKTOTHEHAND

I'm still so irritated.

This morning, Polly was like: 'Phoebe, I'm sorry about yesterday. It's just tha—' And I was like: 'I literally don't want to know.'

And then I walked away from her.

Because her drama is so irrelevant.

There's war, famine, social injustice, climate change, and all everyone wants to talk about is sex. And then when they're finally having it, they don't shut up about it either, because apparently it's not actually as brilliant or life changing as they thought it would be.

Yawn.

And another thing: Polly can do something about that. She can talk to Tristan, but she doesn't, and if people don't even fix the things they *can* fix, how are we ever going to fix the big things?

Rant over.

Today, Emma suggested we should get more creative with the good/shit donations. She was like: 'Why don't we choose an item to be the "donation of the week" every week?'

Kate: Elaborate.
Emma: Something either cool, crap, or cringe. And we all have to upsell it.
Me: Like the picture frames with Mickey Mouse man?
Emma: Exactly.
Kate: Who doesn't need one of those in their life?
Emma: Exactly.
Kate: I think it's a brilliant idea, pet.

Emma and I then chose the chocolate fondue set as our first official donation of the week. Alex is 100 per cent on board with it too, and I swear he spent the rest of the afternoon asking every customer who came to the till: 'Can we also tempt you with a chocolate fondue set?'

Apparently we could not.

FRIDAY 16 MARCH   #PUKE

The cat threw up on my shoes.

I left it for a while, hoping the other cat would eat it, but it didn't, and because Kate wasn't home yet, I had to clean it up myself.

Bleugh!

It's such a good metaphor for my life at the moment. Everyone's literally vomiting all over it.

P.S. I'm even looking forward to going to the charity shop tomorrow.

SATURDAY 17 MARCH   #THEWALKINGDEAD

Today, I overheard Pat trying to bitch to Emma about me.

I was about to walk into the stockroom when I heard them whispering, and so I stood outside the half-open door and tried to listen. And what do you know? Not three seconds later, I heard Pat say my name.

Pat: Why does she have to dress like that? All black and skulls and spooky. It's like . . . the walking dead.

Emma: (LOLing) *The Walking Dead* is a TV show about zombies, Pat.

Pat: A witch, then.

Emma: Pat!

Pat: You know what I mean?

Emma: No, not really. Everyone's got a different fashion sense.

Pat: I'm sorry, but I think that girl is odd. She's always been like that, even when she was little. Quiet. But in an odd way — you know what I mean?

Emma: No, still no. But maybe you only think that because she's put a witchy spell on you?

Pat: . . .

Emma: (LOLing again) I think she's very nice. Maybe she's just a bit sad at the moment because her mum's all the way in Syria.

Pat: Yes, well, that can't be easy. Regardless—

At that point I was like: I don't need to hear another word out of that awful woman's mouth. And so I walked in all like: 'Good morning!' (but extra chirpy).

And, on the subject of everybody having a different fashion sense, some of the girls in my class must be under the impression they get more attractive the less they wear, which is just untrue. Emma was wearing a massively-too-big-for-her multi-coloured jumper and skinny jeans, and her hair was tied up in two buns that were totally askew, and she looked beautiful.

I wish I was naturally pretty. Maybe if I was, I wouldn't want to constantly brush my hair into my face. And then maybe I wouldn't look so 'spooky' either.

God, I hate Pat.

Bleugh!

I swear if I could put a spell on her, I would, which is what I spent the rest of the day imagining.

It was nice of Emma to stand up for me, though. Some people always agree with what other people are saying, even when someone's talking shit. Miriam Patel is a prime example. She's so desperate to be liked, she'd slag off anyone.

Maybe that's why she doesn't have a BFF.

I mean, I don't have a BFF any more either, but even though I hate Polly and the way the synapses in her brain seem to be backfiring at the moment, I'd never slag her off behind her back.

I know I've said it before, but I'll say it again: Compared to everyone else, Emma is pure class.

SUNDAY 18 MARCH   #THEBIRDSANDTHEBEESANDTHENSOME

This afternoon, Kate and I decided to binge watch all the original *Star Wars* movies.

Halfway through, she put one of the preggers designer cats on me.

Kate: Stroke her.

Me: Euw.

Kate: And now talk to me about Polly.

Me: No.

Kate: I still haven't seen her. Why?

Me: She's being a total dick, and I've had enough.

Kate: But she's your friend. Whatever happened to bros before hoes?

Me: Bros before hoes? How old are you?

Kate: (speaking in that stupid high-pitched and slightly

deranged-sounding voice that moves across three octaves) Very. And that's why I know everything and must give you advice.

Me: You seriously don't want to know.

Kate: (still in that voice, batting her eyelashes with ridiculous speed) But I doooooo.

Me: She asked me to meet her at Starbucks, and instead of doing us-things, she told me that her boyfriend is bad in bed.

Kate: (eyebrows hitting hairline) Och, that's terrible. The poor thing.

Me: No, not "poor thing". Poor me. She doesn't talk to me in, like, forever, and when she does, *that's* what she says?

Kate: Phoebe. Who else would she go to with that? Her mum? You should feel honoured that she trusts you with something so personal.

Me: She should go to her boyfriend and speak to him.

Kate: Obviously. But she's probably embarrassed.

Me: How is talking about it any more embarrassing than actually having someone's penis in your vagina?

Kate: I bet you he doesn't even know that she isn't enjoying it. She's probably pretending it's good because she doesn't want to hurt his feelings.

Me: Oh my God, that's so gross.

Kate: A lot of boys, and men, don't really know where things are and how they work.

Me: Things.

Kate: A woman's bits, Phoebe – do keep up.

Me: How difficult can it be?

Kate: Very. Apparently. Trust me, I know. I've been Polly.

Me: Euw!

Kate: A lot of people think sex means a woman making all the right noises while a man is mindlessly thrusting into her from all angles for three minutes, but let me tell you, no woman's ever had an orgasm as a result of that.

Me: (holding the designer cat in front of my face) Stop talking.

Kate: I'm telling you this so you can tell Polly that she needs to show her boyfriend around. (And when she said 'show around', she actually made a presentation-like gesture in front of her vaginal area.)

Me: Please stop talking.

Kate: None of your lesbian friends will ever come to you with this, because women know where things are.

Me: I don't have any lesbian friends.

Kate: You sure about that?

Me: . . .

Kate: Help Polly. She's having a crisis.

Me: You help her.

Kate: Nobody wants to speak to an adult about this, and besides, you're her best friend.

Me: Was.

Kate: Phoebe. Come on – you're better than that. Call her right now and save her from a terrible sex life.

Especially because she's so in love. She needs to at least talk to that boy about the clitoris.

Me: (letting go of the designer cat and literally sticking my fingers into my ears, because have you ever heard a Glaswegian say 'clitoris'?) Oh my God. I'm going to pretend we never had this conversation.

Kate: Oh, pet, if I don't tell you, who's gonna tell you? And the same goes for you, by the way. You need to find a boyfriend or girlfriend or whatever with whom you're comfortable discussing these things.

Me: I swear if you don't stop talking right now, I'm leaving, and I'm never coming back.

Kate: (pulling the dumbest grimace ever, all cross-eyed and cheeks sucked in) . . .

Me: Thank you.

I totally couldn't concentrate on *Star Wars* after that.

Also, when Leia and Luke kissed, I thought of Emma, and then I couldn't look at Carrie Fisher without thinking about Emma, and suddenly *Star Wars* became the Emma show, and it was all very confusing.

I know what Kate's saying about Polly and vaginas, but none of that has got anything to do with me.

Tristan was Polly's choice. She chased him for months. She wanted him more than anything she's ever wanted, including the tickets to One Direction when we were six.

She made her bed and, as far as I'm concerned, she can now lie in it (in the missionary position, wondering what is life).

111

I had a dream that Miriam Patel was giving a presentation on the clitoris.

No word of a lie. There was a chart and everything.

The sex talk with Kate has clearly left me scarred for life.

However, my brain may be sending me subliminal messages, because I reckon Miriam Patel would have no problem showing someone around her vagina, and now I'm wondering if I should send Tristan to her for a quick lesson.

It's funny really, isn't it? Everyone's so desperate to have sex, and it turns out to be the most anticlimactic activity ever.

I'm so glad I'm not obsessed.

Also, the thought of being naked with someone, and needing to nakedly show them around my naked vagina to point out my clitoris is absolutely horrendous.

TUESDAY 20 MARCH   #DIAGRAMS

I'm still not obsessed, but I can't stop thinking about the clitoris. (This sounds weirder than it should.)

The *Illustrated Medical Dictionary* describes the clitoris as a *small, erectile organ*. How grim does that make it sound? I reckon Tristan isn't ignorant, just afraid of it, because a small, erectile organ doesn't sound fun at all. But that's all I'm saying in his defence, because if he'd looked at a diagram, he'd know that it really is nowhere near where the penis goes.

Maybe I'll talk to Polly after all.

P.S. Mum sent an email. They're finally where they need to be.

P.P.S. Alex sold the chocolate fondue set. Turns out offering people random shit at the till does work.

WEDNESDAY 21 MARCH   #KILLMENOW

Gastroporn James from the Goat is on Easter break from uni, and apparently has promised Kate to help at the charity shop every day next week.

Oh God. It'll be like the saga of Polly and Tristan all over again, except this time with grown-ups.

THURSDAY 22 MARCH   #SILENCEISGOLDENEXCEPTWHENITSNOT

I now know why it's so difficult to find out things about Emma. Apart from her seemingly inactive Instagram.

It's a clever little thing she does, and I basically hadn't noticed it until today when I was listening to her talking to a customer. By the time he left the shop, Emma had learned the following:

• He's called Ian.

- He used to work for National Rail.
- He has three children, who all still live locally: one is a teacher, one drives a black cab, and one is a radiologist at St George's.
- He has four grandchildren, and a great-grandchild on the way.
- He supports Tottenham and holds a season ticket.
- He's been divorced for eighteen years but is hoping to find love again (bleugh!).

And here's what Ian learned about Emma:

- She's called Emma.

How is this possible?

Is it rocket science?

No, but it *is* genius: Emma conducts a conversation. She's in charge of it. She's the puppet master. So note to self: if you don't want people to know anything about you, you have to be the one with all the questions.

Seriously, Emma's so brilliant at it, you don't even realize she's doing it.

I'm going to try her own trick on her on Saturday.

P.S. I really hope the casual racist comes back to the shop, because we received the most brilliant donation possibly ever, which meant it got immediately fast-tracked to donation of the week. It's Jesus on the cross. And because it's really good quality, we're asking for £25, which I think is fair.

So guess what happened at the till?

Alex: 'Can we tempt you with Jesus on the cross?'

FRIDAY 23 MARCH   #EASTERBREAK

Today was the last day of school before the Easter break, and I was just like: OK, I'm going to have to talk to Polly about the clitoris, because I'm not going to see her for, like, three weeks, and then the topic will have totally lost its momentum. Also, I wanted to prove to her that I was listening, and that I do still care about her and want her to be happy, even though I despise her boyfriend, and she's erased me from her life like it's nothing.

So at lunch, I walked over to her and Tristan, and I was like: 'Can I talk to you for five minutes?'

Tristan looked proper put out, but I was just like: 'Sorry, mate.' And then I led Polly away by her elbow.

Polly: What is it? Are you OK?

Me: You need to tell him about the clitoris.

Polly: Excuse me?

Me: You have to tell Tristan about the clitoris. He's clearly missing it. And I don't think the penis is designed to do much with it, or to it, and so you have to show him something else.

Polly: Are you insane?

Me: What? No, honestly – him finding the clitoris will help.

Polly: Fuck off, Phoebe. This isn't about the clitoris. Besides, that's not the only way to make a woman come.

Me: . . .

Polly: Why do you have to be so condescending all the time? You act like everyone is stupid apart from you. Maybe I didn't want an instruction manual. And maybe I know about the clitoris. But maybe I just wanted someone to talk to.

And then she just left me standing there.

In an ideal world, I would have shouted: 'Don't be pissed off with *me*. I'm not the one who's shit in bed.'

But obviously I'm not a bitch.

P.S. It's clearly about the clitoris.

SATURDAY 24 MARCH   #BILLANDMELANIE

I was at the charity shop all day today.

Emma and I got so much done, and at one point, she was like: 'I think we should come in every day over the Easter break and properly sort this place out.' And I was like: 'I'm up for it. That's such a good idea.'

Except, of course, it's a terrible idea, because

a) it means spending a whole week with Kate and James, which is basically the one thing I wanted to avoid at all cost; and

b) if I'm at the shop five hours every day, that's five hours of GCSE revision I'm *not* doing.

Oh man.

And, yes, I agree the stockroom needs a good clear-out, but part of me is absolutely horrified about what might be lurking under all those bin bags.

Who actually knows how long some of them have been there? It could be twenty years, because what seems to be happening at the moment is us just going through the new stuff that's on the top. There could be bodies under there.

The other week, there was an article in the *Metro* about an actual dead cat that was found in a donated sofa.

Bill and Melanie brought in pictures of their trip to the Middle East today. They hate Christmas, but instead of complaining about it, they always go away somewhere it doesn't exist.

I obviously love them.

It's also really cute that they went to Boots to physically print off pictures, because who still does that?

Bill: (taking off his hat, then taking Pat's hand and kissing it) Patricia, my darling. I'm always so delighted to see you.

Pat: Oh, Bill, stop it.

Bill: I've brought you a picture of myself floating in the Dead Sea. I know you've been curious to see what I look like in my swimming trunks ever since we first met.

Pat: Bill, really.

Melanie: Careful, Bill, or I'll replace your head with that of Batman.

Then Bill passed the pictures around, and Emma was all like: 'Bill, you're the cutest.' And admittedly, he looked hilarious in his little yellow bathing shorts and straw hat.

He says it's all true about the Dead Sea.

You can't sink.

He says it feels like the water itself is trying to spit you back out. Apparently as soon as you try to go under, you plop back up again.

And then Melanie was like: 'But don't let them fool you into thinking it's saltwater.' Apparently she licked her own arm and was nearly sick. Bill reckons it tastes like battery fluid.

With all that Easter malarkey recently, and my rather delayed realization that my father was an actual human being who was Jewish, I've been asking myself the odd question about religion and Jesus, who was obviously also Jewish (oh, and FYI, Jesus on the cross sold), and I have thoughts: According to the Bible, Jesus walked on the Sea of Galilee that time he walked on water. But the Holy Land (i.e. Israel) is tiny, and the Sea of Galilee runs into the Dead Sea, which isn't even a real sea but a lake, so it's probably more likely for them to have gotten their geography slightly wrong than for Jesus to have actually walked on regular water. And if Bill, who is not a small man, can stay afloat in the Dead Sea, I'm sure someone like Jesus could have walked on it.

Just saying.

I really think I should go to Israel one day. Maybe I'll even find a god, since I wasn't assigned one at birth.

When we closed up the shop tonight, Emma was like: 'Are you still up for Monday?' And I was like: 'Yes, of course.' And then Emma was like: 'Let me give you my number. You can text me so I'll have yours. Maybe we can get Starbucks on our way in?'

I was like: 'K.'

What's wrong with me?

Suddenly I can't speak in full sentences? Or say actual words?

I should have texted her straightaway, because it's now two hours later, and I'm reliving the Instagram-follow-request anxiety.

10.05 p.m.

I still haven't texted her. I'll do it now.

10.10 p.m.

What do I say?

10.13 p.m.

I'll just ask her to meet at Starbucks on Monday because we've sort of agreed we wanted to do that anyway.

10.15 p.m.

When I say we've 'sort of agreed', I mean that I basically said 'K', which doesn't actually mean anything and is a guttural croak at best.

Losing my mind.

10.17 p.m.

Why is this so awkward?

10.25 p.m.

I said:

Phoebe: *Hi, do you want to meet at Starbucks at ten on Monday?*

Done.

Phew.

OMG.

Get a grip.

10.28 p.m.

Emma texted back:

Emma: *Looking forward to it. Goodnight. Sleep well. See you Monday. x*

X! What does that mean?
   Are we *X*ing?
   Should I have *X*ed?

11.10 p.m.

Melanie's wrong, and it *is* actually salt in the Dead Sea.

According to the internet, it's got a salinity of 34.2 per cent, and is one of the world's saltiest bodies of water, apart from Lake Vanda in Antarctica (35 per cent), Lake Assal in Djibouti (34.8 per cent), the Garabogazköl lagoon in the Caspian Sea (up to 35 per cent), and some hypersaline ponds and lakes of the McMurdo Dry Valleys in Antarctica, such as Don Juan Pond (44 per cent).

SUNDAY 25 MARCH   #THEVAGINALORGASM

My search for Polly's orgasm continues, and I'm going the extra mile.

When she said it wasn't about the clitoris, she was talking

about the vaginal orgasm.

And just like the 'small, erectile organ', aka, the clitoris, this is yet another horrendous term that probably puts people right off getting into vaginas – like, literally.

I couldn't find anything in the *Medical Dictionary*, so I looked online, and there's loads.

So, apparently, some people believe there's no such thing as the G-spot, because what it is is basically just an extension of the clitoris, but many sexperts (not Tristan, LOL) say it's definitely a thing, and the easiest way for a woman to achieve a vaginal orgasm is for her to lie down flat on her back, and tilt her hips upwards. That way the penis (regardless of size, apparently) can hit the right area inside the vagina.

Now, I could forward this article to Polly, but then she'd probably be all like: 'Don't be so condescending, Phoebe – it's not about the vaginal orgasm.' (Even though it definitely is this time.)

I swear some people need to take more responsibility for their lives.

It's all well and good Polly just wanting to talk to me about it, but that's not going to solve her problem.

Also, if you have a conversation with someone – a conversation being a two-way sort of thing – why would you be offended when the other person gives you their opinion? I mean, did she just expect me to sit there and nod? Seriously, next time go and talk to a wall or something.

P.S. I'm so dreading tomorrow.

I mean, I'm looking forward to Starbucks, even though, note to self, I'm going to have to remember not to order a soy chai latte, but a vanilla latte. Else Emma may think I'm a weird stalker.

But then I'm going to have to face the Kate and James show.

Bleugh!

P.P.S. I spoke to Mum tonight, and I told her about working at the charity shop like every day now, and she was just like: 'That's such an epic thing to be doing, Phoebe. I'm so proud of you.' But then she launched straight in to: 'Don't forget you need to make a lot of time for revision as well. So if it gets too much, you'll have to tell Kate no, OK? She'll understand.'

I think her comments ticked at least two parenting-goal boxes. Well done, Mum. Excellent work.

Emma and I met at Starbucks at ten, got drinks to go, and then we conquered Donation Bag Mountain.

We pulled out all the bin bags and hoovered underneath, where you can still see the original colour of the carpet.

The thing about tidying, is that at first it looks even worse than before you started, and for a moment we were like: *What have we done?*

We checked for quality stuff in the older donations, and Kate was like: 'If it's completely unsalvageable, just put it in the rag bin.'

We chucked a lot. Here's a list of some of the shit we found:

- A sports bag full of white Y-fronts (not new ones).
- Sheer tights. Used, and laddered.
- One yellow flipper with a picture of Donald Duck on it.
- Totally Plantbased eyeshadow pallet with actual mould on it.
- A wallet with actual mould on it.
- *The Ten Best Walks on the Isle of Wight* with actual mould on it.

Needless to say, none of these items qualified to become the new donation of the week. We're still to decide on one.

James was mainly on shop floor today, reorganizing the entire books and media section. I watched him for a while, all biceps and dimples, and then I imagined kissing him, but literally nothing happened to my insides.

Emma and I are going to have proper breakfast at Starbucks tomorrow, so I'm meeting her at 8.30 a.m.

She's bringing us matching pairs of gardening gloves. Apparently they have a fancy lining. We don't want to put our bare hands into a bag full of unwashed pants again by accident.

TUESDAY 27 MARCH   #EASTERCARDHELL

Emma and I had breakfast at Starbucks this morning. It was brilliant. We both had a croissant. At the shop, the Easter card situation is getting out of control. I wrote a long email to Mum about it, and I told her that she's so lucky she's in a country that doesn't believe in Easter.

At one point today, there was a queue to the door of people wanting to buy cards, and one woman was getting proper aggressive when someone was like: 'Excuse me, can I please get past you and leave the shop?'

Isn't it funny how it's always the old people, who have all day every day to do things, who end up waiting until the very last minute, and then complain that they have to queue? I mean: We've had Easter cards for weeks. Why do you need to buy them three days before Easter? And we all know when Easter is, because it says it in *all* the calendars, unlike Eid, which is only ever in the posh ones you get at, like, Paperchase or John Lewis.

P.S. Kate says the runaway designer cat is due to have kittens this week.

Turns out cats are only pregnant for nine weeks. Who knew?

9.04 p.m.

I just googled animal pregnancies, and dogs are on average pregnant for only eight point five weeks.

Tristan grew inside his mother for nine months. And yet I've seen a dog ride a bicycle. Just saying . . .

P.S. again: Polly hasn't texted me, or called, or anything.

Today, she posted a picture on Instagram of her and Tristan kissing, captioned *So much love*.

I didn't comment, because apparently when you haven't got anything nice to say, you shouldn't say anything at all.

WEDNESDAY 28 MARCH   #DONATIONOFTHECENTURY

Emma and I made the discovery of the century.

We pulled a *Return of the Jedi* movie poster out of a fungus-riddled Nike golf bag, and I was like: 'Cool.'

Then we rolled it out on the big table to have a proper look, greatly inconveniencing Pat and her bric-a-brac in the process, and I saw that it's got MARK HAMILL's actual real-life signature on it.

People are selling things like that for hundreds and hundreds of pounds online.

I told Kate to set up an account straightaway, because we can't have some OAP spending, like, £1.25 on something so totally brilliant.

Alex was like. 'The Force is with us.'

When we were all standing around the table, I was next to James who was like: 'Wow, Phoebe, what a find. This is something special.' And then Kate pushed in, so she was literally on top of us, and I had no choice but to migrated to my left until I was practically sitting on Pat's lap, who went: 'Phoebe, mind yourself.'

Oh, and get this. As we were talking about *Star Wars*, I went to Emma: 'You must be a fan. I mean, because, you know, your Instagram picture.' But she was just like: 'How much do you think we'll be able to get for the poster?'

I said to Kate that we should probably compare similar items online. Imagine us getting something like £300 for it. That would be immense. An average book at the charity shop costs £2, and an average top maybe £3.50. We'd have to sell one hundred and fifty books to make that money. Or eighty-five point seven tops.

I'm totally psyched about our find.

7.15 a.m.

The runaway designer cat had her kittens underneath my wardrobe.

I honestly can't believe it.

Kate even made it a kitten box in the living room with blankets and everything, but it must have thought: Hmmmm, where in this house would be the most annoying place to have my kittens? Oh, I know, in Phoebe's room, under her wardrobe, where people can't get to me.

Kate was under there for, like, an hour.

She was like: 'Who's a good girl? Who's a good mama? Look at your lovely babies.'

Apparently there are four.

I now have a designer cat and her illegitimate kittens living under my wardrobe.

I texted Emma about it, and she was all excited and asked when she can come and visit them.

I told her she's going to have to crawl under the wardrobe if she wants to see them, but she was like: 'OK.' And when I told Kate, she was like: 'Just ask Emma round for dinner. I can drop her home after.'

Now Emma's coming straight after the charity shop tomorrow, and we're going to make pizza and salad.

9.00 p.m.

All we talked about at the charity shop today was the kittens.

Suddenly everyone wants to come to our house, and I swear Kate was one millisecond from inviting James too.

He went up in my estimation today because he and Alex had a proper bonding session, with Alex explaining to him how to work the till, and when Alex had to go get his bus, James was all like: 'Thanks for today, man. I really appreciate that.' And they high-fived.

Should I tidy my room before Emma comes tomorrow?

I don't want to get the hoover out in case I suck up a kitten by accident.

Why do they have to be under my wardrobe?

FRIDAY 30 MARCH   #GOODFRIDAY

I hardly slept because those bloody kittens were making rustling and suckling noises all night. And suddenly I couldn't hear them at all, and I was like: Oh no, they can't die before Emma has seen them. And so I crawled under the wardrobe using my phone as a torch to check, but turns out they were just asleep; except then they woke up.

It's a bank holiday today, so the shop was only open from eleven until four thirty, and of course people were buying Easter cards until four thirty.

They must be hand-delivering.

I honestly never realized Easter cards were even a thing.

Mum sent an email this morning to say she's OK, and that all she wants for Easter is to have a hot bath and a glass of wine.

I'm not being funny, but she could have that every day, so I've got zero sympathy for her.

I took a picture of the kittens and sent it to her, but it's shit because it's too dark, and the kittens look more like furballs than kittens.

Emma came home with us after work, and we made pizza.

Kate wasn't as crazy as usual at dinner (i.e. not talking about sex or vaginas or James in order to embarrass me in front of others), which makes me think that she knows something about Emma that I don't. I really hate that: when you know that you don't know something.

The cats are still under the wardrobe, and so Emma had to crawl underneath. The kittens were making strange gargling noises, and Emma was just like: 'This is the cutest thing I've ever seen.'

Kate was like: 'Maybe you should adopt one. Or four.'

Kate then agreed to setting up an online account to sell the *Star Wars* poster, but apparently she has to have it signed off with her line manager first. She was also like: 'If we bother with this, I think we need to try harder to locate novelty items and designer clothes in the future.'

Emma and I are going to take charge because, let's face it, Pat would've probably binned the poster, and she probably doesn't even know who Mark Hamill is, even though she's old, and *Star Wars* is old, but Pat's like zero into anything cool. She's actually zero into anything.

At nine, Kate was like: 'Shall I take you home, Emma?' But Emma was like: 'No way! I'll walk – it's only fifteen minutes.' And then Kate was like: 'Phoebe, walk Emma home.'

No one ever worries about me.

Emma can't possibly go home on her own, but Phoebe's OK to go there and back.

On her own.

In South London.

Even though she's only fifteen, and Emma's already sixteen, and really doesn't need a chaperone, because even though she's very lovely, she's feisty AF.

Obviously I didn't mind. I like Emma a lot. She's got this laugh she only does occasionally, and it's proper wicked, and it doesn't match her face, but when she does it, it's like someone's struck a match inside her eyes.

Back to work tomorrow.

Emma reckons we should call ourselves the 'Female Fortune Finders' and have our own TV show.

The Female Fortune Finders are on fire.

We found a twenty-pound note in a donated handbag.

It was a shit one too, with a broken strap, and I was just about to chuck it in the rag bin when Emma was like: 'Have you checked inside?'

Now, I'm even checking inside trouser pockets, because you really never know.

The donation of the week this week (apart from the *Star Wars* poster, obvs) is an orange space hopper. When we pulled it out of the bin bag, it was mostly deflated, and so Emma tried to inflate it by blowing into the tiny hole, but that didn't do anything, and then Kate remembered that someone had donated a foot pump once upon a time. It took us, like, an hour to find it, but when the space hopper was inflated, we took it out for a spacey hop on the shop floor. Emma did three big bounces before she faceplanted in front of the till.

We were literally dying with laughter, but Kate just shook her head and was like: 'And thus concludes this little interlude.' She took the space hopper away and put it in the window.

It sold three minutes later, and when the man left with it, Kate was like: 'Certain things only have one outcome.'

Emma: Eternal fun for the whole family?
Kate: A&E, pet. A&E.

Happy Easter.

I got a giant Easter egg from the designer cats, and a selection of small eggs from the kittens.

Kate's so strange.

I felt bad because I didn't get her anything, but we ended up sharing the giant egg right after breakfast.

Then we moved the kittens from underneath my wardrobe into the kitten box in the living room.

They're not doing much yet, just stalking around making high-pitched squealing noises.

I reckon we need to sell them ASAP because people like cute things. Maybe we can put them on eBay?

I've decided Easter is my favourite holiday.

Kate and I did literally nothing. Then we WhatsApped Mum. We showed her the kittens, and she was all like. 'Ahhhhhh, we can have one, Phoebe, if you like. They're very cute.'

When she said 'we', she didn't mean us, she meant me, because who's going to end up looking after it? Not her. And then the kitten and I have to live with Kate, and suddenly there's, like, three cats in this house, and everything will smell of cat piss, and then Kate and I may as well kill ourselves straightaway, because where do you go from there? Besides, I don't even like cats.

Note to self: Never actually get a job in retail, because you're going to have to always work when everyone else is off.

Like today, on Easter Monday.

We took £75, and Kate said that was terrible.

It was just Emma, Kate and me today, because Pat insists on 'observing Easter' (even though I don't think anything happened to Jesus on the Monday), James is visiting his family in Kent until tomorrow, Bill and Melanie are still in Marrakesh, and Alex is attending an Easter fundraiser for which he has baked a Victoria sponge cake, which apparently is actually called a 'classic Victoria sandwich'.

Emma and I found a book called *The Woman's Guide to Cookery and Household Management*. We were going to make it the donation of the week, but it's too good, so we're keeping it.

It's the thickest, heaviest book I've ever seen, and it's proper hilarious. There's a whole chapter on how to 'handle' staff, and one chapter is about how to cook for 'invalids', which basically means cooking for sick people. There are ten pages on how to make different types of soufflé. Having been a woman a hundred years ago must have absolutely sucked.

What even is a soufflé?

In other news, we can see the kittens' distinct colouring now. There's one tortoiseshell, one grey one, and two tabbies.

Emma's coming around as soon as their eyes are open so we can make them pose for pictures, and then we'll set up an Instagram account and share their pictures with #catsofinstagram.

Exciting times ahead.

TUESDAY 3 APRIL   #PASSOVER

James is back from his Easter break.

On our way in, Kate was like: 'Phoebe. I know you're beside yourself about James being back, but you really need to calm down.' And then she put on actual lip tint.

Seriously, *she* needs to calm down.

When he got in, he was like: 'Hi, Phoebe. Did you have a nice Easter?'

Me: 'I don't believe in Easter. I'm Jewish.'
James: 'Fair enough. Did you have a nice Passover, then?'
Me: 'Great, thanks.'

I immediately downloaded the Jewish Festivals app, because quite frankly, I had no idea what James was on about.

PASSOVER
Commemoration of the Jews' liberation by God from slavery in ancient Egypt, and their freedom as a nation under the leadership of Moses.

Apparently you're not allowed to eat anything that rises. Like bread. Which means I failed Passover this year because, apart from the chocolate egg, I ate toast all day on Sunday.

When I was taking down the Easter cards in the charity shop this afternoon, it occurred to me that we had zero Passover cards, and bearing in mind that approximately two hundred and sixty three thousand, five hundred Jews live in the UK, that's pretty shit.

Even if 50 per cent of the Jewish population bought a card at, let's say, £2.99, that would mean the charity shop card people could make £393,932.50.

So why aren't they?

Also, get this. The millisecond the last Easter card was packed away in its special box that we have to send back for special recycling, this old woman comes into the shop and goes: 'Excuse me. Have you got any Easter cards?' I was like: 'Are you actually kidding me?' She carried on like: 'I always buy them just after Easter for next year.'

I swear these things only happen because people have too much time on their hands.

While I was on the shop floor dealing with every weirdo in Wimbledon, James was in the back (alphabetizing the books I had already alphabetized a few weeks ago), hanging out with Emma.

By the time I returned to the stockroom, they were BFFs, which annoyed me.

James: Emma, where do you go to school?

Emma: Wimbledon High.

James: Do you like it?

Emma: Yes, it's OK.

James: Do you play any sports there?

Emma: I play hockey.

I stumbled over my own two feet then, because: Why didn't I know this?

I mean, OK, I've never asked that question specifically, but I've known Emma for a few months now, so why don't I know that she plays hockey?

I seriously need to get into the habit of asking better questions.

Emma must have been like: 'Oh, wow – James is really interested in my life. And look, that's indifferent Phoebe over there, dragging a box of Easter cards to the back door.'

10.41 p.m.

Here's a list of questions for Emma tomorrow:

- What's your favourite thing about school?
- What's your least favourite thing about school?
- Have you by any chance started revising for GCSEs?
- Who's that boy in your profile picture?

Epic fail on the question front; I didn't ask Emma a single one.

Emma showed James *The Woman's Guide to Cookery and Household Management*, and she and him and Kate had a proper laugh over it.

Is nothing sacred? That's mine and Emma's thing.

And then James was all like: 'We've come such a long way in the last hundred years when it comes to the role of women.' And Emma was like: 'I know, but there's a long way to go yet.' And James was all agreeing and talking absolute bollocks about wanting to smash the glass ceiling.

Normally, when people are being pretentious idiots, Kate would be like: 'Now, now. Enough of being pretentious idiots.' But she just stood there, listening to James going on and on, and she was like: 'Oh, James is so right. James is so wise. Everyone should be like James.'

Bleugh!

Seriously, when does his uni start again?

And why can't he work day shifts at the Goat? I know for a fact they're open for lunch.

At dinner, Kate said that she's going to ask him to go on the till more often, because he's so beautiful, and that the power of delicious biceps shouldn't be underestimated.

That's totally sexualizing him.

The Woman's Guide to Cookery and Household Management discussion has taught her nothing.

Yay, Alex is back, so I basically hung out with him all day.

Everyone else couldn't get enough of worshipping James, who found a crinkly old book of First World War poetry and was all like: 'Blah blah blah, blah blah blah, blah. Isn't this profound?' And Kate, Emma, and even emotionally void bloody Pat were all like: 'This is the most profound poem I've ever heard. Its profoundness is so profound it literally aches with profoundity.'

Come on!

I sat under the till by Alex's feet eating crisps, doing more research into the *Star Wars* poster just in case we happen to hear back from Kate's manager at some point in this life, and get the go-ahead for putting it on eBay.

Seriously, I think some people don't want to make money.

Alex was like: 'You can't sit under the till all day.' But I was like: 'Watch me.'

Just before lunch, three hours later, Kate was like: 'Has anyone seen Phoebe?' And Alex was like: 'Yes. And she thinks poetry's shit.'

Me: Do you tell your parents I say words like "shit" all the
        time?
Him: Why?
Me: Because you're my only ally in this place, and I'd hate
        it if they told you to work somewhere else.
Him: No, they're cool.

I asked if Alex and Emma and I could go to Sprinkles for our lunch, and Kate said yes, but Emma said she didn't want to come because, apparently, 'we can't all take lunch at the same time'.

Why didn't she just say she wanted to spend time with James?

At Sprinkles I ordered the Peanut Butter and Jamsplosion, and Alex had Chocolate Extreme again.

Me: Do you think James fancies Kate?
Alex: I haven't really thought about it.
Me: Do you think James fancies Emma?
Alex: I haven't really thought about it.
Me: Do you think Emma fancies James?
Alex: I haven't really thought about that either.

And then I realized that *I'd* thought about it way too much, which almost made me want to not finish my lunch.

P.S. People need to calm down about poetry.

P.P.S.

> *Under the till,*
> *Listening still.*
> *But what's most profound*
> *Makes no sound.*

Big deal.

We got the go-ahead for the *Star Wars* poster.

James suggested we should put it in a frame, and then he went out and got a cheapo one from Wilko, which made the poster look proper amazing.

We took a picture, and then we uploaded it.

I suggested starting at £350, and at first Kate was like: 'It's a poster, Phoebe, not a Monet.' But then James reckoned that would be the right price, and suddenly everyone was like: 'Oh, OK, yes. Three hundred and fifty pounds.'

Not two minutes after it went live, ten people were already watching it, and an hour later, someone had offered £375. How amazing is that? So we'll definitely get £375 for it, but it's got like a whole other week to gather momentum.

We'll make so much money.

Maybe it'll be known as the movie poster that cured cancer.

Imagine.

Today, Emma was like: 'Are you OK, Phoebe?' And I was like: 'Yes, thanks.' And then she went: 'How are the kittens? Can we take the pictures yet?'

I honestly thought she'd forgotten about it, and I was so surprised that she brought it up that I was like: 'Er, I think we need to wait a while yet and allow for their personalities to come through a bit more.'

What am I even saying?

That's such bullshit.

They're cats.

I honestly don't know why I say the things I say sometimes. It's like they literally fall out of my mouth without having been through my brain.

Emma must think I'm completely ridiculous.

I need to ask her if she has a boyfriend. But she hasn't asked me, and usually that's like one of the first things people ask.

Maybe Emma just really isn't like other people.

SATURDAY 7 APRIL   #THEPLOTTHICKENS

So this is what I accidentally/on purpose overheard today:

Bill: And how are you, my darling?
Emma: Really well.
Bill: And Mum and Dad are all right too?
Emma: Yes, thanks.
Bill: You still going to your meeting?
Emma: Yes, of course.
Bill: You wonderful woman.

When I walked back into the stockroom where they were, I felt like such an outsider.

What meetings? What's going on with Emma? And why is he calling her 'darling' and 'wonderful'?

Is everyone trying to drive me insane?

11.19 p.m.

Maybe Emma's an alcoholic.

SUNDAY 8 APRIL   #TOLOSEALEG

Kate reminded me that the other designer cat's kittens are due later this week, so I may want to keep my door shut.

This is the full-on designer litter, so they really need to be born in their designer cardboard box (that Kate nicked from the neighbours' recycling).

I WhatsApped Mum just now, and she told me about treating a little boy who had lost a leg.

I wonder what they do with cut-off body parts and dead bodies there. I can't imagine them having a crematorium at a field hospital. I wonder if it all just gets burned out back.

I can't imagine losing a leg.

And what's that phrase all about?

How can you lose a leg?

You lose your wallet.

But your leg?

The *Star Wars* poster has reached a whopping £401.

How totally amazing is that? And we've got until Friday, and there's like seventy-eight people still watching it.

It was a stroke of genius putting it on when people/people's children are on holiday, because I bet everyone's just sat at home, bored, wondering what they can possibly spend money on next.

Emma and I are getting through donation bags with almost absurd speed now. Turns out, we're a brilliant team. With everything starting to clog up the rails in the stockroom, Kate spontaneously decided we should have a sale. We're going to do Buy One Get One Half Price on all clothes.

I spent all day putting signs up.

Pat thinks it's a terrible idea (of course).

She reckons charity shops should never give in to high street pressures.

I disagree. Not out of principal or because I hate her, but because it's better to make £3.00 than £2.00: If ten people spend £3.00, we make £30; but if ten people spend £2, we only make £20.

It's not rocket science, Pat.

Also, Emma and James are literally doing my nut.

James: I used to row at school.
Emma: Oh, cool.

James: It was intense. There's so much pressure. And one day in Sixth Form, I woke up and decided I didn't want to do it any more.

Emma: Oh, I know. Rowing takes over your life. And your weekends are busier than your week.

Why is she suddenly a rowing expert?

I also don't understand why it's so easy for everyone else to talk to Emma, and I'm just like: 'I think we need to allow for the kittens' personalities to come through a bit more, K?'

I hate myself.

I swear I want to crawl out of my skin and be like James all cool, calm and collected.

And I'm feeling like I'm running out of days with Emma, because we're back at school this time next week, and then I only get to see her twice a week again if that, because GCSEs are getting real.

8.30 p.m.

I'm going to text Emma and ask if she wants to come round and take those pictures.

I know the kittens haven't opened their eyes, but I want to see if she prefers my kittens to James's rowing-arms.

P.S. I know that's immature.

P.P.S. I know they're not my kittens.

P.P.P.S. I know it's not a competition.

9.58 p.m.

Emma texted to say she can't come tomorrow.

Here's what she says:

Emma: *Would love to, but I'm not free Tuesday evenings. Another time?*

Maybe. But I don't want to text her now.

TUESDAY 10 APRIL   #CARDIGANGATE

The funniest thing happened today, and now Emma is my favourite person in the whole world.

She was pricing clothes all day, which involves taking steamed items off the rail/pile and shooting a price tag through the label.

In her defence, the stockroom is in an absolute state, despite our efforts to tidy it. Anyway, so Emma is happily pricing away, and when Pat gets up from her chair to go for her tea break, she's like: 'Has anyone seen my cardigan?'

Turns out, Emma accidentally priced it, put it on a hanger, and Kate took it out to the shop to be sold.

LOL.

We checked every hanger, but couldn't find it anywhere, so it appears that we sold Pat's cardigan in the Buy One

Get One Half Price deal.

She was furious, Emma was mortified, and I wanted to never stop laughing.

Kate told her to choose another one from the shop, but of course that wasn't good enough for Pat, because she wanted *that* one.

I didn't say anything to Emma all day about the text message, but just as we were leaving, she kind of nudged my shoulder and was like: 'Do you want to take kitten pictures on Sunday maybe?'

I nudged her back and was like: 'Yeah, OK.'

WEDNESDAY 11 APRIL   #MINDBLOWN

Here's why people think the moon landing was a hoax: the average customer at our shop is too stupid to comprehend the Buy One Get One Half Price offer.

Here's what the signs say:

Buy One Get One Half Price on All Clothing

And here's what happened:

Customer 1:   The sign says buy one get one half price on all clothing.

Me: Yes.

Customer 1:   I'm just a bit confused as to what that means.

Me:	Buy one get one half price on all clothing.
Customer 1:	Even the jackets?
Me:	On all clothing.

Customer 2:	What does your sign mean?
Me:	That it's buy one get one half price on all clothing.
Customer 2:	Even books?
Me:	On all cloooothinnng.

Customer 3:	So when I buy one, I get another one half price?
Me:	. . .

Minds are literally blown. Not to mention the number of people who come to the till and haven't realized.

All day, Kate's been going: 'And just to let you know, it's buy one get one half price on all clothing.' And the customers are like: 'Is it?' When there are signs EVERYWHERE.

So yes, with scenes like this playing out before my very eyes, do I believe we put a man on the moon? Absolutely not.

THURSDAY 12 APRIL   #SURPRISE

Polly and Tristan came to the charity shop today, which was weird.

Kate completely overreacted to their arrival, all like: 'Gosh, pet, look at you – *I* miss you.'

Whatever.

They were like: 'We just wanted to say hi to Phoebe.'

Why?

To rub their relationship in my face?

The situation exponentially improved the moment they *did* say hello to me, because when they walked into the stockroom, I was just passing books to James, who was up a ladder, his 'delicious' denim-clad bum right in my face.

Polly's eyes literally rolled out of her head, and I swear she was thinking: Why can't *I* have an attractive boyfriend?

Tristan looked like such a child next to James.

I introduced Emma, and Polly was all like: 'Hi, I've heard so much about you.' Which is a total lie, because I swear I've mentioned her maybe once.

Polly and Tristan said they were on their way to some festival on Wimbledon Common, and I was like: 'It's so nice when you don't have to have a job.'

I know that was

a) bitchy, and
b) a lie, because I know I'm actually just as privileged as them, and I don't *have* to have a job.

But I was just like: Why are you all in my face with your new life?

Also, does she think she can just ignore the fact that we

clearly fell out over the clitoris?

I'm still mad at her for being mad at me when all I did was say what needed to be said.

I mean, of course I could have been like: 'Don't worry about it, Polly. Just keep doing what you're doing, and I'm sure one day an orgasm is going to happen to you that will make the twenty-five years of no-orgasm sex with Tristan so worth it.'

I was Polly's best friend, so I think not only should she *expect* my honesty, she should *demand* it.

But what do I know?

When she was leaving, she was all like: 'Text me, Phoebe, if you have a day off over the weekend and want to get coffee or something. Or I'll see you Monday.'

I was like: 'OK.'

Now the ball's in my court again.

I hate that.

What does she want me to say to her?

Also, I don't actually have time.

So I'll see her Monday.

P.S. I hope it bothers Polly that I've moved on.

P.P.S. I've just re-read this entry, and I clearly haven't moved on.

P.P.P.S. I wish so much that I didn't care.

P.P.P.P.S. I just googled *How not to care*, but the results are all rubbish because they're all about how not to care about what other people think about you, but I don't care what people think about me, I just want to feel nothing.

I can't believe the internet is letting me down with something so basic.

P.P.P.P.P.S. I just messaged Polly, and she messaged right back.

Me: *It was nice to see you today.*
Polly: *And you. Miss you xxx*

FRIDAY 13 APRIL   #GOINGGOINGGONE

Friday 13th is our lucky day, because the *Star Wars* poster sold for £530.

It was insane.

Seriously, all those people 'watching' suddenly crawled out of the woodwork, and for the last two minutes, it just went up and up and up.

We knew this afternoon that it would sell for at least £470, and even Pat was eating her words that we'd 'better not' branch out to sell things online.

But I reckon it would've been even better for the auction to have ended on a Sunday (statistically, auctions that end on a Sunday night are the most lucrative), but I guess £530 is still pretty decent.

I told Kate I'd go to my room to finally do some revision, but instead I messaged Emma about the £530.

She couldn't believe it.

I wonder if she's revising.

It's a month until our first exam, and I'm not going to lie, I feel a bit sick.

SATURDAY 14 APRIL   #HEATWAVE

Today, James was like: 'We should all meet up and watch *Return of the Jedi.*' And instead of going: 'Why would I want to see you people on my one day off?' Kate was like: 'That's such a brilliant idea. We really should celebrate.'

So now everyone's invited to ours tomorrow, which is so annoying, because Emma and I had planned on taking the kitten pictures.

I swear James is ruining my life.

It was so hot in the stockroom today, it was disgusting.

Emma wore a floral summer dress and brown Doc Martens. She was like: 'I need sturdy footwear in this shithole. You never know what you're going to step in next.'

I really wish I could be stylish like her.

Also: Bill and Melanie are back from Morocco.

Melanie usually does the books, and they've only been in such a state because she's been away a lot, and today she was

152

all like: 'Kate, your James is a gem. He's done this beautifully. He's even separated the hardbacks. I think it's time that I retire.'

Then they all laughed, because apparently Melanie retired from the shop once before when she turned eighty, but three weeks later, she was so bored at home that she demanded to be reinstated.

I'm going to be exactly like that when I'm her age.

After work, Kate and I went into Morrisons to get food and drinks for tomorrow. We bought so much that she ended up having to get the car, because we couldn't carry it all.

Me: Who's going to eat all this?
Kate: You.
Me: And who's going to cook all this?
Kate: (looking at me, smiling, fluttering her eyelashes) . . .
Me: Oh man.

So I'm going to have to get up early to make salads and stuff.

The Woman's Guide to Cookery and Household Management would not approve of such an impromptu get-together. It suggests starting with the preparation for a Christmas dinner in September.

We're also having to cordon off the designer cats and kittens so that they don't get distressed. It'll be like a zoo.

I'm so unbelievably tired, I'm almost hysterical.

Forget *The Woman's Guide to Cookery and Household Management*, Kate and I rocked the catering. We made garlic bread, two quiches, mini sausage rolls, potato salad, mixed green salad, brownies, chocolate chip cookies, a massive pot of chilli con carne, and a smaller pot of chilli sin carne (because James loves animals so much that he could never eat one). I was like: 'If he gets a vegetarian option, can I have a kosher one?' But Kate just looked at me.

Most of the food obviously didn't need *making* but simply taking out of a packet and heating up or pouring into a nice bowl, but still, it all had to be prepared.

The only person who couldn't come was Alex, who always spends Sundays with his family.

Bill and Melanie brought a whole box of actual champagne. They were like: 'You must always celebrate in style.'

They are so posh, it's hilarious.

Bill was wearing shorts, a cricket jacket and a pink cravat. He looked totally LOL sitting on one of Kate's old plastic garden chairs. And Melanie looked like a movie star from the 1920s. She had on huge Gucci sunglasses that pretty much covered her entire face.

Pat, of course, looked horrendous in a floaty floral knee-length skirt, comfortable old-lady shoes, and yet another beige cardigan.

I was thinking, you know, she's only sixty-five, and

Melanie is eighty-six, so she's young enough to be Melanie's daughter, and yet she looks like Melanie's grandmother.

Emma arrived together with James, which didn't put me in the best of moods straightaway, obviously. She'd bought a card and a £5 M&S voucher for Pat to say, *Sorry for selling your cardigan in the Buy One Get One Half Price deal*, and I think Pat finally felt bad for having been so vile about it, and she was like: 'Don't be silly, Emma. And take that voucher back.' But Melanie grabbed the voucher and shoved it into the pocket of Pat's cardigan, going: 'Nonsense, Pat. Have the voucher. Emma wants to do something nice for you, so accept it.' And then Pat hugged Emma for like a whole minute saying thank you.

She wouldn't have forgiven me that easily.

Everyone had a glass of champagne to say well done for raising all that money for the *Star Wars* poster.

I spoke to Bill and Melanie loads about their travels. I reckon they're doing it right. They're going everywhere, but are staying at hotels – not like Mum, going to all these exotic places and having to build your own shelter and then dig a hole 200 metres away for a toilet.

Because it was so hot, everyone was in our tiny garden pretty much all day, and we didn't watch *Return of the Jedi* after all.

Kate found a badminton set she'd bought when I was little, and Emma and James played for hours until they got so hot that James simply had to take his shirt off.

They were proper laughing, and high-fiving and everything,

and when Kate and I were taking stuff back to the kitchen I was like: 'Do you think James fancies Emma?' But Kate was just like: 'What makes you say that?' Like she hadn't noticed they'd arrived together, sat next to each other on the grass when we were eating, and that they've been playing badminton together with James literally in the nude. If I fancied him, and I know Kate fancies him, I would have been bilious.

Anyway, luckily James had to go to work at five, and Pat decided to leave as well, and then Bill and Melanie said they were going too, and so it was just Kate, Emma and me.

Emma was sunbathing, and she followed the little patch of sun across the garden until it disappeared over the fence. Kate was like: 'Just knock next door, pet. They've got sun for another five minutes at least.'

Kate went inside at, like, seven, then came back outside, threw a big blanket at us, telling me to walk Emma home no later than nine.

I'd completely forgotten we're back at school tomorrow, and I'm not going to lie, all the GCSE revision that *didn't* happen is making me feel nauseous.

Emma and I sat on the towel on the grass under the big blanket, and you know that feeling you get when the sky turns orange and purple, and it's Sunday night in London, and everything seems to just stop?

We watched the planes coming into Heathrow, and we didn't actually talk very much, which was so nice, because you don't have to be constantly talking in order to have a nice time with someone. I also wondered if Emma and James could be silent together like that.

Suddenly it was nine, and we were still sitting there.

Me: I better walk you home.
Emma: You don't have to come with me.
Me: I said I would.
Emma: OK.

And then she smiled at me and winked.

We didn't talk much on the way home, either, and when we did, we whispered, which was odd, but maybe that's what people do in the dark.

When we got to hers, all the lights were on.

Me: (blinking) Wow.
Emma: (sounding exasperated) My parents stress so much when I'm out. I'm surprised they haven't called.
Me: But you were at Kate's. It's not like you're out clubbing and drinking.
Emma: We were drinking.
Me: Half a glass of champagne.
Emma: (all reluctant) I've never had a drink.
Me: Are you actually being serious?
Emma: (shrugs) . . .
Me: There's no way Kate would have allowed us to get pissed or anything.
Emma: I know.

Me: You've seriously never had alcohol? Not even at Christmas.

Emma: My parents don't drink.

Me: What about when you're out with your friends?

Emma: I don't really go out.

Me: Not even to house parties?

Emma: (shrugs) . . .

Me: Wow.

Emma: Wow what?

Me: It's just that people like you usually have busy social lives.

Emma: People like me?

Me: Hockey-playing people.

Emma: (looking at me like: WTF?) . . .

Me: Pretty people.

And I swear that came out before I'd finished thinking it, which shouldn't be possible, but happened, and suddenly I was literally dying on the inside.

Then Emma (not being socially inept like me and obviously trying to make light of my hasty comment) was like: 'You need glasses.' Then we laughed, and I leaned right into her face, pretending to try to look at her, and then I could feel her breath on me, and her laughter moving my hair, and she smelled of SPF 30, and I honestly don't know why that smell made me feel all funny, but my stomach was fluttering like crazy.

Me: Bye.

Emma: Bye.

Me: See you Thursday? We need another donation of the week.

Emma: (nodding, then) Thursday. And, I had fun this holiday.

Me: Me too.

Emma: OK.

Me: OK.

Emma: Bye.

Me: Bye.

10.30 p.m.

I don't want to go back to school tomorrow.

I don't want to do GCSEs.

I don't want to do anything.

I will never be a friend of early mornings, and I will never be a friend of having to take the bus, and I will never be a friend of people making out outside the school gates.

Bleugh!

Judging by Instagram, Polly and Tristan can't have spent a single moment apart during the Easter break, and yet, there they were, at it again, pretending the sex is so great that they literally can't stop having it.

Polly has become the victim of the lies she tells herself.

I seriously need to talk to her about the vaginal orgasm, but I didn't want to open with it.

Also, Polly and I are really not OK, but we've established some weird state of 'we used to be friends, but now we're not' relationship.

I wonder if that's what it's like when people get divorced.

That sense of a person being both familiar but also awkwardly unknown at the same time.

Miriam Patel showed everyone her revision timetable. It's literally a nightmare. Every day is broken up into hourly slots that are colour-coded: *Maths* is red, *English Language* is dark green, *English Literature* is lime-green, etc, etc . She's even scheduled in *Sleep* (baby-blue). I hope for her sake she feels tired between 11.55 p.m. and 6.15 a.m. because that's literally the only chance she gets.

Everyone loved the timetable, of course, and I bet they're all sitting at home right now making one.

I can't be arsed.

I really wanted to text Emma today to ask if her parents were mad about Sunday night, but then I don't want her to think I'm a weird stalker who needs to know every detail of her life. Even though I clearly am, and I clearly do.

I've just spent an hour on her Instagram again looking for that boy.

I also checked Snapchat, but she doesn't seem to be on it (and who can blame her?). The last time I was on it, Steve O'Reilly had posted a picture of his erect penis. And I know that posts delete themselves, but there are some things you can't unsee.

P.S. I totally thought for all those days that Emma may be an alcoholic, and that her secret meetings are AA meetings, but that clearly isn't the case because she said that she'd never had a drink . . . Unless that was a massive lie, and we've accidentally fed her addiction.

P.P.S. No, she's definitely not an alcoholic, because Bill definitely knows about the meetings Emma goes to, and he therefore would definitely not have brought a whole box of champagne.

P.P.P.S. Why is life so confusing?

P.P.P.P.S. I should talk to Polly.

P.P.P.P.P.S. Mum WhatsApped tonight. She looks like she's living in a war zone. Oh, wait, she *is* living in a war zone.

She asked me a gazillion questions about GCSEs.

I reckon she's feeling guilty about not being here to do all the parenty stuff it says to do in the brochures, like: *Make sure your teenager has a hearty breakfast. They may not feel like eating, as nerves often manifest as feeling queasy or having an upset stomach, but eating even a slice of dry toast is advisable.*

Kate's going to be like: 'Eat yer breakfast, ye total drama queen.'

I secretly totally love her.

I don't understand how I'm not her child. We're so much better together than Mum and me.

TUESDAY 17 APRIL   #UNVOLUNTARYBIRTHINGPARTNER

When I got home from school, the second designer cat was having kittens in the kitchen.

There was half a kitten hanging out of its vagina, and one was already lying on the tiles, and twitching, and I proper panicked.

I called Kate's mobile, but of course she didn't answer. Then I called the shop, and Pat answered.

Me: Where's Kate?
Pat: Oh. It's you.
Me: Where's Kate?

Pat:	She's popped out to do a change run.
Me:	When will she be back?
Pat:	How long is a piece of string?
Me:	Ask her to call me immediately, because it's an emergency.
Pat:	I'll let her know as soon as she gets back.

At this point, the cat was licking the half of the kitten that was hanging out, and I was just like: OMG!

I didn't know what else to do, and so I called Emma, who answered straightaway.

Me:	The designer cat is having kittens in the kitchen, and I think one is stuck.
Emma:	(laughing, and I totally get it, because it must be hilarious if someone calls you about that, but it wasn't funny) . . .
Me:	Can you come and help?
Emma:	Where's Kate?
Me:	I don't know – but seriously, what do I do? I can't exactly call 999.
Emma:	(laughing again) I'm on my way.

And then time stopped, and it was 4.49 p.m. for literally an hour.

I kept watching the cat, and suddenly the stuck kitten plopped out and onto the tiles just like the other one, and then the designer cat was all like: OK, *let me lick this clean for a moment.*

I tried to edge closer to see if it was breathing, but then my phone rang. It was Kate.

Me: The cat's having kittens in the kitchen. There's two.
Kate: Does she seem distressed?
Me: I don't know.
Kate: Are you sure there's only two?
Me: I don't know.
Kate: Check under all the furniture for me.
Me: (checking under all the furniture) Nothing. I think.

Then, finally, the doorbell rang.

Me: Emma's here.
Kate: OK. I think it's best to leave the cat for now, because they don't like being disturbed. It's her second litter, so she should be absolutely fine, but keep an eye on her for me, and if she seems distressed, just give me a call back, and I'll be right there.
Me: OK. Bye.

Emma was just like: 'Oh my God, how tiny are those kittens?' But all I could think was: Why me? I didn't sign up for this.

After a few minutes, the designer cat carried one designer kitten by the scruff of its neck into the living room to the kitten box, and when she came back to get the other one, I was like: 'What the hell?' Because there was a third kitten coming out of her.

I was like: 'This is so stressful.'

Emma and I watched it emerge one millimetre at a time, and when it was out, the designer cat quickly gave it a few licks to get all the gross membrany stuff off of it, but the kitten didn't move at all, unlike the other two, and I was like: 'What's happening?' And then Emma went: 'I don't think it's breathing.'

I felt like I was going to be sick, but I went to have a closer look, and Emma was right, the kitten was just on the floor like: dead.

I didn't do anything, I just sat there on my feet, not moving. Emma knelt down on the floor, touched the tiny kitten with her finger, and started rubbing it a bit, but then she was like: 'Phoebe, seriously, it's not breathing.' I was like: 'I don't know what to do.' And then Emma bent down and put her mouth over its face and literally gave it mouth to mouth! And the dead kitten came back to life, all twitchy and pulling faces.

I was like: OMFG.

No one is ever going to believe any of this, but the bloody designer kitten lived, and the designer cat just looked at us like: OK, *cheers, I guess I'd better look after this one too, then.*

When Kate got home, Emma and I were so hyper, we were literally bouncing off the walls, and Kate was like: 'OK, I think we need to leave Mum and her babies in peace for a while.' And so she took us out to Pizza Hut.

On the way back in the car, she was like: 'I'm sorry you're missing your meeting tonight, Emma.' And I swear there was suddenly this massive proverbial elephant in the room/car, and you've never heard a more quiet silence. But instead of me being like: 'Oh, what meetings are they, then?' I said nothing. And instead of Emma being like: 'Oh yeah, I go to these meetings about blah blah blah,' she just went, 'I can't believe I resurrected a kitten. It was one hundred per cent DOA.'

And then we all laughed, because the funny temporarily outweighed the awkward.

11.17 p.m

The designer cats and all seven kittens are doing well now.

What a day.

WEDNESDAY 18 APRIL   #THERUNTOFTHELITTER

Today in Religious Studies, Mrs Turner went through the GCSE-marking hoo-ha with us 'just to reiterate'. You get zero points if there's 'nothing worthy of credit' in your answers/if there are no answers.

Polly looked at me, pointed at herself, and mouthed: 'Maths!'

I just rolled my eyes at her, because I find it hard to believe you'd know nothing, but at the same time I can imagine Polly just looking at the paper and her brain being like: Tristan. Tristan. Tristan.

In order to get seven to nine points, you have to 'show reasoned consideration of different points of view with clear reference to religion' (i.e.: Blahblahblahblah, but with Jesus/Allah/Buddha).

I think the teachers are more stressed about all this than we are. They're getting proper aggressive when they catch you not listening.

P.S. The designer kitten that Emma brought back to life is definitely the runt of the litter.

It's really small compared to its two brothers/sisters, and I swear it looks like it doesn't quite get life. It's full-on ginger, except for its feet, which are white, so it looks like it's got fluffy socks on. The other two are white with beigey ginger all over.

I took a picture of it and sent it to Emma.

She replied straightaway and suggested we call it either Elizabeth or Richard, because giving animals people names is cool.

THURSDAY 19 APRIL   #RESULT

The Buy One Get One Half Price promotion has finally finished. Thank God.

I was literally starting to lose my mind over stupid people.

Alex brought in a whole coconut cake he'd baked, and I ate at least four slices because it was delicious. And apparently you have to use coconut milk instead of actual milk like it says in the recipe, because that makes the cake

a) super sweet,
b) super fresh, and
c) super moist (which is 100 per cent the most awful word ever, especially when uttered by everyone, including Pat).

Alex is honestly such a nice person, and he makes me want to be a nice person too, but then someone'll walk in like: 'What does buy one get one half price mean?' And I'm just like: 'I hate you.'

So today, spurred on by the unprecedented success of the *Star Wars* poster, Emma and I were on a mission to find the next big money-maker. We thought we'd found a genuine Louis Vuitton handbag for a minute, but it was only a cheap replica, probably from Tooting Market. We still made it the donation of the week and put a sign on it saying *Original Fake*.

I know it's a horrible thing to say, but we need more sci-fi fans to pop their clogs, because all that vintage *Star Wars* shit, and *Doctor Who*, and even *Battlestar Galactica* is making proper money on eBay.

Kate said since I'm not really a people person, I can be in charge of the shop's eBay account.

P.S. I'm not *not* a people person.

People just don't like to hear that they're idiots.

FRIDAY 20 APRIL #CATSTAGRAM

Emma came over tonight, and we finally had a photo session with the non-designer kittens.

You know that saying about herding cats? You don't fully understand its meaning until you've actually had to do it.

When we'd arranged one, another one had escaped, and when they were finally all sitting together and kind of looking into the camera, one fell asleep.

It took an hour to get a decent picture.

Because they are half-designer cats, Kate reckons we may still get half the pure-breed designer-cat money for them.

Emma and I made an Instagram account for Kate and posted the pictures. The caption reads:

Four kittens, half Persian. £250 each. All jabs included.
#catsofinstagram #persian #halfpersian #kittens #cats
#Wimbledon #alljabsincluded #cutekittens

It's quite stressful all this cat-selling business.

Also, two of the kittens look identical, so we're going to have to put tiny little different-coloured collars on them to tell them apart.

Emma and I put it on our Instagram accounts too, so

maybe we'll get results from that.

I haven't posted anything in months, and Polly liked it straightaway. She was all like: *Aww. They're so cute.*

I hope she noticed that Emma was tagged in the picture.

P.S. Why do I even care about what Polly thinks when I know she doesn't care about me?

P.P.S. Mum just liked my Instagram post. Is she checking up on me from within a war zone? Why did I think it was a good idea to allow my mother to follow me?

P.P.P.S. I wonder if Emma will still want to come over once the kittens have moved out. I wonder if she likes spending time with me when I'm definitely not as fun as badminton-playing, topless James.

SATURDAY 21 APRIL   #SALSAFORSENIORS

Bill and Melanie signed up to Salsa for Seniors a few weeks ago and are proper into it.

We were given a little taster of what that looks like in the stockroom, and it wasn't funny because they're old, but because Bill was so serious. He did the face and everything while gyrating his pelvis. I was crying. And then he was like: 'Come on, Patricia, my darling. Dance with me.' But Pat was all like: 'Oh, Bill, you know I've got two left feet.' But he pulled her off her chair and senior salsa-ed her up and down the stockroom, dodging books and bags and bins.

We all laughed and clapped, and for the first time since I've known her, Pat actually cracked a smile.

Emma was like: 'We should all go.' And then she winked at me, and I think I was pulling a really stupid face at the time.

Why am I like this? Every time I feel like I'm getting more natural when I'm talking to Emma, something like that happens. I'm literally a car crash.

9.03 p.m.

Maybe Emma only winked at me because James wasn't in today, so she couldn't wink at him.

Maybe it's a nervous tick.

Maybe I'm overthinking it.

SUNDAY 22 APRIL   #HEATWAVETAKETWO

The heatwave is real, and I stayed indoors all day.

Loads of comments on Instagram on the half-designer kittens, but no one has asked to visit, and no one has made an offer.

I just looked at a Sociology GCSE example sheet. Get this: *Describe what sociologists mean by a same-sex family.*

Sweet Lord Jesus.

What could *anyone* possibly mean by a same-sex family?

Same.

Sex.

Family.

Why is the government wasting my time with this?

It's Sunday, and Mum hasn't called. ~~She must have more important things to do. I honestly don't care if she never calls again.~~

Kate got a 'courtesy call' from Médecins Internationaux today informing her that 'Doctor Davis and her team haven't been in contact for thirty-two hours', but that there was 'no immediate reason for concern'.

This has never happened.

Kate says it's protocol to contact next of kin.

I wish they wouldn't, because what's the point? It

a) doesn't locate the missing, and
b) worries people who can't do anything about it.

Once, when Mum and I were on our way to visit Nan and Granddad in Hong Kong, due to a 'technical fault with the aircraft', the flight was delayed by two hours, and the whole time I was thinking: Why would you tell us the plane we're about to get on is currently broken? Say anything, make something up, but don't say *that*.

I think a good lie is hugely underrated.

I was like: 'Mum's OK, isn't she.' And Kate was like: 'Of course she's OK.' But later I caught her stroking two cats simultaneously, and that's not a good sign at all.

I wish I could call Polly, but there's no way I'm going to beg for her time or friendship.

P.S. I just searched online for people like Mum going missing (war doctors, journalists, aid workers, nurses, etc.), and the fact is that most of them are never found. And if they are found, they're usually dead.

I'm so angry with Mum, I can't even.

TUESDAY 24 APRIL   #48HOURS

Dear Miss Anderson,

This is a courtesy communication to inform you that despite our best efforts, we have not been able to make contact with Doctor Amelia Davis and her team in forty-eight hours.

Please rest assured that we are using all available resources to establish contact.

I would like to stress to you that we have no reason to believe Doctor Davis and her team have come to harm or are in any immediate danger.

As per our procedures, we are going to circulate a courtesy email every twenty-four hours.

In the meantime, should there be any developments, we will contact you immediately via telephone on the emergency number you have provided. Please make sure to update your contact details should these have changed.

Sincerely,
Anneke Stromberg
MÉDECINS INTERNATIONAUX, London

When Kate read me the email, she didn't sound Scottish at all, which is, like, the worst sign ever.

I tried WhatsApping Mum a million times, but I can't get through. She's going to have a heart attack when she sees the number of missed calls.

I once read that spy satellites are so brilliant, they can find a match lying on the ground anywhere on planet Earth and tell if it's been lit or not.

a) How amazing is that?
b) Don't tell me you can't zoom in on a field hospital in Syria that's run by an international aid agency.

8.30 p.m.

I could fly out of Gatwick tomorrow at 12.20 p.m. with Ukraine International Airways (via Kiev) for, like, £329.61. That would get me to Ankara at 10.10 p.m.

Kate caught me looking at flights, and she was just like: 'You listen to me now, Phoebe. Your mother is OK.'

But the truth is, Kate doesn't know that. Nobody knows that.

I don't even know why I care, because it's not that Mum didn't have it coming. And because Mum had it coming, I had it coming. We all had it coming.

9.05 p.m.

I just know she's dead.

9.20 p.m.

I wonder what kind of a funeral Mum would want.

We never talked about that, which seems really odd to me right now, considering I always knew deep down it would come to this.

Maybe Kate knows, but I don't want to ask her about it yet. She's still all like: 'We must stay positive.'

But must we? How could our attitude possibly have any influence on Mum's situation?

I don't think Mum is religious, so I don't think we'd go to a church or anything. I reckon she'd want to be cremated. That way, we could scatter her ashes all across the globe; take a spoonful to all the places she loved.

Actually, knowing Mum, she'd probably want to use her remains to feed the hungry. I know that sounds disgusting, but she totally thinks she's all that.

I don't want to be shipped off to Hong Kong to live with Nan and Granddad. Mum better not be dead.

10.00 p.m.

I wonder what Dad's funeral was like.

I wonder if Mum has been to Israel.

I wonder if she still misses him.

I wonder if there's an afterlife, and if so, what would Dad say to her if she showed up now?

Can you still be in love when you're both dead?

WEDNESDAY 25 APRIL   #PLANS

We got yet another courtesy email this morning, and I literally felt so sick that I couldn't go to school.

I searched the internet for the most popular funeral poems.

The first one Google found is called 'Don't Stand at My Grave and Weep'.

How stupid is that? People aren't exactly going to be like: YAY!!

The whole poem is like: Don't cry at my funeral, because I'm not even there, but I am the sunshine, and the wind, and this and that, and something else as well, blah blah blah, so really, I'm with you all the time.

That's the kind of made-up shit people tell other people when they want them to feel better. In fact, Mum's been saying this to me for years. She's always like: 'Whenever you think of me, I'm already thinking of you.'

That stupid poem actually made me proper upset for a minute. Not because it's supposedly deep and meaningful, but because I realized that if Mum were dead, our relationship would be exactly as it is right now, except without the WhatsApping.

I don't understand why she decided to have me.

Polly texted me at lunchtime to ask if I was OK, but I didn't reply.

When Kate got home from work, I was still in bed, staring at the wall. She opened the curtains, pulled the duvet off of me, and went: 'Right, little missy. Fresh air and exercise are good for the body and the soul. So chop, chop – let's go.'

She told me she'd choose my outfit and put it on me if I wasn't ready in five minutes. Then she dragged me up the hill to Wimbledon Common without saying another word.

After twenty minutes of Kate marching along like a proper soldier, and me sulking like a proper dick, Kate was finally like: 'Phoebe. Talk to me.'

Me: If Mum's dead, will I live with you?
Kate: She's not dead. But yes, of course you would. That was all worked out years ago already, though, so your concerns are a bit late to the party.
Me: Worked out when?
Kate: When you were a baby, and Amelia decided she couldn't sit on her skinny arse for more than five minutes and had to go and try to heal the sick and lead the blind, et cetera, et cetera.
Me: How did you know you'd be best friends forever?
Kate: We didn't know that. We still don't. But I'd say the chances are good. Twenty years and counting.
Me: But how did you know you'd want to look after me?

Kate: (cackling, pushing me towards a ditch) Phoebe. I personally pulled you from your mother's vagina. I was the first person who held you. I couldn't love you any more if you were my own child. In fact, I probably love you a lot more *because* you're not, because let me tell you, you pretty much ruined your mum's fanny.

Me: Oh my God, stop talking.

Kate: (insanely Scottish) Oh, try not to think about it, pet. She's all right now. They sewed her back up straightaway.

Me: (gagging) . . .

Kate: Anyway, so of course you would live with me should anything ever happen to her, but right now, she's fine.

Me: OK.

Kate: Good. And keep reminding yerself of that.

When we got back, Kate made us cheese toasties, and we sat with the cats and kittens on the floor. It was like a picnic in a petting zoo.

P.S. I can't believe I broke Mum's vagina. I wonder if she's reminded of it every time she looks at me. No wonder she's away a lot.

P.P.S. I had three missed calls from Polly, and she left a voicemail, but it only said: 'Are you alive or what? Call me.'

I didn't.

I only texted her to say I'll be back at school tomorrow.

P.P.P.S. Kate's been on the phone ever since we got back, calling friends who still work at Médecins Internationaux to see if they know something more than what we're being told, but apparently nobody knows anything. How's that possible? People don't just disappear.

P.P.P.P.S. I feel sick.

THURSDAY 26 APRIL   #NEARDEATH

People only get called out of lessons when someone's dead. Right?

So today, when Miss Curtis called me out of French, my stomach literally dropped.

Everything was suddenly happening in slow motion, and I couldn't hear properly, like when you're underwater.

I sort of stumbled over my own feet and the straps of my backpack, and Miss Curtis actually took me by the arm and led me out of the classroom.

In the hallway, I dropped my bag, and all my books spilt out, and my knees just went, and all I could think was: Why am I shocked? I already know Mum's dead.

Miss Curtis was talking to me, and I could see her lips moving, but I couldn't hear what she was saying until she took my face between both her hands and told me to breathe.

Miss Curtis: Phoebe.
Me: . . .
Miss Curtis: Phoebe. Can you hear me?
Me: . . .
Miss Curtis: Miss Anderson's here to collect you.
Me: Oh my God.
Miss Curtis: It's about your mum. They are setting up a
               phone call.
Me: She's dead.
Miss Curtis: She's fine. Go, talk to her. Miss Anderson is
               waiting in my office. Can you get up?
Me: (picking myself and my things off the floor,
               stumbling) I'm OK, I'm OK, I'm going.
               Thanks.

And then I bolted all the way down the stairs, past the old
building, across the courtyard, into the main house where
Kate was waiting. She was grinning from ear to ear, but I was
like: 'Are they calling the shop?' And when Kate nodded, I
kept running, and I was like: 'Let's go!!!!!'

She'd parked on a double-yellow line, and Alex was in the
car, and I was just like: WTF?

Kate: (fastening her seat belt) Yeah, Pat's called in sick,
        and I know I could have left Alex in charge of the
        shop, but the last time we received too many letters

congratulating us on his excellent customer service.

Alex: (laughing in the back) That didn't happen.

Me: Drive!

Then, because the world hates me, every light was red, old people were taking like an hour to shuffle across zebra crossings, and Wimbledon was gridlocked.

Me: When did they say they'd call?

Kate: (checking her watch) Well, they called an hour ago to say that they were setting up a satellite call within the hour.

Me: Shit.

Kate: (pulling the shop keys from her pocket and shoving them into my hand) Go.

I got out of the car and ran all the way from outside Sainsbury's to the charity shop.

Emma was waiting outside, and she was like: 'Where is everyone? What's going on?' But I couldn't even speak because my lungs felt like they were about to explode.

I unlocked the door and bolted into the stockroom.

Emma: You OK?

Me: (shaking my head, trying not to suffocate) . . .

Emma: Where's Kate?

Me: (coughing up phlegm) . . .

Emma: . . .

Me: Mum was missing.

Emma: No.

Me: But she's OK.

Emma: Thank God.

Me: They called me out of class. Have you ever been
         called out of class? So stressful. I thought she was
         dead

Emma: (smiling the most unusual smile) I'm glad she's OK.

Me: (staring at the phone) I hope they haven't called.

Emma: I'll put the kettle on.

Kate and Alex came in ten minutes later.

Kate: Hello, team. That was all a bit exciting, wasn't it?
         Let's open up again then, shall we?

Alex: Has she called?

Me: (shaking my head) . . .

Kate: Right. Alex, till. Emma, there's clothes to steam.
         And Phoebe, sit down, because you look like you're
         about to pass out.

Me: I'm fine.

Emma: (putting down a cup in front of me) I've put extra
         sugar in your tea.

Me: I'm OK.

Kate: Sit down, Phoebe. You do look a bit peaky.

I swear I just stared at the phone while everyone was going
about their business for, like, an hour.

Emma made more tea and gave me five Hobnobs to eat.

When the phone finally rang, I literally jumped out of my skin, and everyone sort of froze and looked at it.

Kate (answering it): 'Kate Anderson speaking. Yes. Thank you, I'll hold.'

She winked and passed it to me.

There was a lot of nothing for a few seconds, but then something clicked.

Mum: Hello?

I swear my heart actually stopped beating again for a second before pounding back into action so hard, I almost vommed.

Me: Mum?

Mum: Phoebe! How are you, baby?

Me: I'm fine. Great. How are you? Where are you?

Mum: I'm fine – everything's fine. We're still out here.

Me: Where were you?

Mum: Long and boring story. I'll tell you when I get back. Are you OK?

Me: Everyone was really worried.

Mum: I'm so sorry, baby. It's been pretty bad, and we got cut off for a few days, but we were so busy that I couldn't send smoke signals.

Me: Ha ha, you're funny.

Mum: I'm sorry we had you all worried. How's Kate?

Me: She's great – she's here. She's blowing a kiss.

Mum:	How are things with Polly?
Me:	Great. Polly's great. Everything's back to normal. (Total lie, obvs).
Mum:	I'm glad. Tell her I said hello. We'll hopefully have internet again by the end of the week, so I'll call you as soon as I can.
Me:	Great.
Mum:	I have to go now, baby. There's more people here who need to call their families.
Me:	No, wait – don't go.
Mum:	I'm sorry, darling – I have to go. But I love you, Phoebe.
Me:	OK. Talk to you soon.

And then the line went dead.

I looked down, and my hand that was holding the phone was shaking, and I just thought: Why can't Mum be at home like normal parents? And why couldn't she even talk to me for five minutes? I know her less and less every day, which is probably why I had such trouble imagining planning her funeral.

I felt a hand squeeze my upper arm, and then Kate knelt down in front of me and was like: 'Phoebe, are you OK?'

I looked at her, and suddenly this huge sob travelled up from all the way somewhere down in my innards, and I couldn't not cry. I've never had that before. It was completely out of my control, you know, like projectile vomiting.

Kate hugged me, and told me it was OK to be upset, and then Emma came over too, and suddenly we had a group hug going on, and my face got accidentally buried in Emma's hair, and my nose touched her neck, and then the steamer (which hadn't been filled up with water because Emma had been too busy listening to my phone conversation) made that horrendous *raaaaaaaaaaaaahhhh* noise, and we all flinched, jumped apart, and Kate swore, which made us all laugh.

Then Kate got Starbucks for everyone.

I was like: 'Can I have a shot of vodka in mine?' Kate was like: 'Single or double? Not really.'

I sorted greeting cards for the rest of the afternoon, and when a customer asked if I worked there, I was like: 'No.'

I don't understand how I feel about Mum. I don't understand it like I don't understand Japanese. I can see it written down, but I can't decipher it.

11.15 p.m.

There are two reasons I'm happy I lied to Mum about Polly:

1. She'll finally stop going on about it.
2. She can tick the 'make sure teenage daughter is maintaining positive relationships with her peers' box.

And on that note, I had ten missed calls from Polly, and at 10 p.m. the landline rang, and I know it was Polly because Kate was like: 'How nice to speak to you. Let me just see if she's awake.'

I pretended to be asleep, so Kate was like: 'I'm sorry, you'll have to catch up with her tomorrow.'

I bet everyone this afternoon was like: 'OMG, what happened with Phoebe?'

11.55 p.m.

I can still feel Emma's neck on the tip of my nose.

FRIDAY 27 APRIL   #TEARS

I wanted to stay at home today just so Polly would be worried, and yes, I know how massively immature that sounds.

When she saw me, she physically grabbed both my arms and was like: 'What's going on with you? Are you OK?'

I was just like: 'Yeah, fine. We thought Mum was dead, but turns out she's not.'

Her face . . .

10.00 p.m.

After my minor breakdown yesterday, I researched the mechanics of crying, and according to the internet, there are three different types of tears:

1. The constant tears that keep your eyeballs moist.
2. The tears that come when you have something in your

eye, and your brain is like: Get it out!

3. The tears that happen to you as an emotional response to something.

Apparently the chemical compound is different in every one of them, and the emotional tears actually contain a natural painkiller.

It's like your brain is trying to stop your body from hurting by producing these tears.

Which explains my tear-fest yesterday. My brain must have been like: OK, enough of that dull ache you're feeling about your mother. Here are tears to numb it so you can get on with life.

And today, I actually do feel so much better.

P.S. Miriam Patel is walking around school like she's Little Miss Studious.

She now wears glasses, but not actual ones, but the non-prescription ones you get from Topshop. And she keeps going on about how 'the future starts here'.

I'm not being funny, but GCSEs aren't exactly Oxford entrance exams.

Last year, Rachel Griffin said that she memorized her entire French oral exam, and that she had no idea what any of it actually meant, and that she got an excellent mark. I mean, obviously she's an actory type, but she was just like: 'Darling, it's all about the performance.' She reckons our teachers are actually so shit that they don't understand what we're saying, either, so as long as you babble some rubbish but mention key words like *dans*, *sous*, *devant* and *derrière*, they're like: 'Oh, yes – it's all there.'

Maths is basically the same shit with different numbers.

But of course, Miriam Patel has to make a drama out of absolutely everything.

What's with the glasses?

Seriously, she always thinks she has to dress for whatever part she's playing. It's school, not a fancy-dress party.

SATURDAY 28 APRIL   #LUKESKYWALKER

It's still really warm and sunny, so we had hardly any customers in the shop all day.

Emma and I got ice cream this afternoon. We ate it sitting in the sunshine on the hot concrete ground, just outside the back door.

Emma: I'm really glad your mum's all right.
Me: Me too.
Emma: It's scary when you think you'll never see someone
        again.
Me: To be fair, I never see her anyway.
Emma: Phoebe.
Me: . . .
Emma: . . .
Me: Sorry – that wasn't great.

Then Emma pulled her legs up and rested her head on her knees and looked at me.

Just looked at me, light blue eyes, thinking, licking her ice cream.

Me: What?

Emma: (quietly) I want to tell you something.

Me: (feeling shaky, fearing sunstroke) OK.

Emma: But you have to promise me something first.

Me: Anything.

Emma: Promise me you won't change.

Me: Why would I change?

Emma: Because people always do. And I hate it.

Me: . . .

Emma: (licking her ice cream, looking at me, smiling, not smiling) I had a brother.

Me: (thinking: WTF?) . . .

Emma: His name was Bradley.

Me: (thinking: Fuck!) . . .

Emma: He died. On the seventeenth of July last year.

Me: . . .

Emma: He had leukaemia, and then he died. He was seventeen. He was brilliant.

Me: Emma. Why didn't you ever say?

Emma: Because since he died, everyone around me has been acting differently. And I was scared that if you knew, you'd treat me differently too. And I'm sorry that everyone here knew apart from you. I asked people not to say anything because . . .

Me: . . .

Emma: I like that you never knew me with him, and that you
       never knew me when he was sick, and with you I can
       be normal, you know, just me, just Emma. Not
       Emma with the dead brother, or Emma with the
       parents who lost the plot afterwards.

Me: I . . .

Emma: I'm sorry it took me so long to tell you.

Me: I . . . You don't have to apologize.

Emma: . . .

Me: *I'm* sorry.

Emma: Thanks.

Me: No, I really, really am so sorry.

Emma: (smiling) I know.

Me: I wouldn't have treated you differently.

Emma: (smiling more) You're such a natural bitch, I almost
       believe it.

Me: I'm not a natural bitch. I'm actually quite a people
       person.

The sentence kind of hummed in the afternoon heat for a
moment, and then Emma and I both burst out laughing,
because, really, what bullshit. I literally hate everyone.

Then she pushed her ice cream into my face and went:
'Strawberry?' And I licked it.

I haven't even ever done that with Polly, because licking
someone else's spit is normally disgusting.

Me: Is Bradley Luke Skywalker?

Emma: . . .

Me: Your picture on Instagram. Is that you and Bradley?

Emma: Yeah. It's actually from a long time ago when he wasn't sick yet.

Me: I thought he was your boyfriend.

Emma: Euw. Why would my boyfriend and I dress as brother and sister?

Me: That's what I thought.

Emma: . . .

Me: . . .

Emma: . . .

Me: Have you got a boyfriend?

Emma: (looking at me like I've lost my mind) No. You?

Me: No.

Emma: And for your information, I don't have a girlfriend either.

Me: Oh.

Emma: Because as you can imagine, with everything that's been going on, dating sits pretty much on the very bottom of my pyramid of priorities.

Me: Same.

We nodded in agreement, and then she once again held her ice cream in front of my face, and I licked it.

I don't think I'll ever be able to taste strawberry now without thinking of Emma, and remembering the smell of hot concrete, the sounds of a Saturday, and the blue in Emma's eyes forever changing with the angle of the afternoon sunshine.

SUNDAY 29 APRIL   #RICHARD

This morning I was like: 'I know about Bradley.'

Kate put down a handful of kittens and was like: 'I was wondering why you were being odd last night.'

Me: I wasn't being odd.

Kate: Yes, you were. You were being preoccupied and strange. Anyway, I hope you're not mad at me for not saying anything.

Me: No, it's fine. I get it.

Kate: Good.

Me: Emma said everyone's been treating her differently since he died.

Kate: Yes, I suppose it would be very difficult to not do that.

Me: Do you treat her differently?

Kate: I only met her in October when she came in and asked to volunteer. And I think Bradley died in the summer.

Me: Seventeenth of July.

Kate: (nodding, then) I treated her like a young woman who'd just lost her brother.

Me: It's so sad.

Kate: Yes, it's horrible.

Me: I'm glad I'm an only child. And I'm glad I've never lost anyone.

Kate: You've lost your dad.

Me: That's different because I never knew him, which means I can't miss him emotionally. I only miss him intellectually.

Kate: (looking at me a moment, then laughing): Oh, Phoebe, you're such a strange creature. Come here.

And then she hugged me and kissed my head.

Kate: (still hugging me): I love you – you're wonderful.

Me: I love you too.

Emma is coming over this afternoon, so I'm going to tidy up.

9.47 p.m.

Kate just dropped Emma home in the car because it's absolutely chucking it down.

Kate had sexed the designer kittens earlier, and I could finally reveal to Emma that the one she resuscitated is a boy, and so we now call him Richard.

Obviously that's only his working title, because we won't actually get to name him, because in an ideal world, he's going to be sold, even though I actually doubt that, because his eyes are a bit too close together, and he can't seem to walk in a straight line.

The half-designer kittens are doing much better, but I suppose they're older. And not inbred.

Emma loves them all, of course, but she especially loves Richard, and he loves her. I swear he recognizes her as the woman who gave him life, because he made proper squeaking noises when she walked in.

The weather was grim, so we just sat around and took more pictures of the non-designer kittens, which we then put on Instagram because we still haven't had a single offer.

We had a big thunderstorm at five, and then it rained and rained and rained, and Emma and I went up to my room and just sat on the bed and looked out of the window.

Then Emma started giggling, and I was like: 'What?'

Emma: Remember that day after Sprinkles when Alex suggested you were just like that woman in your class you hate?

Me: Oh God, Miriam Patel. Yes.

Emma: (laughing) Your face.

Me: Fuck off.

Emma: (laughing, slapping my arm) Honestly, Phoebe, your face . . .

Me: (slapping her arm back) . . .

Emma: (slapping mine again) . . .

Then, I stabbed her in the ribs with my finger.

Turns out she's absurdly above-average ticklish, so of course I wasn't going to let that go, and I honestly tickled her until she was begging me to stop and started having the hiccups, which was hilarious.

Then she looked at me through her insanely blue eyes, and everything that had just been wild and chaotic stopped, and it was just us looking at each other.

But like really looking, and all I was thinking was: If I knew what you're thinking, I could say something, but since I don't, I can't.

And then I felt her hand brush against mine, which made me jump.

Obviously not because it was unpleasant, because it wasn't, but because I hadn't expected it, nor had I seen it coming in my peripheral vision. But Emma totally must have thought that I recoiled in horror, because then she was like: 'Sorry – I didn't mean to make you jump.'

And I said: 'Yeah, I know. It's fine.'

But it's not fine.

Nothing's fine now.

Did she want to touch my hand? And what would that mean?

11.02 p.m.

It's still raining.

0.15 a.m.

I'm still awake, but Kate is too. I just heard her crash-banging in the kitchen. Maybe my insomnia is contagious.

Maybe it's the rain.

Kate and James had sex!

When I said I heard Kate 'crash-banging' in the kitchen last night, turns out I heard her actually banging. Banging James.

Oh my God, I'm so glad I stayed in my room. Imagine walking in on something like that.

Bleugh!

It all transpired this morning when I went downstairs.

One of the designer cats was sitting by the front door watching one of the half-designer kittens tear something to shreds.

I was like: 'Oi, get off that.' But at that point, white fluff was already everywhere.

I shooed the kitten away and discovered that it was eating the inside of a bra; the three-quarter-moon-shaped booster bit that gives extra cleavage.

I followed the trail of fluffy evidence down the hallway and into the living room, where another one of the half-designer kittens was asleep on an actual bra. And since it wasn't mine, I was like: It's obviously Kate's.

So I was thinking: Hmmmm, this is a bit awkward. But she shouldn't leave her bras lying around.

A moment later, the plot thickened, because the bra wasn't the only item of clothing that was randomly lying on the floor.

I found a pair of jeans, another pair of jeans, the T-shirt Kate was wearing yesterday, and another T-shirt that looked familiar.

I was just like: OMG.

So I positioned myself in the kitchen where I could see into the hallway, and maybe ten minutes later, I heard Kate's bedroom door opening and closing, followed by quiet footsteps padding down the stairs.

Me: Good morning, James.

James: (jumping up in the air) Oh. Eh. Ah. Uh. Phoebe.

Me: Did you have a good night? Breakfast? I'm having toast.

James: Eh. Yes. Thanks. No.

Me: Why aren't you talking in full sentences?

James: (running his fingers through his hair) Sorry. I . . . I . . .

Me: (shaking my head, because what happens to people when they're in love/lust?): . . .

James: (awkwardly rubbing his manly biceps) Kate and I . . . We . . . It . . . ehm . . . errrrr . . .

Me: What's happened to your speech?

James: (shaking his head): I . . . This . . .

[Enter: Kate]

Me: Tea? Toast?

Kate: You need to go to school.

Me: And miss the afterglow?

Kate: Phoebe . . .

James: (blushing) . . .

Me: This is so great.

Kate: I . . . well . . . it happened.

Me: (nodding in a very understanding way) . . .

Kate: And so . . . now you can go to school.

Me: (looking from one to the other) OK. (Turning to James): See you later.

James: Eh. Oh. Uh. Ah.

I casually walked out of the house, humming, and then I texted Emma.

Phoebe: *Found James in our house this morning. He and Kate had sex.*

She texted back straightaway.

Emma: *Finally!!!*

I was just like:

Phoebe: *Really? You saw this coming?*

And Emma was like:

Emma: OMG, *Phoebe, it was so obvious.*

Was it? Because I thought there was a tragic love triangle going on where Kate fancied James who fancied Emma who fancied Luke Skywalker (who turns out to be her actual brother, who is now dead). And does that make it an incestuous love square? And why am I even joking about it?

I must be broken the way Data from *Star Trek* was broken, unable to even observe the obvious.

I think the only way they could fix Data in the end was to take out the emotion chip. The equivalent for me would be futuristic neurosurgery. But to be honest, at this point in my life, I'm game.

P.S. I wonder what's going to happen now. I mean with James.

Was it a one-off, or are Kate and him all official now? Is he going to move in? Do I have to spend every moment I usually spend with just Kate with James as well? We'd be like the weirdest patchwork family in history.

Maybe I should write a book about it, except no one would believe it.

I wonder what Mum's going to say when she finds out Kate's having sex with someone who could be her own son.

I'm not ageist, obviously, but lots of people are.

I hope Kate doesn't forget about me.

If they get married and have babies, I'll have to give up my room in her house.

Mum's going to have to let me stay on my own, but I'll be sixteen by then anyway.

Kate tried to act all normal tonight, but her pupils are literally blown, and she looks zombified.

P.P.S. I could have sworn James fancied Emma.

P.P.P.S. I think everyone fancies Emma.

P.P.P.P.S. I hope Emma and I are OK after the weird hand-touching incident.

TUESDAY 1 MAY   #STRESSINGNOTSTRESSING

Today, Craig Sullivan told me he was starting to stress about GCSEs, and so I spent the rest of the day wondering if that means it's time for me to start stressing too, because Craig Sullivan never revises for anything because he's got a photographic memory.

At lunch, Matilda Hollingsworth was like: 'I've basically not had time to wash my hair in, like, a week, and so I basically had to buy dry shampoo on my way to school.'

I'm not being funny, but if you've 'basically' got time to go to school via the shops and buy dry shampoo, you've 'basically' got time to wash your hair like everybody else.

She needs to get over herself. Basically.

I think there is, as there always is with people at school, a fine line between justified worry and irrational hysteria.

I've decided that I'm not going to worry about maths, because I know that I know it, and there's no way I will allow myself to be outsmarted by numbers.

In all fairness, the only thing that is actually making me twitchy is English literature.

I don't agree with us having to do GCSEs in English the way

we have to do them. I mean, English Language is fine, because we need more people to know that 'could *of*' doesn't actually mean anything apart from the fact that you don't know how to speak English. But why do I need to interpret a poem?

What's my opinion got to do with GCSEs? And besides, it's not that you're actually allowed your own opinion anyway, because you have to say what the teachers want you to say/what the GCSE revision guide suggests you say.

Everyone always goes on about how it's so beneficial in life to be well read, but mentioning something you've read for GCSEs neither *makes* you clever, nor does it make you *sound* clever, because everyone else has read it too and has the same opinion on it, because that's the only opinion your brain was trained/allowed to remember.

I reckon that's why everyone's so stupid.

And one more thing: no one's ever admitted to hating *Romeo and Juliet*, because you can't possibly say anything against Shakespeare, and I swear you'd fail GCSEs if you did, even if you backed it up with the best arguments ever.

Fair enough, Shakespeare was popular and wrote a lot of plays, but *Romeo and Juliet* is actually a bit shit, isn't it?

It's basically teenagers throwing a massive tantrum.

Sure, it must be totally annoying if your parents don't allow you to go out with someone, but do you kill yourself literally five minutes later?

In my opinion, *Romeo and Juliet* is a crap story well written, which disproves the theory that apparently you can't polish a turd.

But can I say that?

No.

9.05 p.m.

I just texted Emma.

Phoebe: *We've been slack with the donation of the week.*

I mean, we've had nothing since the *Star Wars* poster.

9.10 p.m.

She texted back.

Emma: *Thursday. It's a date.*

She's obviously joking.

WEDNESDAY 2 MAY   #PANICKATTACKCENTRAL

Miriam Patel had a meltdown in maths today.

It was LOL at first, with her literally rocking in her chair, Little Miss Smartass, glasses askew, chanting: 'I don't get it, I don't get it, I don't get it.'

But then she couldn't breathe, even though she was taking in proper lungfuls, and Mrs Adams made her breathe into a paper bag, but that didn't help, and then it wasn't funny any more, and they ended up calling an ambulance, and Miriam Patel was taken to hospital.

Mrs Adams reckons Miriam had a panic attack.

What the actual?

If this is what school does to people, then something is seriously wrong.

I normally think Miriam Patel's, like, the biggest drama queen in the entire universe, but she looked proper shit scared.

I told Kate, and she was like: 'Stress can manifest itself in many different ways.'

Trust Miriam Patel to take it to the extreme and be hospitalized.

Maybe I'm secretly stressed, and that's why I can't sleep.

I've also had a tummy ache for days. Not like period pain, but up, just underneath my ribcage.

THURSDAY 3 MAY   #MENTIONITIS

Kate's actually in love.

Bleugh!

I thought the ridiculousness that comes with it was reserved for teenagers (like Polly – not like me, obviously), but apparently not.

Kate:	James isn't working tonight, so he's coming over for dinner.
Me:	OK.
Kate:	James likes stir fry, so I'm going to make one.
Me:	OK.
Kate:	I think I'm going to get some beers in for me and James.
Me:	OK.
Kate:	I wonder if James likes Cornettos.
Me:	Can you say just one sentence without saying James?
Kate:	(doing the rapid-blinking thing) No, I don't think I can at the moment, pet.
Me:	Can you at least try?
Kate:	I don't think I want to.
Me:	. . .

Then Kate let out a high-pitched squeal, grabbed me, and kissed my face for like thirty seconds, going: 'But you're still my favourite. I love you, I love you, I looooove you.'

She's so crazy.

And now she's even crazier because she's in love.

If this trend continues, I'll be the last sane person standing.

No, it'll be me and Pat, because she literally knows no emotion apart from annoyance and hatred.

P.S. OMG, I'm Pat.

Emma was weird today.

Everything was fine at first. We picked up *A Woman's Guide to Cookery and Household Management*, and I was like: 'Hmmm, delicious. Chicken and vegetables in aspic. Basically cat food.' And we laughed, and then we decided on the donation of the week. We're going for the RockJam professional bongos. TBF, we basically chose them because we want Alex to ask all the old ladies who come to the till if he can interest them in the RockJam professional bongos and see their reaction.

Then I didn't really get to speak to Emma much because she and Kate were changing some of the shop around. And because Pat wasn't in, I had to select, steam and price everything by myself in the back.

When we were leaving, I asked Emma if she wanted to do anything on Monday since it's a bank holiday, but she was like: 'I'm so sorry, I can't. I have to revise this weekend.'

On the way home, I asked Kate if she thought Emma was being unusual, but Kate was just like: 'What do you mean?'

Me: I asked her if she wants to do something on Monday, and she said she has to revise.

Kate: Maybe she has to revise.

Me: She's never had to revise before.

Kate: Maybe you should revise.

Maybe. But I can't concentrate at the moment. My brain feels like a sieve.

Maybe I need sleep. I know I look tired, and I defo should be tired, but I don't really feel tired.

At times, I can feel pure adrenaline running through me. There's a constant tingling in my arteries.

I'm awake all night, and my brain is just like: How about this, how about that, and I don't think Emma tried to hold your hand, because why would she do that, and today she basically told you to go away. And have you noticed your persistent stomach ache?

On that note, I'm too scared to look at the medical book just in case I'm actually dying. And I'm most certainly not googling it, because the internet's always like: *cancer*, *stroke*, *heart attack*, DEATH*!!!!!!!!*

3.14 a.m.

Oh my God, I slept for, like, three hours, but now I'm wide awake, and my stomach hurts again. It's a dull pain that gets worse every time I breathe in.

Maybe I shouldn't breathe in.

This is seriously horrendous.

Maybe I should re-read *Romeo and Juliet*. It usually puts me to sleep.

Or I could watch some idiots on YouTube, or just the news, because the more I watch stupid people, the less I fear death.

Today, I had to go on a mission no fifteen-year-old would ever have to go on if they

a) didn't have a dead father,
b) didn't have an absent mother, and
c) weren't living with an insane Scottish woman, who's now even more insane, and who only knows other insane people.

I'd just got home from school when Kate called me from the charity shop.

Kate: You need to do something for me, but no one can ever know about it.
Me: I'm not buying drugs.
Kate: Don't be ridiculous. Can you come to the shop?
Me: I'll be there in ten minutes.

When I got there, Kate pulled me behind the till.

Kate: (whispering) I need you to go to the Goat.
Me: (thinking: This is a made-up James-related mission) No.
Kate: (giving me a look) . . .
Me: Sorry, go on.
Kate: It's about Pat.

Me: (looking around, noticing she's not in) . . .

Kate: You need to go to the Goat and collect her, and then take her home. I can't close the shop. And no one can know about this. Ever.

Me: Why is she there?

Kate: Look, Phoebe, can you just do this for me now? We can talk about it later.

Me: OK, OK, fine. Where does she live?

Kate gave me a piece of till roll she'd written the address on and £20 so I could take a taxi there and back.

Kate: Don't just drop her off, though, Phoebe. Make sure she gets into her house.

Looking back, I should have realized at that point what was going on, but I didn't. Probably because I tend to only see the best in people.

At the Goat, James was like: 'Hi, Phoebs.'

(I was thinking: Just because you're having sex with Kate doesn't mean I'm now 'Phoebs' to you.)

James: Thank you so much. I'd take her home myself, but my manager wants her gone now, and I don't finish until ten, so I called Kate.

Me: I don't understand.

James: (pointing to one of the booths where Pat was asleep with her head on the table) She's had one too many.

Me: Oh my God.

Pat: *Zzhhhhhhhhhhhh.*

James: Come on, Pat, my darling. Let's get you home.

He hoisted her up, and together we dragged her to the taxi rank out front.

The whole time, Pat was holding on to her little-old-lady shopping trolley, and when she wouldn't let go, we had to push it into the back seat on top of her. I ended up sitting in the front with the driver, who was like: 'Your nan?' And I was like: 'I've never seen her before in my life.'

Why do I say these things?

The driver didn't speak to me again until we arrived at Pat's.

She lives in a ground-floor flat in a really ugly building just by Haydon's Road station.

I tried to get her out of the taxi by myself, but turns out, even smallish people weigh an absolute ton when they're smashed. And then her trolley got its wheel wedged under one of the seats, and in the end, the driver had to help, and together we managed to get Pat inside, and plop her onto the sofa.

The flat was in an absolute state. I was embarrassed, even though it's got nothing to do with me.

It smelt of damp and cold baked beans, and I knew the driver was judging.

At one point, he looked at me like: *How can you let her live in such a total shithole?*

I didn't say anything about the flat or Pat, but I must have thanked the driver like a million times, which probably made me look guilty.

Back in the taxi, I texted Kate:

Phoebe: *Mission accomplished. She was totally pissed.*

Kate was just like:

Kate: *Thank you xxxxxxxxxxxxxxx*

At home, I took a long shower, but I swear I can still smell Pat's flat on me.

I'm trying to revise, but I can't get over it all.

I made a revision timetable, but because it took me forty minutes longer than anticipated to make it, I'm already behind.

Fuck off, Miriam.

And I know Pat is horrendous, and opinionated, and probably racist, and I hate her, but no one should have to live like that.

7.40 p.m.

According to the internet, six thousand deadly accidents occur in the home every year, and having seen how Pat lives, I can totally see why:

a) Sink overflowing with dishes: Risk of *E.coli*.
b) Floor littered with ten years' worth of recycling: Risk of trip/fall, and consequential broken neck.
c) Rats congregating after dark, eating leftovers, spreading diseases: Risk of bubonic plague.

9.15 p.m.

I went downstairs and talked to Kate about the state of Pat's flat.

She was proper shocked.

She said that Pat's husband died of cancer a few years ago, and that Pat still hasn't come to terms with it. Apparently she particularly struggles when it's birthdays or anniversaries or Christmas, and Kate suspects that today may have been one of those (obviously not Christmas). Apparently she doesn't usually drink. Maybe that's why she was so pissed. Maybe she only had one pint and was out cold.

The thing is, you wouldn't know she's in such a state from just looking at her. Her clothes are horrendous style-wise, but they're not dirty. Her hair looks neat, and she doesn't smell. Except today, of course, when she reeked of booze.

Kate was like: 'You mustn't tell anyone else. Pat's a very private person, and she'd be mortified if she knew this was common knowledge.'

Too late.

I've already texted Emma. Not because I wanted to gossip, but because I'm actually proper shocked. We're meeting at

Starbucks tomorrow so I can tell her everything.

P.S. I'm still itchy from being in that flat for, like, two minutes.

SATURDAY 5 MAY   #TOTHERESCUE

We're going over to Pat's house tomorrow to clean.

Kate is hiring a van, and it'll be me, her, James and Emma, who now has time this weekend after all . . .

When I got to Starbucks this morning, Emma was already waiting. She smiled at me from across the room, and it felt like everything was fine. Like: everything.

I told her about my trip to Pat's, and she was just like: 'We need to find out if she's a hoarder, or if she's physically not able to do cleaning, or if there's something else going on.'

I was like: 'How can we know without looking inside her head?' Emma was like: 'You were there. What does your gut instinct tell you?'

I don't believe in gut instinct but facts, but I didn't say that to Emma. I told her that I reckon things got out of hand, and the problem now is that even if Pat decided to tidy a bit, it would make zero difference, because the place is basically a landfill.

Emma was just like: 'We're going to have to go over there and tidy her house.'

I was like: 'We can't. We'd need a skip and heavy machinery.' But Emma was like: 'You can't tell me a story like that and expect me not to act on it. Phoebe, honestly, what sort of world do we live in where people like us can't help an elderly person who's having a hard time at the moment?'

I swear Emma's the real-life Jesus.

Or maybe more like a knight in shining armour?

Kitten: dead. Emma: giving it mouth-to-mouth.

Old lady: drowning in rubbish. Emma: going in, armed with bin bags and bleach.

Later at the shop, Emma spoke to Kate, who spoke to Pat, who then immediately left the shop in a hurry, but called two hours later, and Kate was like: 'I'm glad. We'll see you tomorrow.'

Emma: We're on?

Kate: (thumbs up) We're on.

Kate told us again that we can't tell anyone, but the only people who don't know already are Alex, Bill and Melanie, and none of them were at the shop today, because Alex is staying with his grandparents over the bank holiday, and Bill and Melanie are in Scotland. By the time they get back, it'll be done and dusted (literally).

Don't know how I feel about tomorrow. Last night, I had nightmares about rats eating my face.

SUNDAY 6 MAY   #HARDWORK.COM

Today I

a) decluttered Pat's house,
b) had a fight with Emma, and
c) spent an hour in the bath trying to name every muscle that hurt from all the manual labour.

This morning, we picked up the van at eight thirty and arrived at Pat's at nine.

The flat was even worse than I remembered, and it was obvious that Pat was totally embarrassed. I actually felt sorry for her when she was like: 'Would anybody like a cup of tea?' And we were just like: No thanks – we've seen your kitchen.

Kate was definitely shocked and all like: 'Pat, why did you never come to me? We could have sorted this a long time ago.'

Kate and James volunteered to clean the kitchen, Pat said she wanted to do her bedroom, and Emma and I were assigned to clear the living room, which is where we had the argument.

I was like: 'It's bad enough we all die alone, but do we have to die in a pile of our own rubbish?'

Emma was all defensive like: 'We don't all die alone, Phoebe.' But I was like: 'No, we actually do.'

Emma: . . .
Me: What I mean is, when you're dying, you're the only person in your body doing the dying.
Emma: But you don't have to be alone with it. Someone can be there when your body does the dying.
Me: (thinking: Why am I such a dick?) I'm sorry.
Emma: . . .
Me: I'm an idiot, OK?
Emma: No, it's fine. It's your opinion, and you promised you wouldn't hold back because of me, so it's fine.

I continued to scoop piles of newspapers, magazines and takeaway menus into a recycling bag for a bit, but I felt that I should say something else because Emma looked all annoyed and sad, and so I was like: 'Kate was with my dad when he died.'

I looked at Emma to see her reaction, but apart from her eyebrows going up for a millisecond, there wasn't one. She didn't look at me, either – just kept collecting the gazillion empty Shloer bottles. But in the end, she said: 'I didn't know that.'

Me: They worked at a hospital that got bombed. Mum, Dad and Kate. I only found out recently. Did you know?

Emma: Why would I have known about that?

Me: Just wondering.

She stopped with the binning of the bottles, and the room went all quiet because there was no more rustling or clinking, and she finally looked at me. Dust particles danced in a ray of sunshine.

Emma: What was his name?

Me: Ilan. He was from Israel.

Emma: Isn't it nice to know he wasn't alone?

Me: I guess.

Emma: (all aggressive) No. Not *I guess*, Phoebe.

Me: . . .

Emma: Admit it. It's a nice thought.

Me: Are you telling me off?

Emma: Yes, because sometimes you don't seem to realize what you're saying.

Me: What *am* I saying?

Emma: (shaking her head at me) . . .

Me: No, tell me.

Emma: I'm not having this conversation with you.

Me: What conversation?

Emma: (exasperated now, back to throwing empty glass bottles into a bag for life) Any conversation, Phoebe.

Me: Fuck off, w—

Emma: (leaving the room): Fucking off.

Me: I didn't mean literally.

Emma: (returning for a second) I don't think you can literally
fuck off. Fucking off *literally* doesn't mean anything.

She went into the kitchen, where I heard her speaking to Kate
and James, but I couldn't hear what they were saying, and
then I heard the front door opening and shutting, and I
watched her through the living-room window as she walked
down the path to the road, and I was just like: WTF? Because
I didn't think I had offended her to the point of her actually
leaving.

I felt panicky pins and needles all over my body, and so I got
out my phone and called her, and she answered after two rings.

Emma: Yes?
Me: I'm sorry if I offended you.
Emma: I'm not offended.
Me: Then I'm sorry for upsetting you.
Emma: I'm not upset.
Me: You walked out.
Emma: . . .
Me: . . .
Emma: I'm usually more mature.
Me: Are you actually leaving?
Emma: . . .
Me: Because you forgot your backpack.
Emma: (laughing a bit) No. I'm getting some air. And I'm
        getting snacks. Bye.

And then she hung up on me.

I sat down on Pat's sofa and watched the dust slowly settle until the ray of sunshine carried nothing but sunshine.

Emma returned twenty minutes later and gave me a packet of ready salted crisps and a Dr Pepper.

I don't know how she knew those are my favourite snacks, and it made me feel fizzy on the inside. That could have been the Dr Pepper, though.

For the rest of the day, all I could think was that I wouldn't have known what to get for Emma. She bought herself a bottle of Lucozade Original and a small packet of Minstrels. I've obviously now made a mental note.

James and I took one load of rubbish to the dump at lunchtime, which took, like, an hour, because apparently every single person in Wimbledon was clearing out their flat/house/garden/shed too.

I asked James if he thought that everybody dies alone, but he just laughed and was like: 'You're so random, Phoebe. The things you come out with.'

At four, we were literally starving, and so we ordered Domino's, which we ate outside, sitting on the too-low garden wall. Emma took a selfie of her and Pat, which I think should win the picture-of-the-year competition under the title: *South London: Where Past and Present Shape the Future.*

I sat down on the other side of Emma, and she smiled at me.

She took a big bite of her pizza, and I watched a string of cheese getting longer and longer, and when Emma pulled a really silly face, I helped, and stretched the cheesy, gooey string with my finger until it finally snapped. Then we both laughed.

Me: I thought you were revising this weekend.

Emma: Real life tops revision on the pyramid of priorities.

Me: GCSEs are real life.

Emma: Are they?

Me: Ha ha.

Emma: What do you think you'll remember when you're eighty? Revising for GCSEs that Sunday, or helping Pat, and eating pizza, and being with friends?

Me: Fair enough.

Emma: (chewing) . . .

Me: Are you worried though? About GCSEs?

Emma: (with her mouth full) Shitting it, actually.

And we really laughed.

Emma: I'm terrible at maths. No, I lie – I'm OK at it, but I can't remember formulas very well, so I'm doomed.

Me: I know it's, like, last minute, but I can help you if you like, because I'm actually really good at maths, and I can show you how the formulas are totally self-explanatory.

Emma: Show-off.

Me: No, I didn't mean it like that. All I'm say—

Emma: Oh my God, Phoebe – I'm joking. Thank you. I may take you up on it.

Me: OK.

When we left, Pat was like: 'Thank you so much. I don't know how I can ever repay you.' Kate was just like: 'Och, don't be ridiculous now. We're all here for each other. But you can try to look after yourself a bit better.'

Pat: Sometimes I don't bother because it's just me, you know?

Kate: Well, we need you, Pat. Remember that.

P.S. Kate and James are literally inseparable now. I think they even had a shower together.

P.P.S. Pat's flat looked amazing when we left. All you could smell was bleach, and I hope she leaves the windows open overnight so she doesn't die from toxic fumes.

I am so sore from all the house-clearing, I can barely lift my arms.

It's a bank holiday today, and so I revised for English, but I'd had enough by lunchtime, and so I went to the charity shop. Pat was there, so she isn't dead. Phew! She bought Kate an orchid from M&S to say thank you, and I now wonder if she used Emma's voucher for it.

My stomach pain is driving me absolutely insane.

Maybe I'm allergic to dairy? There was a lot of cheese on that pizza yesterday.

I spoke to Mum this evening, and it was all about GCSEs.

She was like: 'Make sure you get a really good night's sleep beforehand, and prepare your clothes the night before as well, and make sure you take the earlier bus, just in case.'

Whatever, Mum.

If she was really all that concerned, she'd be here. I lied to her about the amount of revision I've been doing because I just can't have that conversation. She was like: 'And remember to breathe, Phoebe.' But I literally don't know how to at the moment.

9.03 p.m.

I spent thirty-five minutes revising geography, and the cost price of a regular banana versus a fair-trade banana. The regular banana producer (i.e. grower) gets 7 per cent of the price; a fair-trade producer (i.e. grower) gets 14 per cent, which is double. But, double of 0.01 pennies per banana is still shit. And if they get 0.01 pennies for a banana, how much can the person harvesting it possibly earn?

I'm going to have to read something less depressing before bed. Something sciency.

TUESDAY 8 MAY   #DRGOOGLE

Last night, I had crazy dreams about leaves, and radioactive rocks, and fair-trade bananas, and trying to say numbers in French.

My brain is trying so hard to hold on to information, it fails to process it in any way, shape or form, and so I'm left with this saturated cloud of knowledge where nothing means anything at all.

In other news, Miriam Patel was back at school today. She looked like shit, and she pretty much kept her gob shut, which means there must be something seriously wrong with her.

Polly was like: 'I think we should talk to her.'

But I reminded her that Miriam Patel may be feeling a bit delicate after her hospitalization, but she's still two-faced, and should therefore not be pitied. And you know what Polly said to me? 'Grow up, Phoebe.'

What have I ever done to anyone?

I'm 100 per cent the only person I know who doesn't talk shit all day.

I don't choose my friends according to who is the most socially interesting, I don't jump on every single band wagon, and I most certainly would never settle for godawful sex with my loser boyfriend just because I'm too worried about hurting his feelings.

I'm the least childish person I know.

My brain isn't complicated like: Oh, I'm saying this, but what I really mean is this.

Everyone can seriously fuck off.

Also, I finally checked online about my stomach ache.

The internet says: *A stomach ache doesn't usually last long.*

Great. I've had mine for weeks.

Suggestions on when to seek medical advice:

- The pain gets much worse (tick).
- The pain won't go away (tick).
- You have unusual vaginal discharge (er, no – my discharge is fine).
- You are bleeding from your bottom (no again).

Here's what it's not:

- Appendicitis (because the pain is too high).

Here's what it could be:
- Stomach ulcer.

- IBS.
- Acute cholecystitis.
- Diverticulitis.

I honestly feel sick just thinking about it. I reckon it must be an ulcer, because I have five out of eight symptoms:

- Dull pain in the stomach.
- Not wanting to eat because of pain.
- Nausea.
- Feeling easily full.
- Heartburn.

Dr Google recommends I visit my GP immediately, but who's got time to see a GP?

I'll just have to monitor my symptoms and go to A&E if I'm vomiting blood.

Great.

P.S. I could also be pregnant. LOL.

WEDNESDAY 9 MAY   #BREAKINGPOINT

Miriam Patel had another hysterical fit today.

She's such a mess.

She started crying at lunch, and Jacob had to pull her into a standing position and drag her to geography. Her teeth were chattering like those wind-up ones you get at a joke shop.

Mrs Holmes was all like: 'Miriam, I think it's best for us to send you home so you can get some rest.'

But Miriam Patel was just like: 'Please don't call my mum. I'm OK – really.'

I looked at Polly the whole time, and I could see that she too thought Miriam was actually going insane.

I mean, I still don't feel sorry for her, but it was very confusing seeing her completely non-bitchy and fragile.

It feels like the entire universe is out of whack.

8.19 p.m.

I texted Emma on the bus home to ask if she's really sore too after the day at Pat's, but she hasn't texted back.

8.45 p.m.

The hardest thing about Physics GCSE is going to be remembering all the formulas. Everything else is basic.

One test question goes: 'Figure One shows how the output from fossil-fuel power stations in the UK varied over a twenty-four-hour period. Explain the variance.'

Now, you don't have to be a genius to work out that at midnight less electricity is needed than at 7 a.m., when it's like: Good morning, Britain, and 66 million people are putting the kettle on.

Glad I didn't schedule in an hour to work out something so blatantly obvious.

P.S. I wish this horrendous stomach ache would go away.

THURSDAY 10 MAY   #KILLMENOW

Emma wasn't at the charity shop today.

Apparently she's ill.

I was steaming clothes all afternoon, and then I yawned, and Pat was like: 'Ah. You're bored without your friend, aren't you?'

I was just like: 'I don't mind. I like my own company.' And then Pat was like: 'I know what you mean. I'm the same.'

Great.

I'm literally Pat.

After dinner, I spent an hour photoshopping a picture of Richard. I made him a speech bubble that reads: *I miss you. Get well soon.*

It looks amazing, but for all the wrong reasons. Mostly because Richard is so cross-eyed.

I'm going to send it to Emma now.

Emma messaged me in the middle of the night last night, but I was asleep.

Seriously, I don't sleep for three weeks, and the one night I do, she messages me, and I sleep through it?

She wrote:

Emma: *Thanks for your picture, Richard. You are the most handsome kitten. When I'm not contagious any more, I will come and visit you.*

I'm really happy she replied, but what have I started? Now she's talking to the stupid designer kitten and not to me.

I wonder what's wrong with her. But I don't want to message her again already, just in case she thinks I'm totally annoying.

P.S. Miriam Patel got through a whole day without crying.

P.P.S. This afternoon, I revised.

Fascinating yet entirely irrelevant fact learned: The most stable thorium isotope has a half-life of 14.5 billion years. Just to put that into perspective, the universe (the universe! Is about 13.8 billion years old.

Emma's still ill.

At the charity shop, Bill and Melanie brought lunch for everyone, which was really nice, but I wasn't hungry, plus my stomach's still hurting.

Bill: Phoebe, my angel, what's got your goat today?

Me: I'm tired.

Bill: You work too hard. School all day — you're here most afternoons and on weekends. You need to give yourself more you-time.

Me: I actually need to revise for GCSEs.

Bill: You need to see your friends.

Me: I've got no friends.

Bill: (laughing that laugh that makes the walls shake) I'm finding that very hard to believe.

Me: It's true.

Bill: We're your friends, but I doubt you'd want to spend your precious free time with old farts like us —

Melanie: Who's old?

And then they both laughed, and he gave her a kiss.

Imagine it. Being married to the same person for sixty years and still finding them funny and wanting to give them a kiss.

I'm such a failure as a human. I couldn't even get my best friend to wish me a Happy New Year.

I know we've been talking about GCSEs for years, and maybe that's why it always seemed like they'd never happen, but now they're tomorrow.

I feel like I'm about to be involuntarily inserted into a hamster wheel that isn't going to stop spinning. I'll eventually be thrown back out of it, dizzy, disoriented, and possibly puking, and only when everything's too late, I'll realize what went on and what was required.

The most terrifying thing for me is the anticipated pace of this exam hell. The pressure that you have to be on top form every day.

And still I can't revise.

Instead, I found this really funny website where people deliberately make poetry shit.

So instead of:

> *I met a traveller from an antique land*
> *Who said: 'Two vast and trunkless legs of stone*
> *Stand in the desert . . .'*

It goes:

> *I met a traveller from an antique land*
> *Who said nothing . . .*

LOL.

7.53 p.m.

I told Kate I wasn't hungry and didn't want dinner, but of course that never works, and so she brought dinner to me.

Kate: (holding a tray with tomato soup) Phoebe. Talk to me.

Me: . . .

Kate: (sitting down on my bed, scooping soup onto a spoon, blowing on it, then pushing it in front of my face) Eat.

Me: (opening mouth, eating soup) . . .

Kate: Better.

Me: . . .

Kate: What's going on?

Me: I've got a tummy ache.

Kate: OK. Where does it hurt?

Me: (pointing to it) . . .

Kate: (feeding me more soup) OK.

Me: . . .

Kate: Do you think you're sick, or could you be worried about something?

Me: Worried about what?

Kate: Tomorrow.

Mc: (shrugging) . . .

Kate: You understand that these exams aren't the be-all and end-all, though, don't you?

Me: But they are.

Kate: No, they're not. Their outcome doesn't change your brilliance or your potential as a person, Phoebe. And don't let anybody convince you otherwise. There are bigger things in life than GCSEs.

Me: That's what Emma thinks.

Kate: And Emma's a very wise woman.

Me: (being spoon-fed more soup) . . .

Kate: You know you're my favourite person in the whole wide world, don't you?

Me: I thought Mum was.

Kate: What? Boring old Amelia? Don't be daft.

Me: What about James?

Kate: Oh, please.

Me: (taking the bowl off the tray and eating by myself) . . .

Kate: And what's happening with Polly?

Me: (shrugging) Don't know. I don't know if she's had a boyfriend-induced orgasm yet.

Kate: (laughing): Well, I think you should definitely check, and if the answer is no, I think we need to have her over for dinner and explain a few things.

Me: I've read about the vaginal orgasm.

Kate: Oh, yes? Good for you.

Me: You think I should tell her about it?

Kate: The trick is to tilt your hips upwards.

Me: I know. But please let's not talk about it.

Kate: You started it.

Me: I'm regretting it.

Kate: Eat.

Me: Fine.

After I finished the soup, we went downstairs, and James made me a cheese toastie.

Kate said I should rest my brain for a minute, and so we watched a David Attenborough programme, and the designer and non-designer kittens literally lost their shit over it.

They all sat in front of the telly, and every time the lioness went for the kill, they stumbled all over each other and meowed like crazy.

Isn't it weird to think that lions and cats have the same ancestors?

To be fair, though, ancient humans used to be able to make fire by rubbing stones and twigs together. I know people who can't light a match.

P.S. Twenty-seven exams over six weeks.

I had Computer Science in the morning, and Religious Studies in the afternoon, and I can already tell that the biggest challenge during GCSEs is going to be to not write on the blank page that says: *Do not write on this page.* And being in the same room with so many people, and trying to ignore their rustling and breathing and fidgeting.

Between exams, Miriam Patel was all like: 'I need to quickly go over some dates for this afternoon.'

I was like: 'Could she be any more ridiculous?' Because little in life is more obvious than the year Jesus was born, but then Polly told me what's been going on with Miriam, because she found out from Tristan, who found out from Jacob, and it's actually so tragic, and maybe I shouldn't have made fun of her.

Apparently it's not Miriam stressing about GCSEs; it's her parents.

Polly said that Miriam's dad is obsessed with wanting her to go to Cambridge, and because he works all the time, and Miriam's mum is at home all the time, he reckons it's Miriam's mum's job to make sure that Miriam gets all the grades, and when she doesn't, her mum goes proper ape shit because it means Miriam's dad is going to shout at Miriam's mum for failing as a mother.

When Miriam did majorly badly in her maths mock exam, she apparently heard her parents having a shouting match in the kitchen over it, and her dad was going: 'You've got one job, Grace — one fucking job,' to Miriam Patel's mum, and then he smashed a glass.

That's proper shit, isn't it?

No wonder Miriam gets panic attacks.

I mean, I still don't like her, but imagine your parents being that horrible to each other because you didn't get a good grade that one time.

I'm lucky, really, because at least every time I don't do very well, I can be all like: 'It's because I'm literally an orphan.' And instead of being angry, Mum just feels guilty.

Polly reckons we should help Miriam Patel with maths.

That means she thinks *I* should help Miriam Patel with maths, because Polly literally can't work out five plus five.

I was going to say no, but I do feel a bit sorry for Miriam, because nobody deserves to have shit parents. Also, if we have a revision session together, I don't have to have one on my own, and I can be like: #RevisedAllAfternoon.

P.S I have French tomorrow, and I seriously need to brush up on my fruits and vegetables.

Did you know that the word *pineapple* is pretty much *ananas* in every other language but English? Even in Hebrew, but of course it's spelled like this: אננס so you'd never know.

I also have to revise the words for *under*, *over*, *in front* and *behind*, *to the right* and *to the left*, because, apparently, when travelling to France, no one has access to Google Maps, and one must solely rely on getting directions from non-English-speaking locals.

Yawn.

Emma isn't taking French. She's taking Spanish, which makes so much more sense, because apparently 570 million people in the world speak it.

Only, like, 220 million speak French.

What was I thinking?

TUESDAY 15 MAY #CONTEMPLATINGDEATH

This morning, I had French 1 and 3, and this afternoon I had Biology 1.

Matilda Hollingsworth had a crying fit during Biology 1 because she had to really, really go to the toilet, but she didn't want to go because she thought she was behind on time.

Mr Kane was really nice about it, though. He went over to her desk and was all like: 'Look, Matilda – go to the toilet, and I promise you'll be able to concentrate much better.'

I went to the charity shop afterwards, which was a big mistake, because I'm now almost certain that I have stomach cancer.

Pat caught me stretching, and rubbing my tummy, and she was like: 'Stomach ache?' And I was like: 'It's OK.'

And then she told me how her husband died from stomach cancer.

Why would you be like that?

Someone: I have a really annoying stomach ache.
You: My husband died of stomach cancer.

OMG.

So when I got home, instead of revising for this week's biggies, French and Chemistry, I just googled *stomach cancer survival rates*, and Google reckons that if it's discovered in the early stages, the five-year survival rate is 65 per cent. That means that thirty-five out of one hundred people die. It obviously also means that sixty-five people live, but still.

If the cancer has spread to other areas, the five-year survival rate is about 30 per cent. That means that seventy people out of one hundred die, and only thirty live.

Maybe I should go to the GP.

If it's cancer, I hope that it hasn't spread.

Kate didn't seem particularly worried when I told her about my stomach ache the other night, and I did feel a bit better after the soup and the cheese toastie. Maybe I'm not intolerant to dairy after all?

I wish it would just go away, because I don't want to die of stomach cancer.

I don't want to die of any cancer.

In fact, I don't know how I want to die.

I wonder if Emma would come to my funeral.

I don't think black would suit her.

Maybe I should insist everyone wear bright colours 'to celebrate my life'.

Bleugh!

P.S. I have no exam in the morning, and Religious Studies 2 in the afternoon, but I refuse to revise for it, because nobody is ever going to give a shit about how I did in that subject.

P.P.S. Actually, maybe I should try to do well, because I read that if you want to convert to Judaism, you have to seriously impress the Rabbi.

P.P.P.S. Polly just texted to say we're going to meet with Miriam Patel at Starbucks tomorrow morning to do maths. I'm only going because I miss the Polly that's all independent, and no-nonsense, and 'this is what we're doing'.

WEDNESDAY 16 MAY   #LESSONS

When I sat down at the table with Miriam Patel, I literally felt the universe twitch.

Miriam wasn't her usual self (at first!), because she wasn't at all bitchy (at first!).

We did a few problems, and turns out, the thing with Miriam Patel is that she really does know the answer, but she thinks she doesn't, and so she confuses everything. It's not like with Polly, who actually really doesn't get it, and even if you tell her the answer, she's still like: 'Eh? Sorry, but my brain doesn't do any of this, but that's fine, because you don't have to be good at everything. If we were all good at everything, we'd have no geniuses, and the world would be without wonder.'

OMG, I love that about Polly so much. She's good at finding wonder. Maybe that's her superpower. She sees things other people don't see. Maybe that's why she's with Tristan.

Anyway, at the end of our pointless extracurricular maths lesson, I was just like: 'Don't waste my time, Miriam. You know how to do this, so don't be an idiot.' And she was like: 'That's easy for you to say. Your mum's not here, so she probably doesn't give a shit about your results.'

I could feel Polly flinch, and Miriam looked like she maybe hadn't meant to say it out loud, but then she was all like: *Whatever, I said it, and it's true.*

I just went: 'Get out of my sight.'

After she'd gone, Polly tried to be all: 'She didn't mean it.' But I was like: 'Of course she meant it. She always means it, only she usually doesn't say it to my face.'

Polly: Thank you for offering to help her, though.

Me: I hate Miriam Patel. I can't believe I fell for her sad story.

Polly: It *is* a sad story, Phoebe. Apparently her dad gets really arsey.

Me: And apparently my mum doesn't give a shit.

Polly: She's just jealous that your mum trusts you to become a responsible adult without her monitoring your every move.

Me: You think that's what she's doing?

Polly: Who? Miriam?

Me: No, Mum.

Polly: Phoebe, hello. Do you think she'd go gallivanting around the planet if you were a mess?

Me: I hadn't really thought about it from that angle.

Polly: My mum would never do what your mum does because she's too insecure. If I hang up without telling her I love her, she calls right back.

Me: I never tell Mum I love her.

Polly: I'm sure she knows without you having to say it every five minutes. And that's why she can do what she does.

Me: I don't think I've ever thought about it that way.

Polly: No, because even though you're the cleverest person I've ever met, you're dumb as fuck when it comes to real life.

Me: Fuck off. Why are you horrible to me?

Polly: You fuck off. I'm right.

Me: How are things with Training Wheels?

Polly: When can we stop calling him that?

Me: Probably never.

Polly: How are things with you?

Me: Great.

Polly: So not great.

Me: I've had a stomach ache for, like, four weeks, and Kate is all loved-up with her new boyfriend.

Polly: Kate has a boyfriend?

Me: Yes. James.

Polly: Who's James?

Me: You know James. The guy who was at the charity
        shop that day you came in. They've been getting it on
        for a c —

Polly: Wait a minute – she's dating that hot guy?

Me: Yes. James.

Polly: He's, like, twenty.

Me: Twenty-three, actually.

Polly: And she's how old?

Me: Thirty-eight.

Polly: That's so cool

Me: . . .

Polly: Good for her.

Me: I'm sure it must be.

Polly: At least you've got someone super hot walking
        around yours all the time . . . possibly in a towel?
        Gosh, (biting her lip) Kate's so lucky.

Me: (thinking about James in nothing but a towel, but
        unable to share her enthusiasm) And what about
        Tristan. You know. Sex. And all that?

Polly: . . .

Me: Seriously? How are you still with him? What's the
        point in even having sex when it's bad?

Polly: Because I love him. Don't be so stupid.

Me: Why can't you just masturbate and tell him to watch?

Polly: (eyes nearly rolling out of her head) . . .

Me: Polly, seriously, what's your problem? You're not
        like that. You're a feminist, and you think it's great
        Kate is shagging someone half her age. What's the

deal with Training Wheels?

Polly: (falling back into the sofa, covering her face) I don't know, OK. I don't know. It shouldn't be awkward, but it's awkward. And I hate that it's awkward, and it's all my fault, because I let it become awkward.

Me: You're going to have to talk to him about the clitoris.

Polly: (sitting up and suddenly proper in my face) Oh my God, Phoebe, can you stop going on about the stupid clitoris?

Me: OK. So if you want a vaginal orgasm, and you're on the bottom, you have to tilt your pelvis upwards.

Polly: (clearly imagining this) I hate my life.

Me: It can't be that difficult.

Polly: You have no idea.

Me: People like you are the reason why women still struggle in the world.

Polly: (looking at me like I've actually gone insane) . . .

Me: Because you don't insist on having what should be yours.

Polly: . . .

Me: So every time you and Tristan do it, he has an orgasm, right?

Polly: I'm sure I've told you this before, but sometimes I wish you sounded less like a textbook.

Me: It's all textbook stuff.

Polly: (sipping her drink) And they say romance is dead.

Me: No, listen. Training Wheels having an orgasm totally

Polly: Definitely not.

Me: So the sex is for fun.

Polly: And because I love him.

Me: But it should be enjoyable.

Polly: I didn't say it wasn't enjoyable.

Me: I'm sorry, but you need to insist you get what you came there for.

Polly: God, I'm a failure as a woman.

Me: Not what I said. But you and Tristan wouldn't make dinner together, and then only he gets to eat it.

Polly: (lying back down on the Starbucks sofa, dramatically throwing her arms over her head) I'm responsible for suppression. Misogyny. The gender pay gap.

Me: . . .

Polly: Because I don't insist on getting what's rightfully mine.

Me: (nodding) Basically.

Talking to Polly felt like the months of awkwardness had never happened.

And for the first time in ages, I saw her as her own person again, not like this total weirdo who just follows Tristan around.

Maybe she's changed back a little bit now that she's more settled in her relationship?

It must be frustrating for her putting in the effort when they have sex and getting fuck all in return.

I honestly don't understand it. Just say the words: 'I'm sorry, but what you're currently doing with your penis is not effective. Please use your mouth.' Or something.

To be perfectly honest, I don't get how people have the energy for it at all. Life's hard enough without a (shit) sex life.

I hope Polly at least remembers to tilt her pelvis next time.

P.S. Religious Studies 2 was fine. I reckon the Rabbi would be pleased. And now I don't have to think about any of it ever again in my life. Phew! Very glad that box has been ticked.

THURSDAY 17 MAY   #NATIONWIDEMENTALBREAKDOWNALERT

Kate left an article from the *Guardian* on the kitchen table for me with the headline: 'Stress and Anxiety: How the New GCSE is Affecting Mental Health'.

I didn't read it, to be honest, but I don't have to because I'm basically living it.

Matilda has now stopped taking in liquids because she doesn't want to have to go to the toilet, which is unhealthy and will give her kidney failure. And just as we were going over to take Chemistry 1 this morning, Jonathon Luo was so nervous that he threw up into a bin in the courtyard, and because apparently Miriam Patel can't watch people throwing up without throwing up herself, she also puked, but in the toilets.

And because everyone was being sick, the whole room

smelt of sick, and I was literally dry-heaving all the way through the exam.

In the afternoon, we had Computer Science 2, and at that point, all I wanted was to be done with it. I know that attitude sucks, but whatever.

Oh, and P.S. On the bottom of the article from the *Guardian*, there's even the number for the Samaritans, should anybody feel suicidal.

That's so bad, isn't it?

P.P.S. I didn't go to the charity shop today because I've got my final French GCSE tomorrow, and *zut alors*, did I have to cram in last-minute revision.

P.P.P.S. Emma texted to say she's going to the shop tomorrow because she's not got exams, and she's feeling much better, and she needs to get out of the house, and so I'm going too.

FRIDAY 18 MAY   #CAUGHT

Emma would say: Today will not be remembered for having taken French 4, but for having taken down a thief.

I was on the shop floor putting out bric-a-brac this afternoon, because Pat couldn't possibly walk the ten steps from the stockroom herself, when, out of the corner of my eye, I saw this little old lady reach into the size-ten rack, pull out a handful of blouses on hangers, and stuff them into her little-old-lady shopping trolley.

Then she turned around and casually shuffled out of the shop.

I was like: 'No, you don't!'

Because you don't steal from charity.

I mean, you don't steal at all, but you definitely don't steal from charity.

You don't nick shit and sabotage the effort of all those people who give up their free time rummaging through dead people's clothes and other crap in order to make a quid here and there so there's enough money for people who want to find ways to stop people like Emma's brother from dying.

No word of a lie, it was like an epiphany, and I ran after her like a woman possessed.

Outside I was like: Right, left, right, left, and then I spotted her walking up towards Morrisons.

It was raining, and I was soaked before I even passed Starbucks, and because the pavement was brolly-central, I ran on the road, dodging buses.

When I caught up with her, I grabbed hold of her trolley, but suddenly I was proper aquaplaning in my stupid school shoes.

I went arse over tit and skidded on said arse all the way to the entrance of the cinema, little-old-lady shopping trolley in hand.

She came hobbling across to me, her a face all like: 'I'm going to kill you.' But I was quicker.

I reached into her trolley, pulled out the blouses, and held them proper in her face.

Me: I saw you take these from the charity shop without paying for them.

Her: Oh, I didn't mean to—

Me: No! You meant to. I saw you. We've got you on CCTV (lie). You're stealing from cancer children. You, madam, can sink no lower. And I'm having these back.

Then I just marched off.

I mean, of course I didn't march. I sort of hobbled, because at that point I was like: OK, so I've broken my hip.

Back at the shop, Alex, Kate, Emma and Pat were all like: OMG!

Because I was drenched, Kate made me change into something dry, and I ended up wearing a pair of bootcut Levi's jeans and a brown and orange V-neck vest.

Pat was like: 'You look just like me when I was young.'

Whatever, Pat – you were never young.

At first, Kate was like: 'I'm saying this to everyone now: We do *not* confront shoplifters. It ended well today, but your health and safety is what's most important here.'

But right after her speech, she hugged me and kissed my

face the way she knows I hate, and I was a proper hero for a minute.

I think Emma was impressed, but because she's Emma, she was like: 'How sad, though. Having to steal. Or wanting to steal.'

I watched Alex contemplate this for a moment, and when he reached his conclusion, he was like: 'But she was very brave.' Then he high-fived me. And Kate got Starbucks for everyone.

Now, I can't sit down, because my arse cheek is honestly so sore, but at dinner, I realized that it had made me forget all about my stomach ache.

Apparently if there are multiple simultaneous painful stimuli, the mind will only feel the sensation of pain from the most severe injury.

9.00 p.m.

Update: My butt cheek is black and blue.

I'm so glad we don't have exams tomorrow or Sunday, because I don't think I'd be able to sit. They'd have to get me a special table you can stand at.

Maybe I can do it all lying on my front, because, let's face it, that's the only way I'm going to be able to recline for the foreseeable future.

9.15 p.m.

Kate just put arnica lotion on it, and she was laughing the whole time. I could've totally done it myself, but she said it was her duty as a certified (ex-)nurse and my guardian to make sure I hadn't actually broken anything.

She gave the all-clear, but she said that as far as bruises go, mine was a particularly impressive one.

I may take a picture.

SATURDAY 19 MAY   #STILLNOTSITTINGDOWN

I didn't have a stomach ache all day, which basically means the bruise pain is still supressing every other pain receptor in my brain. I even had to wear my school skirt to the charity shop because my skinny jeans press right on the bruise.

When Emma looked at me like: *Why are you wearing that on a Saturday?* I was like: 'My bruise is enormous, and this is the only thing I can wear, so let's not talk about it.'

Emma: Is it really sore?
Me: You have no idea.
Emma: Can you sit down?
Me: No.
Emma: Can I see it?
Me: No!

That was literally all she kept saying to me all day: 'Can I see it? Can I see it? Can I see it?'

And then Kate was like: 'You should see Phoebe's bruise.'

And Emma was like: 'Why has everyone seen it?'

And I was like: 'No one's seen it. Kate's seen it. But she's a nurse.'

And then Kate said: 'Go and show Emma the bruise, Phoebs. It's such a good one.'

I looked at Emma, who was smiling, and then my brain went: It's OK – the pants you're wearing are pretty standard. And so I was like: 'Fine.'

I obviously wasn't going to pull my skirt down in front of everyone, and so I went into the changing room, and Emma closed the curtain from the outside, and peeked in through a tiny gap she'd left for her head.

She made the best face ever when she saw it, with her jaw literally hitting the floor, and then she just kept her mouth wide open.

Me: I know.
Emma: Ouch.
Me: I have to sleep on my front.
Emma: Can I touch it?
Me: No. Why would you want to touch it?
Emma: No reason.

And then her face disappeared. Maybe she gets off on other people's pain, who knows.

Today, she smiled a lot.

Maybe it's because I confronted the shoplifter.

Or maybe it's because the donation of the week is a book called *Painting with Cats: How You Can Help Your Felines Express Themselves*.

Kate picked it up and was like: 'Oh . . .' But Emma and I were like: 'No!'

When we were leaving, Emma asked me to send her updates of Richard and the bruise regularly.

I'm currently lying on my front, and Kate's put a bag of frozen peas on my arse.

From hero to zero.

SUNDAY 20 MAY   #BIRTHDAYWISHES

Mum WhatsApped and gave me another GCSE pep talk.

Then I showed her my bruise, and she laughed.

She also said I have to decide what I want to do for my birthday.

I can't believe it's my birthday again. I only just had one literally yesterday.

Looks like I'm going to deliver on my promise to turn sixteen gracefully, as I'm not in love and crazy.

I've got Sociology tomorrow, but I need to actually revise for English Literature, which is on Tuesday.

Get this. The definition of *sociology* is: *The study of the development, structure and functioning of human society*. But I swear all we ever discuss is the destruction, chaos and malfunctioning of human society.

I was directly behind Ben Carmichael in today's exam, and he wouldn't stop bouncing his foot up and down, and it was right in my eyeline when I was writing, and it drove me absolutely crazy. I ended up twisting my body into such a weird angle in order to not see him that I gave myself a back problem and a crick in the neck. Not to mention the agony of having to sit on my bruise.

I was just willing time to hurry up because I couldn't wait to get out of there.

This afternoon, I was supposed to revise for English, but I ended up messaging with Emma.

Me: *Hello.*

Emma: *Hello. How are you?*

Me: *Fine.*

Emma: *How's the bruise?*

Me: *Still big.*

Emma: *What ya doing?*

Me: *Messaging you.*

Emma: *Ha ha.*

Me: *Revising, but I've got brain ache. I'm also thinking about what I want to do in life.*

Emma: *As in what job?*

Me: *Yes.*

Emma: *And?*

Me:	Don't know.
Emma:	I want to do what your mum does.
Me:	Have a child and leave it with your best friend?
Emma:	Harsh.
Me:	Fact.
Emma:	I'd like to help people. Maybe be a doctor. But I don't know if I'm clever enough.
Me:	I think you're clever.
Emma:	Thanks. We'll see. Or maybe I'll become a counsellor or something.
Me:	I hate people, and I don't want to help anyone.
Emma:	LOL.
Me:	I don't mean you, BTW. I don't hate you.
Emma:	Thanks. It's good to be tolerated.
Me:	OMG, whatever. You know I think you're great.
Emma:	And how would I know that?
Me:	Why else would I want to spend time with you, and message you, and take kitten pictures, and walk you home, and show you my bruise?
Emma:	Why indeed . . .

And then she went offline.

No goodbye. No nothing.

Is that weird?

Am I overthinking it?

Maybe I'm overthinking it.

I knew I shouldn't have messaged her. I knew it even *before* I messaged her, but apparently I just couldn't help myself.

It's like eating a whole pack of Percy Pigs. You know it's going to make you feel sick, but you keep shoving them down your throat anyway in some sort of compulsive frenzy.

10.05 p.m.

If I was working to Miriam Patel's revision schedule, I'd still have fifty-five minutes of revision time left, so I *will* look at English.

10.15 p.m.

Get these questions:

1. How does Sampson provoke the Montague servants?
2. What impression does the audience get from the Nurse?
3. What does Lady Capulet think of Paris?

Question number 4 should be: And why does any of this matter?

I'm going to bed. This is stupid.

TUESDAY 22 MAY   #WHYINDEED

I am so exhausted, I can't even.

English killed me.

I think I finally understand what Polly goes through when

she looks at numbers and fails to see how they make sense, because I had to read the questions, like, three times to understand them.

Afterwards, Polly and I went to the park for lunch. We were lying on the grass and I was telling her that I have no idea what to do in life, was literally pouring my heart out to her, and then I realized that she'd gone to sleep.

I bet she doesn't fall asleep on Tristan.

She even started snoring, but I only woke her when it was time to take Geography 1, and she didn't even apologize. She was just like: 'I think I needed that.'

OMG!

Tonight, I was like: OK, so instead of making an endless list of all the things I hate, why don't I make a list of things I actually like in regards to long-term employment prospects. And here it is:

- Solitude.
- People not talking at me about meaningless crap all day.
- Numbers.
- Clever people/possibly the absence of stupid people altogether.
- Being allowed to have original thought.

Let's see where this leads me.

Everyone at school is suddenly like: OMG, if I fuck up my GCSEs, life is going to be over, and I'm never going to be able to go to university (even though, why does everybody need to go to university anyway?).

Bill said that anyone who wants to train as a plumber has more of a lifetime guarantee of having a decent income than someone who goes to university and studies some meaningless bollocks like: Post-Second World War Japanese Felt-Tip Pen Art.

Sadly I can't be a plumber because I'd have to speak to people all day, and that's like the first thing on my list of things to avoid.

The search continues.

WEDNESDAY 23 MAY   #NASA

Result.

I'm going to become an astronaut.

This occurred to me during Physics 1, which pretty much kick-started my gone-sluggish, sieve-like brain, and I have a feeling I aced that exam.

Because under no circumstances can you be rubbish at physics when you want to be an astronaut.

I checked NASA's website as soon as I got home, and turns out they're always looking to recruit people who are willing to go on long-duration space missions. Like a mission to Mars.

I mean, no one is going there just yet, but current missions are perfect simulations of what such a journey could look like, and you spend eighteen months in isolation with your crew. Which is brilliant, because you get all the excitement of interstellar travel without the threat of your body exploding in the vacuum of space by accident.

And you eat space food the whole time, so my stomach ulcer/cancer could just shut up.

The pain is totally back, FYI.

P.S. Mathematics 1 tomorrow. Bring it!

THURSDAY 24 MAY   #SPACE

OMG, this morning in the toilets, Polly sank the lowest by succumbing to the oldest trick in the book and literally shoving a scroll with mathematical formulas down her pants. I swear it must have been the most intellectually complex thing to ever have touched her vagina. And of course she didn't go to the toilet during the exam to casually peruse it, because who actually does that?

When we were waiting to go in, Polly was like: 'Miriam looks like she's about to pass out.' And something unexpected (sentiment?) happened to me mid eye-roll, and I went over to Miriam and said: 'You know you can actually do this, don't you? And besides, you're not doing this for your parents.' And Miriam Patel went: 'How insightful of you to assume there's more to my life than just my grades and my parents.' I think she was being sarcastic, which is totally passive aggressive, and so I didn't reply to her, just walked straight back to Polly, who was completely nonsubtly adjusting her pants/vaginal scroll.

Anyway, I think I did well again. Seems all I needed was the prospect of silent spacey solitude, and my synapses were falling all over themselves to make it happen.

P.S. Apparently your body doesn't actually instantly explode in a vacuum, but it's something that science-fiction writers made up for dramatic effect. According to the internet, you may be able to survive a one- or two-minute exposure to the vacuum of space.

What's also fascinating is that apparently the liquids near your body's surface would evaporate instantly, like the moisture in your eyes, and even your spit.

Imagine your spit evaporating.

P.P.S. You can buy space food at the Science Museum. Maybe I should go and buy some.

P.P.P.S. *Painting with Cats* is gone, and apparently nobody remembers selling it. Bet Kate's reading it right now.

FRIDAY 25 MAY   #ENGLISHIITHELL

Today occurred the horror that was English Literature 2.

I had a nightmare last night that I couldn't find the right room, so when I sat down at the desk this morning, with the paper in front of me, I felt a certain sense of achievement already.

Apart from that, I never want to speak about Romeo or Juliet ever again. They're dead to me (LOL, I'm so funny).

It's officially half-term now.

This week has been so stressful.

9.05 p.m.

I took a picture of my bruise and sent it to Emma.

She wrote back: *Tease*.

And then she said that she's planning on revising in the mornings next week and working at the charity shop in the afternoons.

I think I'll do the same because I need to not go insane from revision.

SATURDAY 26 MAY   #TREEPOLLENGATE

My brain feels foggy.

Maybe it's hay fever.

According to the internet, symptoms for hay fever are:

- Runny nose and nasal congestion.
- Watery, itchy, red eyes (allergic conjunctivitis).
- Sneezing.

- Coughing.
- Itchy nose, roof of mouth, or throat.
- Swollen blue-coloured skin under the eyes (allergic shiners).
- Postnasal drip (LOL).
- Fatigue.

I'm actually not displaying any of these symptoms, apart from fatigue, but the tree pollen count was high today, and I ended up with actual pollen in my hair. Which may have caused the fogginess.

Emma and I went on a Starbucks run for the shop this afternoon.

It was really hot, dry and sunny today (hence the high pollen count), so Starbucks was literally Frappuccino-central, and we had to wait for ages. I was casually leaning against the cake and muffin counter, just a little bit in front of Emma, and all of the sudden, I felt her hand in my hair.

Emma: You've got tree pollen everywhere.
Me: . . .
Emma: Did you sleep outside or something?
Me: I have no idea. I mean, no.
Emma: (laughing, picking yellow bits out of my hair): . . .
Me: Are you laughing at me?
Emma: Why would I laugh at you?
Me: Because I'm always such a mess with bruises and tree pollen and having to wear shit from the charity shop.

Emma looked at me.

Just looked at me.

And I noticed that I hadn't noticed her eyes in a while, and I blamed it on the exam stress, and then I noticed that they look different now it's almost summer.

She smiled and took a strand of my hair and twisted it around her finger, pulled on it slightly, and I didn't know whether I should pull back or let her pull me forward, and so I gave in to her until our faces were so close, I could feel how warm she was.

And then she said: 'I don't think you're a mess.'

I looked at her mouth, because I couldn't look at her eyes any more, but that didn't help, and I ended up saying something like: 'Hmngh.'

I watched Emma smile and lick her lips, and I was just like: 'I forgot what we were talking about.'

Emma let go of my hair, nodded, and said: 'Yes.'

Yes.

Yes what?

Yes?

When we got back to the charity shop, Kate announced that we (as in the shop) will be given a special honour for raising all that money for the *Star Wars* poster.

The overall boss person of the cancer charity is going to come to the shop to give us a certificate or rosette, or whatever.

To be honest, I was only half listening, because all I could hear in my head was Emma's yes.

11.14 p.m.

I don't understand why things with Emma are so different. I mean, Polly picks shit out of my hair all the time. It's nothing special. I don't even think about it.

LOL, if I told her about what happened with Emma, and how it made me all speechless and ridiculous, she'd be like: 'Phoebe loves Emma.'

Ha ha.

11.55 p.m.

OMG!

SUNDAY 27 MAY   #WTAF

I've got a crush on Emma, and I don't have time to have a crush on Emma.

And how did it take me so long to realize that's what was happening? Especially when I've so *obviously* been displaying all the classic signs of this insanity:

- Incessant social media stalking.
- Jealousy.
- Sleepless nights.
- Constant adrenaline high.
- No appetite.

- Brain ache.

I'm not Pat; I'm Polly. And I think that might actually be worse.

This is *not* happening to me.

Just no.

I feel like I'm in the wrong brain.

I did a yoga-like headstand against my wardrobe this morning because apparently it's good for your organs to gravitationally rearrange themselves every once in a while, and I was hoping that the pressure on my head would somehow awaken the few sane synapses I may have left in my brain.

I stayed upside down until I was about to pass out, and it *did* help, because two minutes later, I was like: You can do better than this, Phoebe.

So here's the plan:

- Don't fancy Emma.

Also, there's no point in fancying her, because even though she's hinted she may be into girls, it's not like she'd ever fancy me back, because

a) I'm socially awkward,
b) I'm ridiculous,
c) I'm not funny, and
d) I'm the idiot who goes on and on about how we all die alone to people with dead brothers.

How funny that it never occurred to me that I could be into girls, even though I realized today (while standing on my head) that, as a lifelong fan of *Doctor Who*, I never actually fancied the Doctor until she was a woman.

I've never had a crush on a real-life girl before.

To be fair, I've never had a crush on a real-life boy before, either, so that's neither here nor there.

What's happening to me?

I'm going for a walk. I can't cope.

4.40 p.m.

Walking didn't help.

I don't have time to have crushes on people; I'm busy with exams. My brain is working at full capacity; I don't have room for fluffy shit like this.

I'm too confused to revise, so I'm going downstairs to watch crap telly.

6.56 p.m.

When Kate and James got back from their day out, I was still lying face down on the sofa.

All the kittens had climbed up on top of me and gone to sleep, Richard was pressing right on my bruise, but I couldn't even be bothered to make him move.

It took Kate and James fifteen minutes to notice I was even

there, underneath all the kittens.

Kate just sort of looked at me and went: 'Phoebe. Are you feeling OK?'

All I was thinking was: I'm literally in hell. But what I said was: 'I'm fine.'

Kate: Have you eaten?

Me: Not today, no.

Kate: Have you spoken to your mother?

Me: Not today, no.

Kate: (observing me like I'm an alien, or someone about to spontaneously combust): Why don't you try calling her, and then you can help James make dinner.

Me: I'm not hungry.

Kate: Tough shit, pet, because you're eating.

Classic.

9.05 p.m.

I ended up having to give Mum a summary of every exam I took this week.

Halfway through our conversation, I remembered about my plan to work for NASA, and Mum was like: 'I think that's very ambitious and a brilliant idea, baby.'

I wish I could sign up already, because a mission to Mars is exactly what I need right now.

11.09 p.m.

My brain wants me to think about kissing Emma, but I reckon once I've gone there, I'm doomed. I'm trying to not finish that thought, even though I can see its outlines already lurking in the shadows.

11.11 p.m.

You know when you're trying to not think about something? It basically doesn't work.

11.23 p.m.

I suddenly realized that I haven't actually ever kissed anyone I fancied, and that time Toby Daniels tried to suck my face off in Year Eight pretty much scarred me for life, because

a) his tongue was enormous, and
b) he tasted of cheese and onion crisps.

11.44 p.m.

Maybe I should revise all day every day this week so I don't have to see Emma.
   What am I going to do?

There's an article in the *Metro* today that may just save my life:

'Five Tips on How to Get Over That Annoying Office Crush'.

When I got on the bus, it was on the seat I was about to sit on, so I think it's the divine intervention I'd been hoping for.

Here's what to do:

1. Avoid being alone with them (for example, in a lift or in a meeting room).
2. Avoid taking the same lunch hour.
3. Say no to after-work drinks.
4. Remind yourself that you have a life outside of work that is worth living for.
5. Is this person actually your type, or do you simply enjoy flirting around the water cooler?

OK, so the first three can obviously be easily achieved.

Number four is a problem because I *don't* have a life outside of work worth living for. And five is entirely unclear to me, because I don't think I have a type, and I wouldn't say I enjoy flirting, because I basically don't know how to do it.

Since this list is a bit general, I decided to make my own How-to-Fall-out-of-Love-with-Emma list based on the one from the *Metro*:

1. Avoid being alone with her (stockroom, Kate's house).

2. Avoid going to Starbucks/Sprinkles.
3. Say no to after-work activities (i.e. kitten time).
4. Remind yourself that you do have other friends (sort of: Polly).
5. Could you actually live with the embarrassment of coming on to Emma and her recoiling in horror?

I think number five is the key to regaining my sanity here. I think I'd rather die knowing Emma respects me than knowing I've made an absolute tit of myself, and that Emma is now going to never stop laughing.

Also: Emma's ill and wasn't at the charity shop.

I'm quite impressed she managed to schedule her disease for half-term, because imagine having to take exams while being mucus-central.

TUESDAY 29 MAY   #CHICKENSOUP

I took a picture of a recipe in the 'Cooking for Invalids' section of *The Woman's Guide to Cookery and Household Management* and sent it to Emma.

It's for chicken soup, and because in order to make that soup you also need to know how to prepare the stock, which is in a different section, I sent her that too.

She replied straightaway:

Emma: *Not actually that ill. I'd kill for a Lucozade or a Starbucks, but my mother insists on fennel tea. Help!*

I'm going to her house tomorrow to bring her Lucozade (and Minstrels).

I'm also bringing her Starbucks.

Not because I fancy her (I'm 100 per cent committed to sticking to my list), but because she reached out to me as a friend.

WEDNESDAY 30 MAY   #MRSEMMA

Emma's mother is unfriendly AF.

That was unexpected.

I went over to their house around eleven and rang the doorbell.

I thought it would be just Emma, because it's the middle of the week, and everyone's at work, but Emma's mum opened the door and looked at me all like: *What do you want?*

Me: Hello. I'm here to visit Emma.
Her: And you are?
Me: Phoebe.
Her: . . .
Me: A friend. Obviously.
Her: . . .
Me: From the charity shop.

Her:	I'm afraid Emma isn't well enough to have visitors at the moment.
Me:	She said she's not really ill.
Her:	I think I'll be the judge of that, Phoebe. If you don't mind.
Me:	(thinking: Aggressive much?) . . .
Her:	I'm sure Emma will be back at the charity shop next week.

And at that point, I saw movement just at the top of the stairs, and so I moved to the side a bit to see. It was Emma, and she was waving at me, and mouthing *I'm sorry* and pointing at her mother.

Me:	(a bit louder, so she could hear me too): I got Emma Starbucks, and Lucozade, and Minstrels.
Her:	That's very thoughtful of you, but not very good for Emma.
Emma:	(on top of the stairs, mouthing): *Noooooooooooooo!!!!*
Me:	(trying to look at Mrs Emma with an equal amount of understanding and hatred): Fine. I'll give it to her next time I see her.
Her:	I think that would be best.
Me:	Bye.
Her:	(suddenly all nice and chatty because I'm leaving): Goodbye, Phoebe. Nice to meet you.

I hate people who are so obviously two-faced.

Fuck off.

I walked back to the charity shop, and when I saw Kate, I was just like: 'That could have gone a lot better. Emma's mum's a proper cow.'

Kate: I think the word you're looking for is *overprotective*.

Me: Have you met her?

Kate: Only once. But I'm aware that she worries about Emma a lot.

Me: Well, I wasn't trying to poison her child. I was trying to make her happy.

So then I sat by the steamer for, like, half an hour and drank two gone-cold soy chai lattes, and I couldn't even be arsed to decide on the donation of the week. All I could think about was Emma, and whether she would taste of soy chai latte. All sweet and cinnamony and creamylicious.

I'm really worried that I can't stop fancying her.

I know I've only been trying for a couple of days, but I need to try harder.

I wonder if you can fancy someone without wanting them.

Fancy someone . . . What does that even mean?

P.S.

> *fancy* [verb]:
> In British English, the verb *to fancy* is a transitive verb, the primary meaning being to like, love, feel attracted to, have a taste for, etc.

So it's basically the same as saying, 'I fancy cake': I like cake; I love cake; I feel attracted to cake; I have a taste for cake.

BUT that doesn't mean I have to have the cake.

Fine. I can work with that.

Or maybe I can simply treat my feelings (bleugh!!!!!) like a chronic illness, or like diabetes: Accept they exist, appreciate they are annoying, understand them, and manage them.

THURSDAY 31 MAY   #STILLNOTINLOVEWITHEMMA

Emma sent me a text in the middle of the night.

Emma: *I wanted to say sorry my mum didn't let you in. She overreacts. One sniffle, and the house is on lockdown for a week. Hopefully see you Saturday?*

Me: *Don't even worry about it. All parents are strange. Anyway, it's better than having a mum who forgets you exist.*

Emma: *I'm sure that's not true.*

Me: *It actually is.*

Emma: *My mum doesn't even trust me to have a sleepover anywhere any more.*

Me: *Why?*

Emma: *She's always stressing that something could happen to me.*

Me: *Why?*

Emma: *In case I die too.*

Me: *Sorry.*

Emma: *It's fine.*

Me: *We should run away together.*

Emma: *I'm packing my bag.*

Me: *My grandparents live in Hong Kong. They're a bit odd, but we can stay for free.*

Emma: *I'm climbing out of the window.*

Me: *I'll have the flights booked by the time you pick me up.*

Emma: OMG, *I so wish.*

Me: *Me too.*

Emma: *Sleep well.*

Me: *You too. And make sure I see you Saturday.*

Emma: *Can't wait.*

Me: *Me neither.*

Emma: *x*

Me: . . .

Of course, I was wide awake for hours after, and this morning, instead of revising, I looked out of the window at nothing, and this afternoon at the charity shop, I dropped everything, because apparently having realized you fancy someone messes with your basic motor-neuron functions.

I smashed a shitty crystal jar of potpourri, and the whole shop stank of chemically manufactured lavender, and Pat was like: 'Oh, Kate, I'm getting quite a migraine. I don't think I'll be able to be on the shop floor today.' (Like she ever is – OMG, could I hate her any more?)

I rolled my eyes, and Kate was like: 'What's the matter with you today?' And I was like: 'Why? Have you never dropped anything?'

Alex was behind the till, and he just laughed.

Kate was like: 'All right, snappy – why don't you and Alex take lunch together?'

So Alex and I sat in the sunshine by the back door, eating our sandwiches, and then we wandered up to Sprinkles to get some ice cream to go. I got mango, strawberry and peach, and Alex got three scoops of chocolate, and halfway down the Broadway, I looked at Alex, and he had chocolate ice cream all over his face, and I was just like: 'I should have got chocolate.' And Alex was like: 'You should always know what you want so you don't have regrets.'

What do I want?

P.S. Sticking to my list is going well so far. But to be fair, I haven't seen Emma.

FRIDAY 1 JUNE #LIFEONMARS

Today, I came to the conclusion that the only feasible solution to my problem is entering NASA's space programme.

I can't live my life trying to ignore the fact that I fancy Emma, because that would make me as crazy as everyone else, only in a different way.

So I've been looking into possibly studying Astrophysics at university.

At King's, you can study Physics with Astrophysics and

Cosmology, which sounds exactly right.

But, if you want to work for NASA and go on a manned interstellar mission, you have to be fluent in both Russian and English.

I wish they'd tell you these things when you're choosing a language for GCSEs. Why did I want to learn French? Who's ever needed French to do anything? I don't even think you need French when you want to work for the European Space Agency.

They should offer Russian for all those people who are considering a career at NASA, because I'm going to have to learn Russian in my own time now, and I'm already five years behind anyone who went to a school with forward vision, and obviously Russian people, who already speak Russian as well as English, because everyone speaks English.

I spoke to James about it, who, FYI, seems to have moved in, even though he's in the final stages of his dissertation and should be writing or painting or doing whatever nonsense fine art students do. But anyway, he reckons if I get into a decent uni, and if I'm serious about it all, I can probably take a foundation course in Russian then.

But it's going to take that much longer because of their bizarre alphabet.

Like bloody Hebrew.

But who knows, maybe I've inherited weird-alphabet genes from my dad, and it's actually going to be a piece of piss.

Maybe instead of driving lessons like everyone else, I'll ask for Russian lessons for my birthday. After all, who needs a car in London — or in deep space, for that matter?

Emma was back today, and she looked like she hadn't even been ill.

I didn't know what to say to her, mainly because most conversations I've been having with her took place in my head this past week, and so I pretended to be busy and was just like: 'Hi,' from across the stockroom.

She walked straight over, and for a second, it looked like she was going to hug me, and I swear my whole body went rigid.

In the end, we just stood there, and she was like: 'How's the bruise?'

Me: (clearing my throat, because apparently I do that now) Fine, yes, great, OK, much better. How are you?
Emma: Finally out of prison.
Me: Oh.
Emma: Sorry again about my mum.
Me: (shrugging) . . .
Emma: . . .
Me: I saved your Lucozade.

I got it from the fridge and gave it to Emma, and then I was like: 'And I got you Minstrels.' And Emma was like: 'Oh my God, I love you.' And then she did hug me.

You know when you're at the dentist, and they tell you

that you need a filling, and they're going to do it straight away, and you're unprepared, and helpless, and reclined, and your stomach is fluttering like it's actually trying to break out of your body?

That.

She smiled at me, and her eyes were pale blue, which basically means that she was focusing on something, and her pupils had contracted, which had made the retinal tissue expand and therefore appear lighter. Like when you stretch a balloon.

Then she opened her Lucozade and was like: 'How have you been, Pat?' And Pat was like: 'Oh, you know me. Same old. Flat's still looking nice, mind. And it's nice to have you back too. I had no one to talk to all week.'

I HATE that woman. Because I was there. Every day.

P.S. I don't understand how I feel about Emma. One moment, I want to message her; the next moment, I want to never see her again.

P.P.S. I wish I could talk to Polly.

P.P.P.S. But Polly would be all romantic about it and no help at all with me trying to not feel anything.

SUNDAY 3 JUNE   #BUSTED

Mum wanted to know everything about my upcoming GCSEs

and my career with NASA tonight, and I was so not in the mood to talk about it, and so I was like: 'Have you met Kate's boyfriend yet?' And Mum was just like: 'Kate has a boyfriend?'

I took the laptop downstairs, with Mum still onscreen, and totally busted Kate and James on the sofa.

I mean, they weren't having sex or anything, but it was so awkward that it was great.

I was like: 'Mum, this is James. James, this is Mum.' And James was like: 'Hi, Mum.' I could tell that Kate was dying on the inside, and she was like: 'Amelia, I'll email you. Go away, Phoebe!'

Mum then became proper LOL, because she was like: 'No, no, wait a minute, Phoebe. If you take me away now, I'll disown you.'

And so I just left the webcam on Kate and James.

Mum: Hi, James.

James: Hi again.

Mum: Are you and Kate an item, then?

Kate: Ameeeeeeliaaaaa!

James: (smiling, dimple-alert) Yes, we're seeing each other.

Kate: We are?

James: Of course we are.

Mum: (smiling) Congratulations. I'm happy for you both. Well, I'm happy for you, James, because my friend's pretty epic. What is it you do, James?

Me: (silently LOLing) . . .

Kate: Amelia, go away – I'll email you.

Mum: But we're having such a nice time.

Kate: Amelia!

Mum: Fine. But email me tonight.

Kate: I will.

Mum: And I want details.

Kate: Go away!

Afterwards, Mum started going on about the astronaut thing again, and how King's is a very good university, and that I should definitely look at their entry criteria right away.

Thing with Mum is, I never know if she says these things because she actually engages with me, or because she wants me to like her.

P.S. I got side tracked during revision and discovered that all that standing on my head business was the worst thing I could've done to get rid of my infatuation with Emma.

Apparently when we fancy someone, the blood flow to the pleasure centre of the brain increases, which is the same part of the brain implicated in obsessive-compulsive behaviours. So I've been accidentally feeding my obsession by making all the blood pool in my brain.

I'm now aiming to reverse the effects by remaining upright 24/7. Which probably means I'm going to fail all future GCSEs, because of my brain's intentionally reduced blood flow.

Life! It's all swings and roundabouts.

This morning before History 1, Polly pulled me into the toilets.

Polly: I tilted my pelvis, and hey presto.
Me: . . .
Polly: The vaginal orgasm.
Me: We're about to take a history exam.
Polly: I just wanted to let you know. It didn't work for ages, and it's only happened once so far, but you know . . .
Me: We're about to take a history exam.
Polly: Yeah, I know. It's great. Love you.

Then she winked at me, and sort of floated out of the toilets and down the hallway.

I know it's all my fault, but
  Oh!
  My!
  God!

On the bus home, I texted Emma

a) because I subconsciously know that I've lost Polly to Tristan forever, and I should therefore, in the most pathetic way possible, start clinging on to the people who are still in my life, and

b) because I'm stupid.

I was like:

Phoebe: *Are you revising, or do you fancy coming over and seeing Richard?*

And she was like:

Emma: *I'll be over at five.*

And because my brain was having a bus-nap, I asked her if she wanted to stay for dinner, and she said yes.

So then I had to check with Kate if it was OK, who told me not to be so daft, and that Emma could come over whenever she wanted to, but that she couldn't stay long because of tomorrow (English Language 1, Geography 2).

When I opened the door, Emma was like: 'I'm here to see Richard, please.' And I was like: 'Right this way, madam.'

Emma played with him for a little while, and then he fell asleep on her. I told her to stay where she was, and I went into the kitchen to help Kate make dinner.

Me: You can't sell Richard. Emma saved his life, and she
        should have him.
Kate: . . .
Me: He thinks she's his mother. He loves her.

Kate: Does he now?

Me: (grating cheese) Why do you say it like that?

Kate: Like what?

Me: Like I'm making it up?

Kate: Phoebe. Take a deep breath.

Me: (taking a deep breath): . . .

Kate: And another.

Me: (taking another): . . .

Kate: (whispering): I think *you* love Emma.

Me: (taking no breath): . . .

Kate: . . .

Me: . . .

Kate: (still whispering): OK, fine, moving on. But, anyhow, you can't just give her a kitten. Her mother's going to have a fit. The woman's a total germophobe, and I don't blame her for it.

Me: (whispering, but in a shouty way): I don't love Emma.

Kate: (shouty whispering too): I'm talking about the kitten now.

Me: And what if I did?

Kate: Nothing.

Me: I'll never speak to you again if you say anything.

Kate: (pretending to be locking her mouth with an invisible key, and then tossing the invisible key over her shoulder): . . .

When I walked Emma home after dinner, it was all weird.

Like I didn't know what to say to her, and like I had to think about how to walk. By the time we got to hers, I'd additionally lost the power of speech, and so I just stood there, like a stranger in my own life.

Emma: (looking at her shoes, then looking at me, smil ing, possibly mocking me) Good night. And good luck tomorrow.
Me: What's tomorrow?
Emma: (laughing, definitely mocking me) GCSEs.
Me: Oh yeah. Fine. OK – I almost forgot. Night.

If you could die from awkwardness, I'd be dead.

TUESDAY 5 JUNE   #THELOVEFACTOR

I'm exhausted.

I didn't sleep very well after yesterday, and everyone stressed me out this morning, asking stupid last-minute questions, so by the time I sat down to take the English exam, I couldn't remember how to spell my own name.

In other news, the person from the cancer charity is coming to the shop on Friday night to give us the fundraiser award.

Someone from the *Wimbledon Gazette* is coming too, and Kate wants us all to be there so we can be in the picture and raise awareness.

I wish this school year would hurry up and be done with, because I'm over everyone and everything: GCSEs, Polly, Tristan, kittens, the charity shop, Emma.

I don't think I have the tolerance for heightened emotions.

When Polly first had a crush on Tristan, she ran with it. She loved being in love, and she loved how it consumed her.

But I'm not like that. I feel like I've fallen into quicksand, and now I'm unable to move, and I'm sinking, and I can't breathe, and I hate it.

Being in love is ridiculous, and it makes people do ridiculous things.

Look at Romeo and Juliet: Ridiculous.

WEDNESDAY 6 JUNE   #NOEXAMWEDNESDAY

Today, all the clever people (like Emma) who took Spanish instead of French had their exam, and I had the day off.

I revised for Maths all day, which was strangely soothing. I appreciate the structure of it. Everything makes sense, there's only ever one right answer, and my thoughts don't drift so much when I look at numbers.

Mum sent an email to say she'll definitely be back for my birthday, and that we should have a big party in our garden and invite all my 'new' friends. And James.

I wonder if she'll ever find a new boyfriend.

Maybe she doesn't want one.

Or maybe she's got one. Maybe he's like my dad: Israeli, and funny, and gorgeous.

THURSDAY 7 JUNE #MATHS

I took Mathematics 2 today, pretending it was the entrance exam to NASA's Mars Exploration Programme.

I think I did really well.

I was done before everyone else, and I was like: Hmmm, shall I sit here and go over it like a thousand times even though I know it's right, or should I just hand in?

So I handed in.

Afterwards, Miriam Patel said that it wasn't as bad as she'd thought.

Drama queen.

Emma texted me asking if I'm coming to the thing tomorrow night, and I said I was, and then she was like, great, because Alex is coming too, and now the three of us are going to Sprinkles before, and one half of my brain was going: Remember the list, Phoebe. But the other half was just like: List? What list.

P.S. Tomorrow we've got English Language 2 and History 2.

I honestly want to sleep for a week. My whole body aches. And speaking of aches, my bruise currently looks like a love bite.

It was so hot today.

I was literally melting during English, and even though they'd opened all the doors and windows over lunch to air out the room, it was absolutely boiling in the afternoon, and instead of history, all I could think about was the future, and how much I wanted to get out of that room alive. The Jew in me kept groaning: Oy vey! the whole way through.

Afterwards, I rushed home because I wanted to have a shower before meeting Emma and Alex, and after spending half an hour trying on all sorts of outfits, I ended up back in my black skinny jeans, and by the time I got to Sprinkles, I was sweating again.

I once read somewhere that you know exactly how you feel about someone when you see them again after a prolonged period of absence.

When we met outside Sprinkles, it had been ninety-three hours since I'd last seen Emma, which isn't all that prolonged, but I couldn't stop looking at her, and it took me, like, five minutes before I could form a full sentence, which basically means I don't just fancy her the way I fancy cake, and can therefore take it or leave it, but that I'm actually completely in love with her.

Me: Hi.
Emma: Hi. How are you?
Me.   Fine.
Emma: (smiling) . . .

Me: (possibly not smiling) . . .

Emma: (smiling more) . . .

Me: (possibly still not smiling) . . .

Emma: How did today go for you?

Me: It was hell.

Emma: Same. So hot.

Me: If I fail, I'm not retaking anything.

Emma: (nodding) I think we all feel like that.

Me: I'm not joking, either.

Emma: (smiling at me like it was funny): . . .

Me: . . .

Emma: Any sign of Alex?

Me: Not yet.

Emma: He's the one who didn't have exams today, and he's late. Such a diva.

Me: Totally.

And then I finally dragged my eyes away from Emma's face, and I realized that she was wearing a cute little pastelly summer dress and Vans, and that her hair was down, and that she'd put on some lip gloss that didn't turn her lips into a different colour but made them look naturally juicy delicious.

Me: I should have made an effort.

Emma: What do you mean?

Me: I look terrible.

Emma: (laughing) You don't look terrible. You look like . . . you.

Then Alex appeared, and even he'd put a dress shirt on, and even though it was proper hot outside, he was wearing his smart coat. Both Emma and I watched him walk up to us, and I was like: 'Nope, I definitely should have made some sort of effort.' And Emma laughed and was like: 'Wear something from the shop then.' But I was like: 'Please don't take the piss.'

I had Peanut Butter Extreme, and all the sugar and protein made me feel light-headed. We sat in one of the booths, and I was sitting next to Emma, and Alex was sitting opposite us, and halfway through my meal (I say 'meal', but it wasn't really; it was basically a whole week's worth of calories in one bowl of ice cream), I felt Emma's leg against mine, but instead of shifting and repositioning myself, I just stayed, and I even pressed against hers.

What is wrong with me? This is not helping. Maybe I'm a masochist.

And the thing is, I don't even think Emma noticed it, because she didn't say anything, or look at me in any sort of way that would suggest it could have been deliberate, and then I reminded myself of her pyramid of priorities, and I was like: Of course it doesn't mean anything.

Luckily we had to be at the charity shop at half six, so I didn't really have time to think about it too much, except I was thinking about it too much. Like a computer running background checks while letting you write an essay.

The rest of the evening ended up being quite hilarious because of the old people.

Pat looked like the Queen was coming. She'd put on this most bizarre two-piece flowy skirt-and-blouse combo, and when the charity guy shook her hand, she curtsied.

We had to take the team picture, like, 3 million times because Bill kept telling jokes, making us all laugh.

Melanie was just shaking her head, going: 'Goodness, Bill. You're such a child.'

At one point, Emma pulled me further into the frame by my wrist, and I literally fell into her, and then she flung her arm around my shoulder, and I felt awkward in my own body.

Emma and I stayed until the end, and when Kate was locking up, we were standing on the pavement, and I looked at her, and she smiled, and all I could think was: You're *everything*.

SATURDAY 9 JUNE   #SPEECHLESS

This morning, Kate knocked on my door at seven.

Me: Mum's dead.
Kate: (sitting down on my bed, hand reaching for my leg) No, pet. Your mum is fine. But Melanie had a stroke.
Me: What?
Kate: Melanie had a stroke. She's at the hospital, but it doesn't look like she's going to recover.
Me: What?

Kate: (rubbing my leg): Pat just called me to say that she's at the hospital with them.

Me: OK.

Kate: She says it's not looking good for Melanie.

Me: What do you mean?

Kate: She probably won't survive.

Me: But she was OK yesterday.

Kate: I know, pet, but a stroke can occur suddenly, and very unexpectedly. It's important to get to the hospital quickly to save as much of the brain as possible. Bill didn't realize something was wrong until he found her in bed early this morning, and she wasn't able to get up.

Me: And now?

Kate: I'm going to go to the shop and put a sign up to say we'll be shut today, and then I'm going to go over to the hospital. Can you text Emma to say not to come?

Me: Of course.

Kate: Do you want to come to the hospital?

Me: I don't think I like hospitals.

Kate: I understand. Hospitals are shite. Do you want me to text you with news?

Me: (nodding): . . .

I sat in bed and waited for the front door to shut, and then, instead of texting Emma, I called her.

Emma: (answering straightaway) Hi, Phoebe.

Me: Melanie had a stroke.

Emma: What?

Me: I know.

Emma: Oh my God.

Me: She's at Kingston hospital. Kate's gone over, and Pat's there too. Kate said they don't think she'll live.

Emma: Oh my God.

Me: I know.

Emma: Are you going?

Me: I don't like hospitals.

Emma: I don't think anybody likes hospitals.

Me: We could get the bus.

When we met at the bus stop, Emma hugged me, and it wasn't even awkward. Weird what bad news can do to people, I thought, and on the bus, we talked about Bill and Melanie and how cool they are.

I texted Kate to say we were on our way, and she met us at the entrance.

When I was little, I had to go to A&E once because I fell backwards off a rocking chair, bashed my head open, and needed stitches. I oddly can't remember if it was Mum or Kate who took me at the time, but I remember being terrified because the lights were too bright, and everything was the opposite of comforting.

In the lift, I saw that Emma was shaking, like she was cold, and Kate went over and hugged her, and rubbed her arms real fast, like, to warm her up.

Kate: Is this where Bradley—

Emma: No.

Kate: (hugging her again) You OK, pet?

Emma: Yes, sure. Thank you.

Kate: Because you don't have to be here.

Emma: I want to be here.

Kate: All right.

Pat was sitting in the hallway outside Melanie's room, and when she saw us, she was like: 'How good of you both to come. It's important to say goodbye.'

I was like: 'I'm here to say hello.' But she just smiled that hideous smile she smiles when she wants you to know that she knows everything, and you know nothing.

Emma asked straightaway if she could go into the room, and Pat went inside to ask Bill, and then two seconds later she came back out and said it was OK.

Emma: (to me) Do you want to come?

Me: (shaking head) . . .

Emma: OK. I'll tell them you're here.

I sat down opposite Pat, and Kate sat down next to me.

Kate: You've never seen anyone at this point, Phoebe, have
        you?

Me: At this point?

Kate: When they're dying.

Me: She's not dead.

Kate: (taking my hand and looking straight at me) No. But she's dying. We're not sure how much damage happened to her brain, but she's not conscious, and her kidneys are failing. If Bill decides to not put her on life support when the time comes, she will probably die later today, or maybe tomorrow.

Me: How do you know that? You don't know that.

Kate: (taking a deep breath in, and a long breath out) I'm sorry, Phoebe. But I know that.

Me: But she could recover.

Kate: The brain is a very complex organ. When so much of it dies, it is highly unlikely a person can come back from it. Not all the way, not really.

I just sat there for, like, a thousand minutes, and then the door opened, and Emma came out, and I thought that I should really pull myself together, because if anyone had a reason to feel a bit sick about it all, it was her. Well, and Pat. And Kate, I guess.

Kate: Are you OK, Emma?

Emma: (nodding) She's not in any pain.

Kate: No, she isn't.

Me: How can you know that? Just because she isn't saying anything, doesn't mean she isn't in pain. She could be screaming on the inside.

Pat's eyes literally rolled out of her head, and I swear she would have said something if Kate hadn't beaten her to it.

Kate: No, Phoebe – we know. OK? I can tell you right now that Melanie is currently not in pain. And if you insist on the stone-cold truth, I will give you that too.

Me: Please.

Kate: This isn't about Melanie. She's not really here any more. She probably doesn't know Bill, or Pat, or Emma, or anyone any more. This is about us now. It's about whether we want to be with her body as it stops functioning. Do you understand? The Melanie we knew is already gone.

At the end of the speech Pat was sobbing, and Emma was crying, but she wasn't making any noise. It was as if tears were just flowing out of her eyes while she got on with life.

I mumbled something about not wanting to be there, got up, and left.

I walked out of a sterile hospital into the hot June afternoon, and I stood in the car park for a minute, and I swear I couldn't remember how I even got there.

I sent Kate a text to say that I was taking the bus home, and when I got there, all I could think about was that I probably should revise for next week's science extravaganza, but I didn't.

I didn't even make it upstairs.

I just played with the designer and half-designer kittens in the front room, and when they got bored and wanted their mums, I just lay on the floor and stared at the ceiling.

James came in around midday, and he was like: 'Hey, Phoebe – what's up? Where's Kate? She's not answering her phone.'

Me: Melanie's in hospital, and she's dying, but I left.
James: I'm sorry, what?
Me: Melanie had a stroke, and everyone's at the hospital, but Kate said that she's basically dead already, so I left because what's the point?
James: (looking at me like I hadn't been speaking in English) That was a lot of information about a lot of things in just one sentence.
Me: Keep up.
James: I'm going to try calling Kate again.

I held up my phone for him to use, because I knew she'd pick up, and James disappeared upstairs.

Ten minutes later, he came back down, and he was like: 'I'm going to get an Uber and go over to the hospital. Do you want to come?'

Me: No.
James: Bill signed a form to say Melanie shouldn't be resuscitated. So . . . Well, you know what that means.
Me: . . .

James: . . .

Me: Imagine having to do that.

James: I can't, actually.

Me: Imagine if you had to sign one for Kate.

James: I couldn't. But if it were the other way around, I'd wish she would. It's fucked up, isn't it?

Me: Totally fucked up. And Emma's just there like it's the most natural thing in the world.

James: (thinking, then) I suppose it is. Dying is part of life, isn't it?

Me: It scares me.

James: Me too.

Me: Do you know about her brother?

James: (nodding) Yes – she told me I remind her of him. We both used to row at school.

Me: (feeling like a massive idiot) . . .

James: You sure you don't want to come?

Me: (getting off the floor finally after, like, three hours) I'm going to get everyone water and hoodies first. In case she doesn't . . . you know . . . die, like . . . soon.

James: I'll wait for you out front.

When we got to the hospital, they'd moved Melanie to another room close to an operating theatre, because apparently she's an organ donor, and the transplant team were basically waiting for her to stop breathing and clinically die so they could take all the good bits ASAP and save other sick people.

It was all so grim and so ridiculous.

James enveloped Kate, and I sat down next to Emma.

Emma: You OK?
Me: Not really.
Emma: (nodding): . . .
Me: You?
Emma: Not really.
Me: . . .

We sat for ages, not talking. Pat went into the room to be with Bill, and the rest of us just sat in the uncomfortable chairs.

Kate and James got everyone sandwiches from the cafe at one point, but no one was hungry.

Emma ate half of hers and passed me the other half, and I only ate it because it was there.

Kate came over and kind of knelt in front of Emma and was like: 'Are you sure you're happy to be here? Nobody would think less of you if you went home.'

Emma was like: 'I'm fine. I want to be here, and my parents say it's OK.' And then Kate was like: 'All right, but if you change your mind, you let me know, OK? James or I can always take you home.'

Emma was like: 'Thank you.'

Nurses went in every half hour or so to check on Melanie, even though they weren't actually checking on her but on the condition of her organs.

Emma and I went for a walk at one point because I was

freezing and getting twitchy just sitting there. We walked all the way to the entrance to Richmond Park without saying a word, and then we turned around and walked back.

Emma: Are you thinking about Melanie?

Me: No.

Emma: What are you thinking about?

Me: Bradley.

Emma: Me too.

Me: Was he in hospital when he died?

Emma: (nodding) . . .

Me: . . .

Emma: I was there.

Me: . . .

Emma: . . .

Me: How did you know what to do? I mean when he was, you know, dying?

Emma: (shrugging) I didn't. Not really. I just kept stroking his arm. And I told him that I loved him.

Me: . . .

Emma: But in a really silly way, you know, like: I love you more than I love a Domino's Cheese Feast. I love you more than I love Christmas. I love you more than, I don't know, life.

Me: I hate that you had to do that.

Emma: I hate that he's dead.

Me: . . .

Emma: My mum lost it the day we knew he was going to die.

She wanted new drugs, new consultants, a new hospital. She just couldn't accept it. I think I kept so calm because the whole time I was thinking what I would want if it were me instead of him. You know, you'd want someone there for your parents.

Me: I suppose so.

Emma: I know Melanie would want more than anything for someone to be with Bill right now so he doesn't have to feel like he has to make really impossible decisions alone.

Me: Yes.

Emma: The worst thing is the emptiness after. It feels like someone has physically ripped your heart out, and you can't breathe, and you can't think, and all you know is that you're lying on the floor, drooling.

Me: . . .

Emma: I still have dreams about him, you know. He's alive, but because I know he's going to die, I don't want to see him, because I'm like: No, I watched you die already, I'm not doing it again. And sometimes when I wake up, I'm glad that it's already over.

I didn't know what to say to that, and so I took Emma's hand and kissed the back of it, the way Kate sometimes does it to me.

Emma was like: 'Stop being weird.' But I was like: 'Fuck off – I'm not being weird. I've been wanting to kiss your hand for ages.'

She laughed, but that wasn't even a lie.

Me: Do I have to go in and see Melanie?

Emma: No, of course not. It's like Kate said, it's about you now.

Me: I really don't want to see her like that.

Emma: And that's OK.

Me: Are you sure? Because I don't want people thinking
        I'm a horrible person.

Emma: I don't think anyone would think that.

Me: Pat would.

Emma: She already thinks you're a horrible person.

Me: . . .

Emma: (giggling, then) Love you.

Me: Fuck off.

When we got back to the hospital, nothing had changed.

Bill came out briefly, and I gave him a hug, and then we just kept waiting.

At eight, they moved Melanie again because she hadn't died in time for her organs to still be of any use to anyone. Apparently her entire body had been under-oxygenated for too long. So she went upstairs into a nicer room without much machinery.

I didn't look when they wheeled her past me.

James took Emma and me home at nine even though we don't have school tomorrow.

I'm waiting to hear now.

I can't sleep.

I don't want to sleep.

To think that a person is in the process of leaving this life is so complicated.

I think I love Emma.

SUNDAY 10 JUNE #DEATH

4.24 a.m.

Melanie died.

Kate just rang. She's going to help with things at the hospital, and then she and Pat are taking Bill home.

I still can't believe any of it.

Melanie was fine.

Her picture is going to be in the *Wimbledon Gazette* tomorrow.

9.15 p.m.

Kate finally came home at nine this morning and went straight to bed.

James visited for a few hours, but went to work at four, so I made dinner and woke Kate at six.

Kate said it's always very difficult when old people have been together for such a long time and one of them dies, because they are entirely co-dependent. She said she hopes that Bill doesn't die of grief.

Melanie would be so disappointed if that happened. Or maybe she'd be flattered?

I had to take Biology 2 this morning, and Geography 3 this afternoon. After yesterday, I honestly don't know how I did it.

I told Polly about Melanie after lunch, and she was just like: 'I'm so sorry. I can't believe you're even here.' And then when we walked to Geography 3, she held my hand, not Tristan's.

Polly is brilliant.

Melanie's funeral is on Friday.

How strange to think that her body is lying somewhere all dead and cold until then.

I wonder how many more dead people are currently lying around waiting to be buried or cremated.

I've never been to a funeral, and I actually don't know if I want to go. It's going to be all sad and horrible, and I think the coffin with Melanie in it will be in the church/room.

P.S. Our picture in the *Wimbledon Gazette* looks hilarious.

Next week, Melanie's obituary will be in it.

P.P.S. I just tried googling *How many dead, unburied people are currently on Earth?* But Google doesn't know, which is confusing, because Google knows everything.

I suppose I could always try to work it out by looking at how many people died last year, then dividing that number by the number of days of the year, and then working out an approximate number, but I'm too tired.

11.43 p.m.

There are approximately 151,506.85 dead, unburied, and uncremated people on planet Earth right now. And Melanie is one of them.

Goodnight.

TUESDAY 12 JUNE #MATHS3

I had anxiety dreams all night about showing up for Mathematics 3 without a calculator despite having plastered sticky notes all over the house to remind me to take it.

The exam was fine.

Polly (again with a fanny full of formulas) just grinned like an idiot, and I was like: 'Did it go all right, then?' But she was just like: 'It's over, Phoebe. That's all that matters right now. A dark cloud has shifted, a heavy weight has been lifted – oh, I'm such a poet.'

I never should have told her about the tilting of the pelvis because, quite frankly, she's even more in love (aka insane) now.

She asked me about Melanie, though, and wanted to know how I was doing, and I just shrugged, because sometimes things are what they are, and it sucks. So Polly gave me one finger of her KitKat and told me she loves me.

I'm sad about Melanie dying, but I'm mostly sad about Bill feeling sad.

WEDNESDAY 13 JUNE   #CHEMISTRY

I was surprisingly motivated this morning, because I was like: OK, superb knowledge of chemistry and chemistry-related problem-solving is going to be vital when exploring outer space.

All last night, I was willing my brain to take a mental photograph of the periodic table, but it never happened/developed, which is fine because it wouldn't actually have been helpful.

The exam went fine, and tonight we had Bill over for dinner.

I hadn't seen him since the hospital.

It sounds like Pat has taken over his life, which is great, because there's so much ridiculous stuff people want you to get on with, like death certificates, cancelling bank cards, insurances, etc.

How awful having to deal with all that crap when all you really want to do is curl up in a ball and cry.

One of the non-designer kittens loves Bill. It came over, licked his shoe for ages, then it clawed its way up his yellow corduroy trousers and went to sleep in his lap.

P.S. I have concluded that emotional attachment is not a good thing.

I understand that through the history of evolution, humans were better off in groups, and forming emotional bonds made sense, but we're not exactly hunter-gatherers any more.

I don't ever want to be like Bill or Emma, so heartbroken and sad.

P.P.S. I have no exams tomorrow, so I am going to sleep until I'm no longer tired. Emma has Spanish.

THURSDAY 14 JUNE   #DUSTTODUST

So the one day I could sleep in, I was up at seven.

Life.

I revised for Physics 2 in the morning and went to the charity shop in the afternoon.

It felt all wrong with one person now forever missing.

Emma came in after her Spanish exam. I hadn't expected to see her, so that was nice. She now hugs me every time she sees me, and I'm wondering if that will stay the same once we stop being sad about Melanie.

Alex, as always, had all the answers to life's greatest question saying that we come from dust, we become dust again, and that even the earth is going to crumble to dust one day.

I didn't have the heart to tell him that it'll actually go up in flames first when our sun goes supernova, mainly because Melanie is being cremated.

I suppose he does have a point, though.

Kate's picking me up after my exam tomorrow, and then we're getting Emma. The funeral is at two thirty.

I don't want to go.

P.S. My stomach ache is back.

I swear it's psychosomatic.

FRIDAY 15 JUNE #FUNERALS

Emma and I held hands today.

At the funeral.

Which means that I don't know what it means.

Before we went into the little chapel at the crematorium, I was like: 'I really don't want to go.' But Emma was just like: 'Phoebe, unlike at the hospital, this isn't about you. This is about Bill, so you need to get over yourself. And I'm sorry if that sounds harsh.'

So I sat on a bench, and the whole time I was thinking: Don't be sick, don't be sick, don't be sick, because I felt like I was going to vom.

I sat against the wall in the third row from the front, and Emma sat to my left, then Kate, James, Alex's dad, Alex, Alex's mum and Pat.

My stomach was fluttering like mad, and I was shaking, and when I looked over at Emma, she was crying again, even though the service hadn't even started, and then I wanted to cry too because it made me so sad.

Bill looked very smart in a three-piece suit, and he nodded at us when he saw us. There were a gazillion old people there, and the place was absolutely heaving, and at one point, I turned around and saw that people were even standing in the back and in the aisle because there was nowhere left to sit.

Me: (whispering to Emma) 'I think I'm going to be sick. What if I have to be sick, and I can't get out, and I throw up all over these people?'

Emma: (unzipping her Topshop handbag and holding it open for me) . . .

Me: No way.

Emma: You're not going to be sick, but yes. Just in case.

Me: Thank you.

And then Emma took my hand, and interlaced her fingers with mine, and kissed it the way I had kissed hers the day Melanie died.

I noticed that Kate noticed, but she didn't say anything.

The whole funeral took no more than half an hour.

Because I hadn't been to one before, I don't actually know how good it was, but I thought it was nice.

The only awful part was at the very end when the coffin gets transported out on a conveyer belt and they played 'Fly Me to the Moon', and everyone who wasn't already crying burst into tears and watched Melanie leave the room. Then the curtain shut behind her, and the funeral narrator person was kind of like: OK, everyone – show's over. And so we weren't allowed to sit there and digest what had happened, because the next funeral party was already outside, waiting to come in.

I can't get over the fact that Melanie's whole life was reviewed in less than half an hour.

Imagine it, you live for eighty-six years, then you die, and a stranger narrates the highlights, before gently yet firmly ushering your friends out of the chapel because he has to do the very same about another dead person he never met five minutes later.

I'm not being funny, but emotional detachment is potentially the greatest superpower of our time.

After the funeral, we went on to Bill's sailing club to have designer canapes and drinks, and Bill just said: 'Thank you, everyone, for coming.'

This time last week, he was giving a roaring speech about that *Star Wars* poster.

SATURDAY 16 JUNE #PAT

I know Pat's the most horrendous person that ever lived, but turns out she's really good in a crisis.

She's basically living at Bill's house because he's still so shocked, he can barely get out of bed in the mornings.

According to Kate, Pat has repeatedly been threatening to send him into a home, which is a bit harsh, considering Melanie's only been dead for a week, but it's also a bit LOL, TBH.

P.S. It also just occurred to me that GCSEs are almost over. All I have left is the Certificate in Maths 1 and 2, and then it's done. How did that happen?

P.P.S. Polly has Dance GCSE on Tuesday. I don't understand how you can give an academic grade on dance, but best of luck to everyone. LOL.

SUNDAY 17 JUNE   #VIOLENTDELIGHTS

Emma and I accidentally had a nap together this afternoon, and it was the best thing in the world ever.

She has no more exams, and so she decided to spontaneously come over at lunchtime, and we made cheese toasties and cups of tea. Emma played with Richard, and then I was like: 'What do you want to do?' And Emma said that she didn't want to do anything because she was really tired, and so I was like: 'Great, we can just watch some crap on telly.'

We put on old episodes of *Love Island*, and not five minutes into it, Emma was like: 'These people are so redundant.'

I remember thinking about what a great word that is, and then the next thing I knew I was waking up with Emma's bare legs across me. She was asleep, and I was just like: This is nice. And so I went back to sleep too.

We only woke up when Kate and James came back from their romantic brunch date (bleugh!), and Kate was like: 'Phoebe! Emma!'

I felt busted, but I don't think she meant it in that way, because she was smirking at me, and I was thinking: If you say anything embarrassing right now, I'm leaving forever.

Emma's parents were expecting her for dinner, so she couldn't stay, and I walked her home at five.

Just before we got to her house, she took my hand again, and I let her hold it, even though after, like, five seconds, I had a seriously sweaty palm situation going on, and my stomach was 100 per cent literally fluttering, and then I was like: Remember the list. And then I forgot to breathe like a normal person, which made me so dizzy that I nearly passed out.

When we said goodbye, we hugged, and even though I've hugged Emma loads now, I still don't know what to do with my hands, which is ridiculous, because when I hug Polly, I literally don't even think about it.

I was just wondering if my arms felt at all awkward to Emma when she pulled away, and then suddenly her nose brushed along the side of my face, and it accidentally made me flinch.

Emma smiled at me, but her eyes looked like she was trying to work out an advanced Sudoku.

I must have looked like a fish out of water, all twitchy, with huge fish eyes, and a gasping fish mouth.

Weird how much can happen in one second.

10.21 p.m.

If Emma had kissed me, I think would have kissed her back, even though I have no idea how to kiss someone like Emma.

10.50 p.m.

Who am I kidding? I don't know how to kiss *anyone*, but it never mattered, because it never mattered.

I wonder if Emma is feeling any of the things I'm feeling, because there are moments when I think it's impossible I'm the only one who's losing her mind over this.

It's so different in *Romeo and Juliet* because they basically kiss before they even know each other, which not only makes their love story a lot less complicated than people want to admit, but also a lot less heartbreaking in the end.

P.S. I'm going to have to get that list back out if I don't want to go INSANE!

P.P.S. 'These violent delights have violent ends.'
— Friar Laurence, *Romeo and Juliet*, Act 2, Scene 6

P.P.P.S. I also spoke to Mum today, and I realized that sometimes I forget she exists.

Polly and I went to Starbucks this afternoon because

a) we didn't have school, and
b) Tristan had a dentist appointment.

Polly: I can't believe GCSEs are basically over.
Me: I know. I hated it, and I never want to do it again, but it wasn't too bad, looking back.
Polly: I bet you never even revised.
Me: Of course I revised. And the only reason I didn't revise as much as I'd originally planned was because I can't think straight at the moment. But luckily I always paid attention in class – not like you, always thinking about Tristan.
Polly: (staring into the distance, eyes glazing over): I know. I'm so in love.
Me: Please, I'm eating.
Polly: One day, you'll be in love, and you'll be happy like me.
Me: . . .

So for the rest of the afternoon, all I could think of was that maybe I'm *not* in love, because I'm certainly not happy. I'm miserable. I'm a mess. And maybe you can only be in love when the other person is also in love with you. Which would mean that right now, I'm basically one of those freaky fan celebrity stalkers. Except the other person knows I exist.

I'd see a psychiatrist, but imagine going to one with something this stupid.

I'm still hoping it will go away, because Polly was in love with Adam Smith once, and now she's just like: 'Mmmhhhe, he wasn't that great.'

TUESDAY 19 JUNE   #IHATEHUMANS

Further Mathematics 1 was OK.

What I hate most is people doing last-minute revision in the corridor, or on the toilet. Like you're going to have a Eureka moment at that point.

Miriam Patel is the worst for it.

Here's what GCSEs have taught me above all else: I hate people.

Today, someone was doing that thing when they were sucking snot back up into their nose every thirty seconds for the entire duration of the exam instead of blowing their nose once and being done with it.

I could have punched someone.

Maybe I'm not capable of going on a space mission after all. It would be just my luck to be on the same rocket ship as the snot sucker-upper.

Polly and I had a quick Starbucks after school.

We sat outside, and for a moment, it felt like last year's summer holidays, and I took a deep breath, and then I thought how I haven't noticed taking a breath for, like, months.

Polly was like: 'What's different with you?'

I told her that I'm tired, but she looked at me through half-closed eyes, stretching her legs after what must have been an exhausting Dance GCSE, and went: 'We're all tired . . .'

I can't talk to her about it.

Also, what if I said to her: 'Oh, by the way, remember Emma?'

What's the point?

Emma could be with anybody. Why would she want to be with me?

WEDNESDAY 20 JUNE   #HOWTOFIXTHEUNFIXABLE

We need to do something about Bill.

Kate says that Pat says that he's going to actually die of a broken heart.

I've googled it, and even though it seems to be largely a myth, there are recorded occurrences where couples have died within minutes or days of each other. It's odd to think that your body would allow that, because have you ever tried holding your breath? The body proper fights for it.

I messaged Emma to see if she has any suggestions.

Me: *How did you get over Bradley dying?*
Emma: *I didn't.*
Me: *Sorry.*

Emma: OK.

Me: How do you keep going?

Emma: Because of my parents. I don't want them to see me broken. I don't think they could handle it.

Me: Are you still broken, then?

Emma: Yes.

Me: I wish you were happy.

Emma: I am happy. But I'm also broken. But it takes a lot of work to be both.

Me: What about Bill?

Emma: I don't know. I think he needs something to live for.

Me: Pat?

Emma: LOL.

Me: Seriously, though.

Emma: Maybe we need to tell him that he's got responsibilities at the shop. I mean, he actually has.

Me: True. Kate's already complaining that Pat's at Bill's all the time, and nothing in the shop gets done.

Emma: And we haven't been there loads, either.

Me: I know.

Emma: I have to go now. Talk to you tomorrow?

Me: I'll be at work tomorrow. Talk to you then.

Emma: x

Me: x

Further Mathematics 2 marked the end of my GCSEs.

Loads of people were having a get-together in the park after, but I was just like: I need to *not* see you for a while. And so I went to the charity shop as promised.

Kate had bought me a bunch of flowers to say well done for getting through the past six weeks, and she kissed my face for literally five minutes while holding me in a death grip.

Emma just laughed.

Because we've been shit, Emma and I decided to up our game and have an actual donation-of-the-week contest with each other. And this is how it'll work:

Instead of just having the one, we're going to choose one ridiculous donation each, work on the display, try to sell it for at least £10, and whoever sells theirs first wins. We're going to play every week until the end of the school year, and then whoever has won overall buys the other Sprinkles.

This means: More fun for us, more money for the shop, and ice cream at the end.

Also: Alex is not allowed to take sides but must promote both entries equally. He obviously has a lot to say about that, but we told him he can come to Sprinkles, so he's less frowny already.

My first candidate is a pair of bowling shoes I found on the bottom of the hideous-shoes-that-are-never-going-to-sell pile.

They are bright red, totally worn, and have zero grip.

I cleaned them until they looked super shiny, labelled them *Vintage*, and put them in the window for £15.

Emma found a framed picture of pressed flowers that she put in the display cabinet with a sign saying: *A picture is worth a thousand words*. I reckon it's worth nothing, but we'll see.

The shoes are a definite winner.

P.S. I'm a free agent now. No more exams. But now starts the horrible wait for results. Seriously, school is basically an endless string of unavoidable events that make you feel literally sick.

FRIDAY 22 JUNE   #WHATHAVEIAGREEDTO

Today, Polly was like: Have you ever been to Tooting Lido?

Me: Never. Where is it?
Polly: Tooting.
Me: You're funny.
Polly: I know. That's why I'm your favourite.
Me: (thinking: She's right; she *is* still my favourite) Why?
Polly: Because Tristan and I want to go on Sunday.
Me: Have fun.
Polly: And we were wondering if you wanted to come.
Me: And watch you guys make out in a swimming pool? Let me think . . . eeeeehm. No!

Polly: It won't be like that.

Me: You say that now, but when you see him in his swimming trunks with his skinny little legs poking out, you'll be like: OMG, I must lick all that immediately.

Polly: . . .

Me: What?

Polly: That's what you think of me, isn't it? That I'm a sex-crazed maniac.

Me: . . .

Polly: I actually love spending time with Tristan, and I love spending time with you, so why is it so difficult for your smart brain to process that maybe I just want to have my two favourite people in the same place every once in a while?

Me: . . .

Polly: So are you coming or not?

Me: I'm coming.

Polly: Good. Geeez! It's like drawing blood from a stone with you.

P.S. I've just messaged Emma to ask if she wants to go to the lido, and she was like: *Yes. I love swimming.*

Oh my God, I hate swimming.

Kill me.

Saturdays at the charity shop are so weird without Bill and Melanie.

Pat was in today, and it was the first time I'd seen her since the funeral.

Kate: Pat, why don't you go home and get some rest?

Pat: Thanks, Kate, but I prefer to stay busy.

Kate: All right, but don't forget to look after yourself. It's all well and good you looking after Bill, but you're no good to anyone if you end up having a nervous breakdown.

And then Emma was like: 'Do you think I should ask if Bill wants to come to my meetings? I know Melanie didn't die of cancer, but a loss is a loss.'

Kate: (biting her lip, looking into the middle distance) To be honest, pet, I don't think Bill is ready for anything like that.

Emma: Maybe.

Me: (finally) What meetings are they?

Emma: I go to meetings with people who've lost people to cancer.

Me: OK.

Emma: I like going.

Me: OK.

Emma: I think it keeps me sane.

Then Kate wrapped an arm around Emma and pulled her into a sideways hug and kissed the top of her head going: 'I'm so happy at least one of us is sane.'

8.05 p.m.

I want to know what happened after Romeo and Juliet died. I want to know what happened to the Nurse, and to the parents, and to all the shit-stirrers who caused Romeo and Juliet to go crazy.

But nobody ever talks about the time after the great tragedy.

9.10 p.m.

I wish I'd just asked Emma about the meetings sooner. I literally thought it was this huge, secret thing, when it's just her going to talk to people who've been through the same trauma.

SUNDAY 24 JUNE #LIDO

This morning, we took the bus to Tooting. Polly and Tristan were already on it, I got on at Wimbledon, and Emma got on at South Wimbledon.

I had to buy a swimsuit at Primark beforehand because the only one I own is from Year Five and has Minnie Mouse on it.

Note to self: Always own a decent swimsuit, and definitely don't start buying one two minutes before you have to get on the bus.

I ended up with this vile, ill-fitting, bright blue thing.

Why am I incapable?

More reasons a mission to Mars would be brilliant:

- You get your own space-suit.
- NASA-regulation underwear.

Emma looked fantastic in her bright red halter-neck bikini, but to be fair, she looks fantastic in anything.

Emma and Tristan got on like a house on fire, of course.

What is it that makes him so irresistible?

Is it his helplessness?

The fact that he looks twelve?

Honestly, not ten minutes into the bus journey, and Emma and him were laughing and joking like they'd known each other all their lives. And later, they went to get us water, then ice cream, and once they even went for a wee together.

Polly was like: 'This is nice. Like a double date.' And as soon as she'd said it, she looked like she was kind of listening back to it in her head, and then she regarded me through half-closed eyes, and she went: 'Phoebe?' But I was just like: 'Fuck off.'

We went swimming a few times, but I didn't really like it, partly because the water in that lido is absolutely freezing, but mainly because I'm not a very good swimmer. Everyone was doing proper lengths, while I was struggling to stay afloat.

But because it was hot, and we were having a nice time, we stayed until we all were 100 per cent late getting home.

Emma was the first one off the bus, and she kept skipping and waving at us, even though she was no longer looking, and Polly thought it was so funny, she literally cried.

I got off next, and when I got home, Kate was like: 'Any news?' And I was like: 'Like what news?' And Kate was like: 'I don't know. *News* news. You know.'

Me: What are you talking about?
Kate: News.
Me: Can you stop saying news?
Kate: News.
Me: I think you may have actually lost the plot.

I'm not saying Kate was ever *not* crazy, but I swear ever since she's been in love, we're talking a whole new level.

9.04 p.m.

I had the best day, and for some bizarre reason (possibly sunstroke), I even found Tristan mildly tolerable.

And maybe I can be OK with just being Emma's friend.

And maybe that would be better anyway.

Because friendships last.

I think Polly and I are finally OK again.

This morning I was like: What is life?

I hate that, you know, I'm so tired in the mornings, and then in the evenings I'm awake for ages because I'm finally no longer tired.

Tomorrow night, people are coming over to look at the kittens.

Kate was like: 'It's time they go on to their forever homes.'

I'm obviously not their biggest fan, but it'll be weird without them, because even though they've been a pain in the arse, they've been fun to have around.

Mum sent me a long email, because she didn't get to speak to me yesterday because I've been 'having way too much fun with your friends to think of your old mother'.

Why does everything have to be about her?

And I'm sorry, but yes, I honestly haven't been thinking about her very much, because basically I haven't seen her in five months, and I've been busy with GCSEs, the truth about my father, and people dying.

Emma keeps saying: 'Oh, I want to be like your mum when I grow up.'

No, you actually really don't.

I lied about the availability of the designer kittens (mainly Richard).

The first people arrived before Kate was back from work, and so I let them in and showed them the kittens, and I was like: 'Those three are certified pure breeds, but the ginger boy one has already sold.'

So when Kate came in, the man was like: 'We'll have one of the girls. We'd prefer the boy, but I understand he's already been snapped up.'

Kate looked at me like: *What?*

Me: The all-over ginger ones are always most popular.

Man: They sure are.

Kate: *?*

I'm glad she wasn't like: 'What are you talking about? Of course you can have the bloody ginger one.'

When the people had gone, Kate just looked at me, crossed her arms, and was like: 'Explain.'

Me: Please don't sell Richard.

Kate: (deep sigh) Phoebe.

Me: Please. Let Emma have him.

Kate: Have you even asked her if she wants the bloody kitten?

Me: No.

Kate: Well, you need to have that conversation, don't you
        think? And maybe while you're at it, have that other
        conversation too.

I stormed out like a proper dick and went to my room.
    What's wrong with me?
    I need to stop this madness.

8.43 p.m.

I googled *How to fall out of love with someone.*

Disappointingly the internet turned out to be no help at all, because apparently that question can only be asked when you actually were in a relationship with someone.

The suggestion is to *write a list of why things haven't worked out.*

Well, things haven't *not* worked out. Mainly because the person in question has never looked at me in that way / would never in a hundred years look at me that way.

I mean, it's great that you can watch YouTube videos like 'All You Need to Know About Black Holes in Twenty-Five Seconds', but what about the answers to questions that actually have an immediate impact on real life? Like: How do I fall out of love with someone????

Surely there's got to be a way, and surely I can't be the first bloody person to be asking this question.

P.S. Emma and Polly and Tristan are following each other on Instagram now.

I feel my life unravelling.

WEDNESDAY 27 JUNE   #DESPERATETIMES

Today, I thought about the phrase 'falling in love' again, and I finally totally get it. You fall. You trip. And *boom!* It's entirely unintentional, not like a parachute jump (which is called 'jump' not 'fall' for a reason).

Apparently it doesn't matter how clever you are, and I'm very clever, but I'm also clumsy AF, and I think I fell in love with Emma the way I often fall when I trip over my own feet.

I reckon the thing to do is to do nothing and wait until I hit the ground. Then I can deal with the impact, brush myself off, and limp away with as much dignity as humanly possible.

Like that time I tackled the shoplifter.

THURSDAY 28 JUNE   #WINNINGNOTWINNING

Here's how you *don't* do it:

• Try touching them at every opportunity.
• Try making them spend time with you.
• Spend an hour deciding what to wear because their possible reaction to it is suddenly more important than you actually feeling comfortable.

- Re-read *Romeo and Juliet*.
- Give in to mentionitis.

On a positive note, the zero-grip bowling shoes have sold, which means the score is 1:0 to me.

I was like: 'Who on earth bought them?' And Kate said it was the old lady who always comes in wearing her sunglasses and immediately complains it's too dark, and that she can't see anything.

Maybe she didn't see they were bowling shoes.

I seriously hope she's not going to fall over and break her ankle, because that would totally be my fault somehow.

I swear Kate watches me now when I'm with Emma.

Is there anything more embarrassing?

Emma and I moved on from the bowling shoes and the pressed-flowers picture, and this week I'm going with a green, pink and white shell suit from the 1980s, and Emma has put a mouldy old Bible in the display case.

I already know it's not a winner because it's not the season for Bibles.

The game is on again.

FRIDAY 29 JUNE   #BALLSORNOBALLS

Tonight, Kate was like: 'Phoebe.'

Me:	Yes.
Kate:	I'm taking all the kittens to have their jabs and stuff on Monday.
Me:	And?
Kate:	You need to tell me what you want me to do with Richard.
Me:	What do you mean what I want you to do with him?
Kate:	He's a pure-breed tom cat. He could make someone a lot of money.
Me:	You still want to sell him.
Kate:	Of course I do. But. I know what it's like when you feel all mushy on the inside, and you can't imagine giving up something that sweet, especially when the person you looooooooove adores it so.
Me:	Everything is fine with my insides. I just think Emma should have him.
Kate:	I understand that, but have you had a chance to ask Emma?
Me:	No.
Kate:	OK, so that's your mission tomorrow, because I need to know if his future owner wants to use him. If not, I'll have his tiny little balls chopped off on Monday.
Me:	That's horrible.
Kate:	Actually it's more like twisting them off.
Me:	Stop.
Kate:	(shrugging) . . .

I texted Emma straightaway.

Phoebe: *If you were Richard's parent, would you want him to be in working order to make you lots of money, or would you want him to have his balls twisted off?*

Emma texted back.

Emma: *?*

I was just like: 'Never mind, because, in all honesty, I can't have a conversation with Emma about a cat's testicles.'

SATURDAY 30 JUNE   #NOBALLS

Kate says she's going to have to look for more volunteers now that we're one person down.

It's like we're in a war.

I suppose we are in a way.

We need to work harder so we can make more money so more people can do more research and people don't have to die from cancer any more.

It's the war against death, which in a way is stupid, because we all have to die.

But I do think, since I'm not really good with people, and will therefore never be like Mum and Dad, that this is the only way I can help others, and maybe the world/the universe/karma will be pleased.

Lots of customers have been coming into the charity shop going: 'Oh, isn't it terrible about Melanie? But she did have a good life.'

I reckon this is another thing we tell ourselves so we can feel better.

I asked Emma about Richard's balls in person, which was strangely less awkward than in a text, and she was like: 'I wouldn't want him to have his balls twisted off – that's cruel.'

Me: But here's the other side of the argument. What if he goes around and shags all the cats in the neighbourhood?

Emma: I suppose there's enough unwanted kittens in the world.

Me: If he keeps his balls, it would literally be his job to shag other designer cats and make designer kittens.

Emma: My poor baby.

Me: He'd be like a stud horse.

Emma: Have you ever seen horses shagging? The size of a horse's penis is something else.

Me: . . .

Emma: I mean, I didn't watch it on purpose.

Me: . . .

Emma: I say he should have his balls twisted off, then. But why are you asking me about this anyway?

Me: No reason.

Oh my God.

All the other designer/half-designer kittens are girls. The non-designer ones are going to have their tubes tied, and the designer ones are being left intact because the new owners want to use them for breeding.

I hate all that.

Why do we need designer ones anyway?

And even though, according to Kate, they are trying to prevent inbreeding, you just know that sooner or later, some cat is going to have kittens from its own father.

In the Bible, this actually happened to humans when the daughters of Lot decide to have children with their father. I mean, it probably didn't *actually* happen, but this could potentially explain why people today are so stupid.

SUNDAY 1 JULY #GUESTLIST

How is it July already?

I spoke with Mum, and she was like: 'Only two more weeks, baby, and then I'll be home.'

This basically means that in two weeks

a) I'm going to move back home,
b) life as I've known it since January will be over, and
c) I'll be sixteen like everyone else.

I know I kind of agreed with Mum on having a party, but I don't really want to have one now because I'd have to speak to people all day, and I won't be able to just leave when I've had enough, which is usually literally after five minutes.

I mean, obviously Mum would be there, which would mean she'd be the star of the show as usual, so maybe people wouldn't even notice if I abandoned ship.

In fact that would be a bit LOL. Imagine it: Everyone's leaving, and someone suddenly goes: 'Where's Phoebe? I haven't seen her all day.'

Anyway, I told Mum I'd have a think about who I want to invite.

When Miriam Patel turned sixteen, she literally invited everyone because she didn't want to 'discriminate'.

She had an Oscars-themed party, and her parents rented out one of the pubs by the river. There were, like, three hundred people there, and I don't think I spoke to her once all afternoon/evening.

Thing is, though, if I'm going to have a party, I'm going to have to invite her because basically I went to hers.

If I invite Polly, I'm going to have to invite Tristan, especially now that we're like BFFs after going to the lido together.

I'll have to invite Kate, obviously, and maybe James.

And I want to invite Alex.

And Emma.

P.S. There are moments when I wish I'd never met her.

Because Kate had to take all the kittens to the vet this afternoon, Emma and I agreed to help Pat in the shop and lock up.

Going in an extra day means that I'm obviously still not sticking to my How-to-Fall-Out-of-Love-with-Emma list.

Also, we had a play-fight today.

It only happened because Emma whipped me with a tea towel, and so I poked her in the side, and she literally lost her legs like one of those wooden animals you get where you have to press the button underneath, and they collapse in a heap of limbs.

I was laughing so hard that I couldn't breathe, as was Emma, and then I pulled that disgusting donated quilt with the cigarette burns from the donations pile, and threw it over Emma, and she squealed so loudly that Pat was just like: 'What are you doing?'

At that point, I was like: OMG, what *am* I doing?

I feel like my brain is melting.

P.S. Richard had his balls twisted off today, and he seems depressed about it. What have I done?

TUESDAY 3 JULY   #PATHETIC

I should write to NASA and ask to apply to their space programme early.

Imagine it.

NASA: What makes you the ideal candidate for the manned
mission to Mars?

Me: I'm basically in love, and I need to not be, so I have
to leave Earth.

WEDNESDAY 4 JULY   #JESUSMARYANDJOSEPH

Apparently the Bible sold.

The score is now 1:1.

I was like: 'Nooooooo, who buys a Bible in the middle of
summer?' And Kate told me it was someone who is going to
use it for their creative writing lessons by cutting it up into
words and phrases to then make poetry.

Totally wanky.

Also: sacrilege.

THURSDAY 5 JULY   #THEGAMEISON

Emma picked a cow onesie for grown-ups, featuring rubber
udders, as her donation of the week, and I went for the
2,000-piece Ed Sheeran jigsaw puzzle that doesn't look
anything like Ed Sheeran, but more like Ron Weasley in
double denim.

We fought for the best window display place for them, and

Emma ended up falling backwards out of the window into the shop and on top of the mannequin she'd tried to put the stupid cow onesie on.

We were absolutely dying laughing, and Alex looked at Kate like: *Well, they've proper lost it now.*

Also, turns out, Alex knows everything, but says nothing. Which interestingly makes him the polar opposite of Miriam Patel, who knows nothing, but says everything.

He knew about Bradley and never said anything, never slipped up, nothing. I'm not saying this because he's got Down's syndrome. I just mean, people normally blurt out secrets like that all the time because they want to feel important.

I asked him to come to my birthday party, but he said he'd have to ask his mum and dad, and I was just like: 'They can come too.'

I think I'm going to have to start writing things down, because it's in ten days.

FRIDAY 6 JULY   #VINAIGRETTE

I did nothing today apart from watch *Love Island* and cut up a page of *The Woman's Guide to Cookery and Household Management* to make a poem for Emma:

'Basic Vinaigrette Dressing Poem'

One part vinegar to three parts oil

Your beauty is
Basic
Simple

Vary as you wish
I shall always
Add
Take

I follow
At the end
Or
Maybe
Since always

I think it's rather profound. LOL.

P.S. Obviously I'm never showing this to Emma. Or anyone.

P.P.S. I reckon the hardest thing about being an actual poet is having to share shit like this with real people and not die of complete shame and embarrassment at the same time.

SATURDAY 7 JULY   #CHAOSANDKISSES

Today at the charity shop, we had a crisis meeting regarding Bill.

Emma: I went to see him yesterday, but he wasn't
         bothered.

Kate: Bad, bad sign. That man adores you.

Emma: He seems to have fallen into himself. Physically.

Pat: He sits in front of the telly all day, and it's not
         even on. Melanie always said that he was driving
         her potty because he was usually reading up to ten
         books at a time, and he always left them lying
         around all over the house. I haven't seen him read
         anything.

Emma: Maybe we should get him a book token. Then he
         has to get out of the house and browse a
         bookshop.

Pat: But he doesn't want to do anything. Oh, I've
         never known anything like it (wipes her eyes).

Emma: Dad was like that after Bradley died.

(Room goes quiet. Everyone looks at her.)

Emma: It's weird because, at first, there's loads to do,
         with all the paperwork and telling everyone and
         organizing the funeral. And then you have to send
         cards thanking everyone for their kind words, and
         then suddenly it all stops and goes so quiet, and
         you just want to drown in it.

Pat: (weeping) . . .

Kate: (taking Emma's hand) But you didn't drown.

Emma: But I had my mum and dad to think about.

338

Everyone: . . .

Emma: I know that Bradley felt guilty for dying and
            making them sad, and I thought the least I could
            do was to keep going.

Pat: (weeping hysterically now, snotty nose, tears) . . .

Kate: Oh, Pat, I know you've been trying so hard with
            Bill. And you're still coming to terms with your
            own loss.

Pat: I don't know what more I can do, Kate. I want to
            shake him.

Emma: Maybe we should do that.

Everyone: ?

Emma: Not physically, obviously. But what about we give
            him something to do that he can't say no to?

Everyone: . . .

Emma: We could say customers have been asking about
            him. Or we could say that Melanie would be so
            disa-ppointed if she knew he was neglecting his
            duties.

Everyone: . . .

Me: Or we could give him a kitten.

Everyone: (except Kate) Oooooooooooh!!!

Kate: Phoebe, you need to stop giving those bloody
            kittens away for free.

Emma: Why? Who's gone already?

Me: No one. She's joking.

Kate: . . .

Pat: He wouldn't want a kitten.

Emma:	Who doesn't love kittens?
Me:	It'll be like a therapy cat.
Pat:	He did enjoy going on safari. I suppose it's worth a try.

Then everyone just looked at Kate.

Kate:	Oh, all right, ye total fuckwits. We'll take a kitten across to him when we shut tonight. But ye're all coming, and if this goes tits up, Pat's having the bloody kitten.
Pat:	Kate, no, really. I'm not a c—
Kate:	I have spoken.

In the afternoon, Kate made me go to the pet shop and get a kitten starter pack. You don't need much, really: only kitten food, a litter tray, and cat litter, which weighs, like, a ton and took me ten minutes to carry fifty metres to the shop.

We all piled into Kate's car, and I got the giggles, because if you'd told me I'd ever end up in a bashed-up Mazda with Kate, Emma and Pat on a Saturday night, taking a kitten to an old guy's home in Putney so that he could have a reason to live, I would have told you you're totally crazy.

Emma was holding the kitten (one of the non-designer ones, obviously, and possibly the one that had bonded with Bill that one time), and I was holding its accessories.

Before we got out of the car, Pat checked her face in the mirror, and put some more apricot-coloured lipstick on. I didn't know at the time that it was her warpaint, and so I may have rolled my eyes.

When we got to the front door, Kate rang the bell.

Then she rang it again.

And again.

And again.

Kate: (knocking like a mentalist) Fer goodness' sake, open yer bloody door, ye stubborn old man.

Emma: (eyes wide, looking at me) . . .

Me: (whispering) So Scottish.

Kate: Excuse me, are you making fun of me? Because I'm not in the mood. Bill. I'm gonna kick yer door in.

Everyone: . . .

Kate: Of course I'm not going to kick a door in. Don't be ridiculous.

Pat: (knocking) Bill, we're all here. It's rude to ignore people who are calling to check on you.

Emma: Maybe he's out

Pat: He's not out. He's ignoring us. Melanie would be so disappointed. Well, there's nothing for it . . .

And then she started rummaging around her handbag, got out her wallet, opened the change compartment, pulled out a tiny screwdriver, and shoved it into the lock.

Emma: How do you know how to—

Pat: You think because I'm old, I'm incapable?

Emma: No — it's just . . . Never mind.

Pat was rattling the door like mad, poking at the lock, and suddenly there was a *click*, and the door opened. At the exact same moment, Bill appeared just behind it.

Bill: You would break into my house?

Pat: I *did* break into your house.

Bill: I will call the police.

Pat: You will do no such thing.

Half-designer

kitten: *Meowwwwwwwwweeeeeee.*

Emma: (holding it up and into Bill's face) . . .

Kate: And before you say no, let me tell you that I have neither the time nor the patience, let alone the money, to look after any more cats, and this one I can't get rid of because it's not a pure-breed, and it's a cranky little shit, and since you've decided to never leave your house again, I'm giving it to you.

Bill: I can't have animals.

Kate: Don't be ridiculous. This is your house — you can do whatever ye like.

Half-designer

kitten: *Meeeeowwwwweeeee.*

Emma: Please, Bill. Look — she's so sweet.

Me: And if you don't like her, you can always

drown her. But don't tell Emma.

Pat: Are you going to invite us in, Bill? Or shall we leave the kitten on your doorstep?

Me: Like baby Jesus.

Emma: I think that was Moses.

Pat: It was neither.

Bill: You mean Mowgli. From *The Jungle Book*. He was an orphaned human and raised by a different species.

Kate: Great. There you go, then. This is Mowgli, but she's a girl. Mowgli, this is Bill. We've brought cat litter and food – Phoebe, put all that down right here. Any questions, just give me a call. Let's go, team.

Emma put the tiny kitten into Bill's ginormous hand, I put down the litter and the food, and then we all turned around and walked towards the car.

Before I got in, I looked back at Bill holding the kitten, and I could hear it meowing. It was like the opening of *The Lion King*: epic.

Kate dropped off Pat first, and then she was like: 'Emma, do you want to come in for a cup of tea? See Richard?' And Emma was like: 'Sure. If that's OK.'

But I was thinking: Remember the list, remember the list, remember the list. Emma at the house means total disregard of four points out of five.

Unfortunately it was out of my hands, and so I was like:

Well, the only thing I can do is stay on guard.

Richard galloped towards her when he saw Emma/heard her voice, and she picked him up and kissed his squashed-up little face.

I went into the kitchen to make tea.

Kate: (whispering) You know you're going to have to work for me all next year too, to pay off Richard if you want to give him to Emma.

Me: I won't have time. I'll have school.

Kate: You had school this year.

Me: Do you think I can ask Mum to give me Russian lessons for my birthday?

Kate: Are you changing the subject?

Me: No. I was just thinking about when I'm back at home.

Kate: Don't go back home, Phoebe. I'll miss you. Why don't you just live with me?

Me: Mum probably wouldn't even notice.

Kate: Phoebe.

Me: What? It's the truth.

Kate: (hugging me, squeezing me, kissing my face) It isn't, but just so you know, I love it when you're here, and I always hate it when you go back home, because I loooooove you, you wonderful, wonderful human. (Then, whispering again): When are you going to tell Emma you fancy her?

Me: (extracting myself from her iron clasp) Shut up. Never.

Kate: Phoebe. I know you're a bit awkward, but you're not a coward.

Me: (whispering) Oh my God, thanks for the compliment. She wouldn't fancy me back anyway.

Kate: (eyebrows up) . . .

Me: (whispering) What?

Kate: (whispering) She clearly fancies you.

Me: (heart beating totally out of control) Fuck off.

Kate: (whispering) I've known her longer than you have.

Me: (whispering) And that's why you can read her mind?

Kate: (whispering) Fer goodness' sake, Phoebe – stop being such a fuckwit.

Me: (whispering) Besides, even if she did fancy me, which she doesn't, I don't do all that. Because I can't.

So I walked back into the living room, head throbbing, with our cups of tea, and when I looked at Emma, she looked at me with her beautiful eyes, all smiling, and happy, and perfect, and all I could think was: All things aside, I couldn't be with you, because I couldn't be without you after that.

Emma: Are you OK?

Me: Yes, fine.

Kate made me walk Emma home at nine as usual, and when we were outside her house, Emma hugged me, but I was all physically awkward again. Like *Argh!* but with my limbs.

Emma: Have I done anything to upset you?

Me: No. Why?

Emma: Because you've gone all quiet.

Me: I'm always quiet.

Emma: OK.

Me: OK. See you next week.

Emma: Yes, see you.

And as I turned to walk away, she went: 'Phoebe, wait.'

And then she kissed me.

On the lips.

For one, two, three seconds.

Just like that.

I ran all the way home.

P.S. Now what?

P.P.S. I just researched kissing on the internet, which was difficult, because it appears Emma's quick peck on the lips has literally left me visually impaired.

But anyway, there's no evidence that ancient humans (hunter-gatherers/the Egyptians) kissed.

Apparently modern hunter-gatherer tribes even find it revolting.

The most recent kissing-related evidence goes back to an old Hindu text that describes it as inhaling each other's souls.

I mean, that's definitely what Tristan does to Polly. Except he doesn't do it in a deep and meaningful Hindu-style sort of way, but more in an entirely horrific *Harry Potter* Dementor-style kind of way.

The internet reckons humans kiss because our sense of smell is shit, whereas animals can smell each other's pheromones without having to stick their tongues down each other's throats.

Interestingly, women apparently prefer the smell of men who are genetically different from them, which explains so much about Polly and Tristan.

Polly:

- Brilliant.
- Gorgeous.
- Funny.

Tristan:

- Stupid.
- Gross.
- Dull.

Here's what I want to know, though: Why do Emma and I want to kiss each other? Because it's not that we could enrich the gene pool.

How does it all make sense?

Like, biologically?

SUNDAY 8 JULY   #PATHETICPOETRY

I didn't know what to do with myself today.

I think if you add it all up, I spent about thirty minutes standing on my head. I know it's not good for me, but the discomfort makes me think about important things like breathing, rather than confusing things like Emma.

When my arms got tired, I hung upside down from the sofa.

Kate was like: 'Phoebe, if you're bored, I have a lawn that needs cutting out back.'

So I went to my room and cut up that ridiculous soufflé chapter from *The Woman's Guide to Cookery and Household Management* instead and turned it into poetry.

Sweet, light, airy.
Skin is milk.
Soft, delicate, shiny.
Lips are heat.

Maybe I'm too bland?
Maybe she's too vanilla.
To do this right,
Follow the master recipe.

You need to have no qualms about perfection.
Already you're everybody's favourite.
Perfect for luncheon or supper,
In fancy food language.
I'm ready.
To spoon.
To blend.
To hold.

This I demand of you:
Of course, it's different,
Quick and hot.
But essential, necessary.
I'm rapidly beginning to subside.
Give me little space, cover me.
Finish me off.
Watch me
As I fall
To pieces.

Do you think there's a chance people wrote poetry because they were in love with people but didn't want to be?

I wonder if it worked for them.

They'd probably proper roll their eyes at us analysing it for GCSEs. In fact, they're probably glad they're dead so they don't have to witness it.

7.35 p.m.

Mum called to say that she's getting her itinerary tomorrow.

Not sure I'm ready for her to come back, and I honestly don't know what to do about my birthday.

8.45 p.m.

I just realized that the second stanza of the soufflé poem is shaped like a triangle which, to the untrained eye/literary critic may look like a vagina.

If I were to accidentally become a famous poet, school children will forever have to go on and on and on about whether or not this was a conscious choice made by the poet who was, at the time of writing it, a bit of a lesbian.

And the reality is, I'm not even a poet, and these are just words cut from a shitty soufflé recipe and then glued back together in a different order with Pritt Stick.

9.10 p.m.

I haven't heard from Emma.

And I don't know what to say to her.

Maybe it's good Mum's coming back after all, because I'll move back to Kingston, and then I'll never really have to see Emma again. We'd be like Romeo and Juliet. Eternally without each other, except in life, not in death.

I didn't go to the charity shop today, despite the fact that I had fuck all to do.

When I told Kate I'd cleaned the bathroom and hoovered, she looked at me like I was unwell, which I suppose I am.

I think Emma and I only exchanged 20 million bacteria, and now I wish it had been 80 million.

I want to kiss her again so much that I feel like my insides are going to explode if I'm left wanting it for much longer. But I don't want to want it.

Maybe I want it so much because Emma and I are so genetically different that we don't even make sense.

7.45 p.m.

I finally sent everyone invites via Instagram to my birthday because Kate was like: 'Get on with this!'

I think I'm proper broken in the brain because I sent an invite to Miriam Patel 'plus one'.

She confirmed immediately, of course.

If she wasn't so secretly clever, I'd say she should give up school and be a full-time socialite.

I told Kate that I actually have no idea how to organize everything I need to organize in my life right now, and she was just like: 'Don't worry, pet. It's all in hand.'

But is it?

Because the last thing I saw her doing was inhale James's soul in the kitchen.

Emma still hasn't texted me.

I don't know what that means. Maybe she regrets having kissed me. That happened to Polly once after she kissed Pete Abbot, because he thought they were literally married, and Polly was like: 'Oh my God, I can't believe I did that. I don't even fancy him that much.' And then she had to have a super-awkward conversation with him, which broke his heart.

Maybe I should text Emma and tell her to just forget about the kiss.

In other news, Kate says that Pat says that Bill is obsessed with his new kitten. Apparently he's finally left the house and walked to the pet shop to buy Mowgli a collar and get her a tag with his phone number on.

Result.

TUESDAY 10 JULY   #SORRY

Got a text from Emma today:

Emma: *Sorry if I did something you didn't like.*

I don't even know where to start with that.

Except that she obviously doesn't regret it.

OMG, and of course I liked it.

But I don't like how it's making me feel.

I hate that I've become this pathetic human who is looking for her self-worth or some sort of salvation in someone else's eyes.

I hate that I'm unhappy when I'm not with Emma, and I also hate that I feel like I've swallowed a bucket of popping candy when I'm with her.

I don't want someone else to make me happy, because what happens when they are no longer there to do it?

Look at Mum. I obviously didn't know her when Dad was alive, but from what Kate's been telling me, I know that when he died, Mum changed. And now she's running away from everything and everyone all the time, and when she stands still for a moment, she's got to be the centre of attention, and who's actually really like that?

And what would happen to Polly if Tristan left her? Or worse, if he left her for someone else?

I don't want to be that weak.

I can't give that sort of power over my life to another person.

I wonder now what's easier: being in love with your partner, or not being in love with them.

Maybe there's a point to an arranged marriage.

Polly and I had Starbucks in Kingston today.

For some reason, things escalated, and she ended up telling me every detail of her sex life, and now I know what Tristan looks like without any clothes on.

I also know everything about the curvature of his penis, and that the tiny hole on the end is slightly off-centre.

Oh my God.

Then she was like: 'Honestly, Phoebe, I can't wait for you to fall in love. I think it would be hilarious.'

That's the moment I figuratively dropped the ball, and because I didn't say anything straightaway, Polly suddenly shot up from her seat and was all in my face like: 'Shut. Up.'

Me: What?

Polly: You've met someone.

Me: No.

Polly: Don't lie to me.

Me: I'm not.

Polly: Liar. Who? When? Where? Now.

Me: Fuck off. I'm not in the mood.

Polly: Who?

Me: (shaking my head) . . .

Polly: (reaching for my hand) Phoebe?

Me: . . .

Polly: I'm sorry I said it would be hilarious. You know I'd never make fun of you like that.

Me: Maybe you should.

Polly: Tell me?

Me: We sort of kissed, but not really. On Saturday.

Polly: Tell! Me! Now!

Me: Emma.

Polly: FUCK! OFF!

Me: . . .

Polly: How am I that thick?

Me: . . .

Polly: It was totally obvious, and I didn't realize. I'm so
         stupid — of course. You've been hanging out with
         her, like, every free second this year.

Me: Only because you were busy with Tristan and forgot
         about me.

Polly: You didn't call me either, Phoebs. I thought you'd
         gone off *me*! Oh my God, did you fancy *me* by any
         chance? Were you jealous?

Me: (laughing, because, really, what's wrong with
         people) . . .

Polly: (punching me in the shoulder) Rude! Anyway, tell
         me. You kissed her. Oh my God, Phoebs, you big
         lesbian.

Me: Fuck off. And *she* kissed *me*.

Polly: And then what?

Me: Then nothing. It was outside her house. She went
         inside, and I ran home.

Polly: And then?

Me: Nothing.

Polly:	But today is Wednesday.
Me:	And?
Polly:	Are you going to kiss her back?
Me:	No.
Polly:	. . .
Me:	I can't do all that, Polly. I'm not like you.
Polly:	You can't do what? The kissing? Have sex? You don't have to do it all straightaway – don't be stupid.
Me:	No – yes. The whole . . . love thing. I can't do it. It's too . . . I don't know . . .
Emma:	. . .
Me:	Big.
Polly:	(clutching her chest) You're such a romantic, Phoebe. I literally want to cry.
Me:	You and me both.
Polly:	(still clutching her chest, looking at me with pity): . . .
Me:	I don't recognize myself any more, and I hate it.
Polly:	You fancy her, though.
Me:	I don't want to.
Polly:	But you do.
Me:	Of course I do.
Polly:	And you think about her a lot.
Me:	I mainly think about how to un-think about her, but yes.
Polly:	You do realize that you can't help who you fall in love with?
Me:	Apparently not. But at least I'm trying.

Polly: You know, Phoebe, for someone so clever, you are
        remarkably stupid.

10.10 p.m.

I texted Emma to ask if she's coming to my birthday party,
because she still hasn't confirmed on the Instagram group
conversation.

10.30 p.m.

Emma just texted:

Emma: *Not sure yet if I can make it.*

So that's that then.

THURSDAY 12 JULY   #MOWGLISNEWADVENTURES

I wanted to see Emma so much, but I ended up not going to
the charity shop this afternoon for that exact reason.

Just like my brain, Polly won't shut up about it all, and
now I regret having said something, because the last thing I
need is someone else's hysteria added to my already volatile
brain chemicals.

Polly called me at lunchtime and was like: 'Any news?'

Me:	No.
Polly:	You know, Phoebe, being in love with someone isn't a disease.
Me:	Why do I feel sick then?
Polly:	That'll go away.
Me:	Like a headache?
Polly:	(sighing) Emma's embrace will work like paracetamol.
Me:	I don't want drugs.

I don't want to be sixteen and in love and stupid!

Intellectually I know that the best outcome to the whole Emma situation would be if Emma didn't come to my birthday on Sunday.

Because then it wouldn't have to be awkward, and we could just never see each other again.

I can always tell Kate that I have to concentrate on school, and learn Russian, and that I have no time to come to the charity shop once Mum's back. I mean, I'd be really sad not to see Alex again, but I suppose we can still have Sprinkles dates and stuff.

And I can pay Kate the remaining kitten money back at a later stage. Like, when I'm on the mission to Mars.

Hmm. I never thought about it, but I wonder how much astronauts earn. It must be really good money, because it's such a dangerous job, and you have to be highly skilled. And you'd have, like, zero expenses because you'd be in a spaceship. I wonder if it's tax free. I feel like that would be fair.

Anyway, Kate can have back her money then. Plus interest.

P.S. Tomorrow after work, we're going to Kingston to get the flat ready.

Dusting, hoovering, food shopping – the usual. Plus we have to do all the party decorations and food for Sunday.

Can't believe it's been half a year since Mum left.

P.P.S. Most bizarre news from Bill.

He's joined Instagram and now posts daily about #MowglisNewAdventures. Apparently he already has 385 followers.

Seriously, I can't even.

And, because everyone loves him and Mowgli, people have been messaging him to ask where he got the kitten from, and Kate now has ten requests for kitten viewings, and they are all coming on Monday.

FRIDAY 13 JULY   #SURPRISE

Mum isn't going to be here for my birthday after all.

I told Kate that my birthday is cancelled.

We never went to Kingston.

11.07 p.m.

I just threw a massive tantrum.

I'm so embarrassed, and I'm not just saying that.

Kate hasn't tried to talk to me since, which means it was bad. Like, really, really, really bad.

I kicked a wall.

Like, really, really, really kicked a wall. My foot is throbbing.

And then I threw my school shoe against the front door so hard that it left a mark.

And I screamed like I was losing it, calling Mum every name under the sun.

And then I went to my room and slammed the door so hard that the whole house shook.

And then I cried for, like, three hours.

I think that's what they mean when they say 'she lost her shit'.

I can't see myself ever getting out of bed again.

I love Emma so much.

SATURDAY 14 JULY   #WHATEVER

I didn't go to the charity shop today because I'm

a) still too angry with Mum, and

b) too embarrassed to face Kate, and

c) unable to deal with Emma.

I'm not even mad about Mum not coming home for my birthday, even though she *promised* that she would, but I'm mad because I'm mad.

Because I should have expected it, because this is what *always* happens.

I cancelled my party via Instagram, and literally five minutes later:

Polly: *Are you OK?*

Me: *Yes, fine.*

Polly: *Party cancelled. Why?*

Me: *Mum's staying behind for a patient, so she won't be home until next week.*

Polly: *That SUCKS.*

Me: *She sucks.*

Polly: *Why is she staying?*

Me: *Someone's having a baby, and apparently women haven't been able to give birth successfully without her since always, and so Mum needs to be there. Naturally.*

Polly: *But I've got a present for you. Can I at least come over tomorrow?*

Me: *I'm not in the mood for anyone. Sorry.*

Polly: *I respect that. But I'll call you.*

Me: *OK.*

Polly: *Don't be sad. Love you.*

Me: . . .

Then I watched *Love Island*.

Luckily the show is so dumb that my brain literally switched off to protect itself from further deterioration, and I fell asleep.

I only woke up when Kate got back from work, and I swear my whole body felt broken.

Kate (looking down at me lying on the sofa): 'Do you want to talk about last night?'

Me: (new tears rolling out of my eyes) I'm so sorry, Kate.
Kate: Thank you.
Me: It won't ever happen again.
Kate: (nodding) . . .
Me: . . .
Kate: (putting her hand on my forehead like she's checking if I have a temperature) Have you had food today? Water?
Me: No. And yes.
Kate: (sitting down, putting my feet on her lap) I know you find emotions hard, Phoebe.
Me: . . .
Kate: But they make us human.
Me: I hate that.
Kate: I know. But what happened last night is not acceptable.
Me: I know.

Kate:	I know you know, and that's why we don't have to talk about it again.
Me:	Thank you.
Kate:	Emma tells me you cancelled your party.
Me:	So?
Kate:	So, when were you planning on telling Alex? He's not on Instagram.
Me:	Shit.
Kate:	Yes, shit. But don't worry, I spoke to his dad.
Me:	I'm sorry.
Kate:	You're welcome to change your mind, you know? We can go to Morrisons right now.
Me:	(shaking my head) . . .
Kate:	OK. But we *are* going to go out for lunch.
Me:	I'm honestly not in the mood.
Kate:	I wasn't asking you, pet. I was telling you. I feel like telling the story of how your clever little head breached your mother's vagina, and you plopped out into my hands sixteen years ago.
Me:	I guess I owe you that.
Kate:	You do, pet.

10.43 p.m.

I wonder where I'll be in a year from now.

11.15 p.m.

I've never cried as much as I have in the last twenty hours. I thought I was done crying, but then Kate made me a cheese toastie, and I started all over again.

SUNDAY 15 JULY   #HAPPYBIRTHDAYTOME

0.01 a.m.

I'm sixteen.

11.35 a.m.

Thirty-five people have already messaged me wishing me a happy birthday, including Miriam Patel.

Emma hasn't.

Kate gave me a card Nan and Granddad sent from Hong Kong. They say I should visit soon. Maybe I should spontaneously go this summer. It's not that I'm doing anything else. Maybe I'll ask Mum.

She hasn't messaged me.

Kate, James and I are going out to lunch now, but we have to go via the charity shop because Kate left her wallet there, and she'd never let James pay.

So yesterday was basically insane.

We got to the charity shop, which was obviously shut because it was a Sunday.

Kate unlocked and shimmied inside, and James was all rubbing himself up against her back in the process, and Kate was like: 'Phoebe, can you see if my wallet's on the stockroom table?' And I was like: 'Check yourself.' But Kate was like: 'I can't, because I'm kissing James.' And then she went and kissed James, and I was just like: 'Gross.'

So I walked through the shop, and into the stockroom, and suddenly all these people shouted – actually shouted:

'*SURPRISE*!!!!!!'

And I swear I screamed and fell to the floor.

Kate was laughing, and clapping, someone switched on the lights, and opened the back door, and then everyone was singing 'Happy Birthday'.

Everyone was there.

In the stockroom.

Singing.

Polly, Tristan, Emma, Miriam Patel, Alex, his parents, Bill and even Pat.

I think I must have said 'fuck' about a thousand times, but no one was outraged; they just laughed at me.

My eyes kept bouncing back to Emma, and my heartbeat

was all over the place, but that could have been the shock of the surprise. She smiled at me, but I knew straightaway that something was off. Missing. Broken.

My brain was like: What have you done, Phoebe. But there was so much going on that I couldn't process that question properly, and so I was left just looking at Emma, and looking at Emma, and looking at Emma.

Kate must have arranged the whole thing on Saturday when I was having my come-down from that awful meltdown and was literally lying unconscious on the sofa.

The table was set all Halloween-like with skull cups and ghost plates and a string of skull fairy lights along the middle, and skull and rat candles.

People must have brought chairs, and there was food, and presents, and everything.

It's still so strange to think that everyone had made such an effort for me.

I'm also still surprised that Kate had any love left after I almost kicked down the wall that separates the hallway from the kitchen in my blind rage.

I hugged her for, like, five minutes until she was like: 'OK, get off me now, and say hello to your guests.'

I felt like a celebrity, walking down a line of well-wishers, shaking hands and hugging people.

Turns out, Miriam Patel came minus one, because she's jumped onto the suffragettes' bandwagon and therefore no longer believes in the 'plus one'. She sat next to Alex, and they were talking all afternoon. He even let her pick a French

Fancy off of his plate, and he normally really isn't into people interfering with his snacks. I think the whole Emmeline Pankhurst thing actually suits Miriam. That way she can still talk and talk and talk, but without talking actual crap, and sounding like the idiot she isn't.

Alex's parents are super nice too. I didn't speak to them at Melanie's funeral because they didn't come to the party bit at the sailing club. They got me flowers, and Alex baked my birthday cake. It had black icing on it and a white skull wearing a pink ribbon. But the best thing was that when we cut it, the inside was rainbow layers. I was like: 'This must have taken you ages.' And Alex was like: 'Yes. Three days.'

Three days.

He made me something that took him three days.

I almost didn't want to eat it, but it was proper delicious.

Pat was like: 'Alex, you are a magician.' Which is true.

The party turned out to be a barbecue after all because Kate had bought disposable ones and put them just outside the back door. Bill took charge of the grilling, and we could hear him and Pat bickering outside for literally an hour. For the rest of the day, if he wasn't talking about sausages, he was talking about Mowgli. What have we done by giving him that cat? He's now an online sensation: 863 followers to date. And he's got a sponsor for his cat food!

After everyone had eaten, Kate was like: 'Time to open your presents, Phoebe. Mine first.'

She gave me a little box, and I already knew it was jewellery.

I opened it, and inside was a silver chain with a tiny Star of David pendant. I think I must have looked at it for, like, ten minutes. In the end, Kate was like: 'You do know what that is, don't you?' And I was like: 'Obviously.' Kate was like: 'You like it?' But I didn't even know what to say, because I literally loved it so much. Kate helped me put it on, kissed my head, and whispered: 'I love you.' And Bill was like: 'Mazel tov.' And everyone went: 'Happy birthday, Phoebe.'

Polly and Tristan got me cinema vouchers, and Polly's card said: *Happy New Year.* LOL.

Miriam got me a book about inspiring women who have changed history. Honestly, half a year ago, she probably would have given me fake eyelashes or something equally as tedious, but this is actually a really good gift.

Bill, Pat and James got me a Starbucks gift card and a poetry book (clearly James's idea).

When Emma gave me her present, I still hadn't spoken to her, and it was all a bit awkward.

I was like: 'Thank you.' And I went to open the card, but Emma was like: 'Maybe the card is for later. Open the present first.'

I tried to be all careful and not destroy the gorgeous wrapping, but everyone was like: 'Come on!'

It was a T-shirt from Topshop with a picture of a Space Shuttle on the back, and the NASA logo on the front.

I felt her eyes on me, and my chest felt all tight, and I was thinking: Why are you giving me such a well-considered gift when I've been ignoring you because I'm trying so hard to forget you ever happened?

I was just like: 'Thank you.' But it came out all shaky and pathetic.

I was dying to read her card, but I waited for half an hour, and then stuffed it into my trousers and went into the toilet.

I sat down and ripped open the envelope.

It looked more like a Valentine's card than a birthday card because it had just one red heart on it.

Mine almost stopped.

Dear Phoebe,

Happy birthday. I hope sixteen is everything you want it to be and more.

I'm sorry for kissing you without asking you first, and for assuming it was something you wanted too. I must have misinterpreted things.

I hope we can be friends.

Love,
Emma
x

I tucked the card back into my jeans, washed my shaking hands (even though I never actually went to the toilet . . .), and when I looked at myself in the mirror, I was just like: *What are you doing?* Because Kate's right: I'm not a coward. And so before I could rethink anything, I walked out of the toilet, and straight up to Emma, and I was like: 'Please can you come with me for a sec?'

I went out into the shop, and into the changing cubicle.

Emma came in behind me.

I pulled the curtain across, and suddenly it felt like there was only the two of us, and we were on an interstellar mission into the future, and the only air we could breathe was between us because everything else was the infinite vacuum of space.

For a moment, I just looked at her, and it felt like I was seeing her for the very first time.

She smelt of raspberries.

Her cheeks were flushed, and she was biting her lip, and I got all confused for a moment because her eyes weren't blue, but pitch-black, and I'd forgotten what that meant, but then I was like: OK, Phoebe – go!

Me: It's not that I didn't want it.

Emma: . . .

Me: The kiss.

Emma: . . .

Me: I tried to not want it.

Emma: (looking confused) . . .

Me: Because it made me feel physically sick.

Emma: Oh my God.

Me: No, not like that. Obviously not like that. No, not like . . . that. Obviously. What I mean is . . . I . . . You . . . This . . . We . . .

And then I was just like: FFS, Phoebe! Because I literally couldn't remember words, and Emma looked at me the way you look at your phone when it's suddenly stopped working.

She opened her mouth a little to probably say something that would make my previous statements sound less idiotic (because she's good like that), but before she could actually say anything, I leaned forward, and I kissed her.

And that was literally like the end of gravity.

It was all soft lips and tongues, fruity lip gloss and terror, and 80 million bacteria, and the single most delicious thing I ever experienced in my whole entire life.

When we stopped, I felt like I'd swam the whole length at Tooting Lido underwater – dizzy, boneless and breathless.

Then we giggled, and I was like: 'I'm so sorry I'm so ridiculous.'

Emma was like: 'I've never met anyone like you, Phoebe, and I wouldn't change you for the world.'

I was like: Wow. And then I was like: Maybe that's what it's all about?

I don't think I let go of her hand for the rest of the day after that.

Kate knew immediately what had transpired, and I reckon an hour later, pretty much everyone else got it too.

I'm 98 per cent sure that Pat opposes homosexuality, because she kept looking at me like: You corrupted the lovely Emma. But in reality, it was Emma who corrupted me with her beautiful eyes and lips, and class, and funniness. But whatever, Pat.

At one point in the afternoon, I looked at my phone, and there was a WhatsApp message from Mum.

She'd sent a picture of herself and a girl holding a tiny baby.

Mum: *Happy sixteenth. I hope you're enjoying your party ;)You share a birthday with this little man, whom I had the pleasure of welcoming into the world this morning. He is called Salomao, which means Man of Peace. I'll be home on Thursday. I can't wait to see you. I love you, and I'm very proud of you. Mum xx*

Emma was like: 'The mother looks like a child.' And Kate was like: 'Amelia said the girl's only fifteen.'

Emma was like: 'Imagine having a child at fifteen. In a refugee camp.'

I obviously feel like a massive dick now for having been so horrible about Mum not coming home but wanting to help a pregnant girl instead. But if you don't know the whole story, how are you supposed to behave as though you do?

So that was yesterday.

Today everything was back to normal, but I have to say I do feel different . . . Like there's a lot of open space ahead, but I don't hate it.

When Kate got home, she was like: Sit.

Me: What?

Kate: Remember the birds and the bees?

Me: (rolling my eyes so much, I nearly severed my optic nerve) Oh my God.

Kate: It obviously doesn't quite apply.

Me: Obviously. Quite.

Kate: I just want to say to you that I'm here for you should you need anything. Help, emotional support, advice – even though I trust you know where things are—

Me: Oh my God, Kate. I've literally been with Emma for twenty-four hours. I'm not going to have sex with her straightaway.

Kate: All of that is between you and Emma, pet. I only wanted to let you know that I'm here if you need me.

Cringe!

I'm 100 per cent not going to talk to her about my sex life when I have one.

On that note, Emma's coming over in a minute, but we're not going to have sex.

All the kittens are being collected, and we're seeing them off. (Not Richard. He's staying at Kate's for the time being because I still want to give him to Emma, but I think I may have to get into her mum's good books first #pressure #inlaws.)

So I think it's time for me to present to Kate the final financial breakdown of all moneys owed and services rendered. FYI, I'm not including the financial loss of Richard here because Kate agreed to keep him (for now).

I thought I'd end up owing £2,000, because the non-designer kittens were expected to bring in zero pounds.

However, we are selling three of them for £250 each. That's £750.

£2,000 minus £750 equals £1,250.

I'm also going to take off the £530 for the *Star Wars* poster (only fair), so that's £720. Also, minus £15 for the bowling shoes is £705.

My labour over the past four months has definitely been worth £705, so I think this means Kate and I are even.

P.S. I can't believe I'm sixteen.

Turning sixteen was always for other people.

But I suppose so was love.

ACKNOWLEDGEMENTS

The creation of this novel coincided with a time of great change and uncertainty in my life, and I must thank first and foremost the three women this book is dedicated to for pulling/ dragging me through it: My best friends Brittain, Luci, and Sophie. Thank you for your unwavering love and support, for putting me up, for making me dinner, for making me cake, and most importantly for always making me laugh. I love you endlessly.

Thank you Tony, you drove the getaway vehicle back then. Thank you Ruth, you gave me a home. Thank you Dawn, you offered me a job, and casually threw in a handful of amazing new friends for free.

A huge and heartfelt thank you goes to Melvin Burgess for your encouragement, your wisdom, your humour, and for giving me a leg-up.

I would like to thank the Bath Spa MA Writing for Young People community, especially my workshop besties Hana Tooke and Lucy Cuthew. From day one you have been both supportive and critical, and I know I was so very lucky to have landed in your midst.

Thank you to Audrey and Jack Ladevèze for the Bath Spa University MA Writing Award which greatly eased the financial burden at the time.

Thank you to Julia Green and all my phenomenal tutors on the MA, especially to my genius manuscript tutor, and Phoebe's real-life godmother, Joanna Nadin. Your tenacity and hard work is an inspiration to me, and I will forever be grateful for you continuously and savagely pushing me to try harder, and do better.

Thank you to Jo Unwin for forwarding my love letter to JULA to the wonderful, fierce, and courageous woman who then became my agent: Rachel Mann. Rachel, Rachel, Rachel; thank you for loving Phoebe as much as you do, and for telling everyone. Thank you for checking in with me when I've gone quiet, for teaching me what's what, and for always knowing what I want. You are the most wonderful gift.

A big thank you to the hard working team at Macmillan who hosted us and threw a mini party for Phoebe even though it was in fact the Gruffalo's birthday that day. Thank you to my brilliant editors Rachel Petty and Joy Peskin, who always ask the right questions. Your insight, knowledge, and empathy enabled me to make better choices again and again.

ABOUT THE AUTHOR

Wibke Brueggemann grew up in northern Germany and the southern United States, but London is her home. She originally studied acting at the Academy of Live and Recorded Arts but ended up becoming a writer. Wibke has a Master's in Writing for Young People from Bath Spa University, where she was the recipient of the Bath Spa University Writing Award. *Love Is for Losers* is her debut novel.